TROUBLE RESTORED

Trouble Cat Mysteries #13

CAROLYN HAINES

Cover design by Cissy Hartley
Formatted by Priya Bhakta

All proceeds from the sale of this book will be donated to the Good Fortune Farm Refuge.

ISBN: 978-1-7330169-1-9

Black cats have always been an inspiration for me, and I've been lucky to share my home with a few of them. This book is for E.A. Poe, who inspired the original Familiar, and Coal Shaft Haines, who was the "prototype" for Trouble. Now I have the wonderful, petite, Karma, a female black cat. Who knows the mischief she will drag me into.

CONTENTS

CHAPTER ONE

*B*loody Nora! My hometown is in turmoil. As I saunter along the Main Street of Wetumpka, Alabama on this fine fall morning, I find my normally serene village in an uproar. Folks are moving furniture into the street, gathering to discuss how they plan to renovate their homes and businesses, and simply sharing the excitement that has come like a sprinkling of fairy dust over the town since the arrival of the Home Again renovation crews.

The TV cameras are everywhere, filming the original look of some of Wetumpka's classic old cottages and storefronts. In the center of the whirlwind are Hank and Katie Evans, the stars of the hit HGTV home remodeling show that has taken on the entire town of Wetumpka for a facelift. I doubt there's been this much excitement since the meteorite struck the area, flooded a large section of the southeastern United States, and contributed to the death of the dinosaurs. Yes, as a smart, sassy, superior black cat detective, I know my history. So many foolish bipeds never crack a book and fail to learn the true facts of history. Therefore they're doomed to repeat mistakes. But that is too dark and dreary a thought on such a day of promise and optimism.

Ah, I see the local hardware store has been swept up in the madness.

There are saws whining, drills buzzing, maybe a jackhammer. And a three-man crew is peeling off the old roof in preparation for a new stamped tin roof that is more accurate to the time period when the store was built. Even Tammy Lynn, my beloved humanoid, is making some changes at the Book Basket. Not too many changes, I hope. I have my nooks and crannies where I like to lie about for a snooze.

Tammy sees me and opens the front door to allow me ingress to the store, and right behind me comes the famous TV renovation duo, Hank and Katie. At least I'll be able to participate in the decisions being made about the bookstore. I take my perch on the antique sofa near the register and settle in for a bit of eavesdropping. But who is that striking young woman bustling through the door with a look of sheer desperation on her face? I do believe something is going to happen, and it's a good thing I'm about to be called back into action. I'm always sleek and svelte, but a few weeks without a case to solve and I feel my fur is a little too tight! Tammy has been experimenting with a newfangled pressure cooker pot, and some of her creations are...far too tempting.

The home improvement duo has barely said hello to my Tammy before this young woman makes a beeline for Hank and Katie. She's in such a rush to talk to them, she trips over a stack of books and almost falls. She's as tightly strung as a piano wire, and it's clear to me she has a lot on her mind.

Tammy picks up on the young woman's distress—she has a heart of gold and is always eager to help. So what has caused such consternation in a young woman with an alabaster complexion and big hazel eyes? I sense something afoot that will require my unique skills. Rescuing damsels in distress is what I do best.

Let me shift my perch to the countertop so I can more easily eavesdrop on the biped conversation. If something is amiss, I need to know about it.

. . .

Tommie Sykes stepped into the Book Basket and stopped short. Her quarry stood in front of her—Hank and Katie Evans were exactly who she needed to speak with. Her shoe caught on a stack of books on the floor, and she stumbled forward, almost ramming into a slender red-headed woman.

"Are you okay?" the redhead, who Tommie knew also happened to own the Book Basket, asked.

For a moment embarrassment and confusion rendered her silent. Books! Nothing smelled as wonderful as a new book. All her life she'd found refuge in bookstores, libraries, and between the covers of tales of adventure, crime, and romance. Today, though, she didn't have time to peruse the shelves of book titles. She was on a mission. One that would determine her future.

She'd tracked the renovators, Katie and Hank Evans, to The Book Basket because she needed their help. She had a big idea— a really, really big idea. But she needed someone to help her bring it to life. She inhaled deeply, aware that the Evans and the bookstore owner were waiting for her to speak. She was also tuned in to the black cat sitting on the counter who watched her as if he understood all the thoughts and fears rushing through her mind.

"Can I help you?" the redheaded bookstore owner asked a little more forcefully.

"You're Tammy Lynn, right?" Tommie said.

"I am. What can I do for you?"

Tommie pointed to the renovators. "I really need to talk to Mr. and Mrs. Evans. I...uh...I've inherited some property and I need help."

Hank Evans stepped forward and extended a hand. "Happy to offer what we can, but we were about to go over plans for the bookstore with Ms. Lynn here."

Tommie took a step back. She'd come into the store like a

whirlwind and just pushed on top of everyone there. She felt a flush creep up her neck. The truth was, she had to have some answers so she could decide what in the world she was going to do with the rest of her life.

"I'm so sorry. I—" She stopped. "The truth is, I need help. But I had no right to burst in here and just take over your private conversation. I can wait outside." She started for the door, but Tammy's gentle hand stopped her.

"Who are you and how can we help you?" Tammy asked.

"My name is Tommie Sykes. I'm a jewelry maker."

"You're the woman who inherited Loftus Manor," Tammy said.

"That's right. I'm the new owner of Loftus Manor. Samuel Loftus was my great-great uncle."

"Welcome to Wetumpka. What can we do for you?"

Tommie took a deep breath. This was her chance. Right now. "I want to renovate the manor and turn it into a small inn. I think the property is perfectly suited for that, if I can afford the necessary renovations. The bedrooms are in pretty good shape, but the bathrooms and kitchen need work."

"Loftus Manor is a beautiful old place," Tammy Lynn said, as she turned to include the renovators in the conversation. "It's west of town. The property fronts a part of the Coosa River. The architectural details are to die for. I believe it was built in the early 1800s."

Katie Evans wore a grin that would light a room. "Now that's a project I could get involved in. Bathrooms and kitchens are my thing. Hank here will make sure we're true to the historical architecture. When can we take a look? I can't wait."

"Right now. Whenever you're ready." Tommie's smile came from relief.

"We'd actually just stepped inside to talk to Ms. Lynn about the renovations to the Book Basket," Hank said. "How about we meet you at the manor in about two hours?"

"Thank you so much. I'll be waiting for you." Tommie stepped back and opened the door, a tiny flame of hope sparking in her heart. "I'll be waiting. And thank you."

THE ALLEY of beautiful hardwoods that lined the drive to Loftus Manor swayed in the wind, leaves scattering in all directions as Harley Jones sipped a cup of coffee on the front porch of his cottage. He stood and rolled his heavily muscled shoulders. He loved physical work, and Loftus Manor gave him plenty of opportunity.

The small stone house had originally been the groundskeeper's cottage when Loftus Manor was new and filled with Loftus relatives. Harley had been in the cottage for the past five years and considered himself the guardian and groundskeeper, though with the unfortunate death of Samuel Loftus, he wasn't certain what his future might be.

He and the old man had come to an agreement—one that suited them both. Harley, who had no love for the company of others, stayed in the cottage and kept an eye on the manor and on Samuel. Harley took care of the small repairs that Samuel was interested in making, running errands to town, laying in supplies, and sometimes spending an evening over a few whiskeys and the old man's rambling stories about the clever design of Loftus Manor and the rich heritage of the house and name. Samuel Loftus could spin a grand tale and he was a fine raconteur once he gave himself to an audience.

Finishing the last swallow of hot, black coffee, Harley walked to the edge of his porch. He had a clear view of the big house, and for a moment he thought he saw someone glide past an upstairs window. But that was impossible, a trick of the light striking the windowpane. He smiled to himself. Samuel had loved to share ghost stories about the house, tales of lovelorn swains and pretty ladies with spirit. Most of the ghost stories centered around tragedy and the revenants of those lost ones left to linger about the house and property.

Harley stared up at the house. It was too far away for him to be certain of anything, but it could only be an illusion, a curtain blowing or something of that nature. Since Samuel's death, Harley had only been in the cottage or else walking the grounds of the house. He'd avoided the manor. Not a living soul had been on the premises after the police finished their investigation of Samuel's suicide.

His smile deepened. Maybe it was Samuel, checking it over before his great-great niece, the heir, a woman from California, arrived. He knew next to nothing about her, except that she was in her twenties and hailed from the West Coast.

He gave the house one last look and turned to go inside. Changes were coming, and he wasn't a man who liked change. Any change. He'd been content here in Wetumpka for the past five years. He'd found all he needed—a job that required honest work, isolation, the company of a decent man when he needed it, and no one prying into his business, into his past. He'd had a good run at Loftus Manor and Samuel's suicide was the only regret he carried. Time to move on. But he wasn't done yet. Not totally.

The one thing he had vowed to Samuel was to keep the integrity of the manor intact. That had been important to Samuel, that the house and the many architectural wonders incorporated into the estate be honored and respected. Harley meant to make that clear to the young heir, should she indicate she wanted to make drastic changes. Harley would keep his word to Samuel and then move on down the road.

There had already been attempts by local developers to get their hands on the property to create a high-end development on the Coosa River. Paul Rider, a local real estate mogul, had made several offers on the property which, before his death, Samuel had emphatically turned down. Harley could hear Samuel talking—"They want to turn my home into a club house for a bunch of fools and rape my land to build houses for their worthless spawn."

Samuel had been a man of strong opinions, and that scenario wasn't going to happen. Harley had given his word that he would do all in his power to prevent such a thing. Loftus Manor would change with a new owner, no doubt, but the land would not be parceled off and subdivided if Harley could stop it.

The sound of a car motor made him step back out on the porch and walk to the edge where he had a clear view of the driveway curving up to the road. The cottage was situated so that he could make certain no one came or went without his knowledge. When the small red car came down the drive, he knew it was the heiress, the woman who had inherited the estate. He put his coffee cup in the house and started the walk down the driveway to meet her.

He caught sight of her, a slender brunette, as she bent over the car's trunk, tugging at a suitcase. She was a curvy and fit woman, an observation he was smart enough to realize would only earn her ire if she suspected his thoughts.

"Can I help?" he asked.

The woman startled and bumped her head on the top of the hatchback. "Damn!"

She spun around, her hazel eyes wide with surprise.

"Sorry. I didn't mean to sneak up on you." He motioned for

her to step back and he lifted her suitcase out. The woman must have packed bricks. The suitcase weighed a ton.

"Sorry." She rubbed the top of her head. "I didn't hear you."

"Let me get this to the door for you." He hefted the suitcase and led the way. After she'd unlocked the door, he put it inside. "I'm Harley Jones. I helped Samuel with repairs and gardening."

She nodded. "Tommie Sykes. The attorney told me you were living in the cottage."

"That's right." She was pretty. He hadn't anticipated that. "I'll let you settle in." He took a step back.

"I'm expecting some visitors. If they stop at the cottage, could you send them on down here?"

"Sure."

"I hear the property extends all the way to the Coosa River," she said. "Do you know where I might get a map?"

"Samuel had some in his office. If you go poking around the property, steer clear of the river until you're more familiar. There are some treacherous currents." His tone was brusquer than he intended, but it was better for her to be warned. The Coosa, which was not far from the house, looked deceptively calm, but after a rain it could be dangerous.

He saw her shoulders stiffen slightly. She'd taken offense at his comment. "Thank you, Mr. Jones. I'll take your warning to heart. Now if you'll excuse me, I have a lot to do." She closed the door firmly and he was left standing on the stoop.

Yep. There were going to be a lot of changes coming along. And he didn't think he was going to like any of them.

CHAPTER TWO

Tommie stood at the door for several minutes, thinking about the encounter she'd just had with Harley Jones. She'd heard from the lawyer who handled her uncle's estate that Harley lived in the groundskeeper cottage and a young woman, Nina Ahearn, who'd been her great-great-uncle's caregiver, had also lived on the premises. She'd had a suite of rooms in the manor. The lawyer had given Tommie the idea that he viewed both Harley Jones and Nina Ahern as freeloaders.

Harley Jones didn't *look* like a freeloader. He had the body of a man who enjoyed physical labor and did a lot of it. Nina Ahearn, she hadn't met and was very glad the lawyer had moved the woman out of the house after Samuel's death. From what Tommie understood, Nina had rented an apartment in town. One less thing to worry about.

Tommie dragged her suitcase to the stairwell that was a true architectural wonder. She put aside her forebodings and fears long enough to really look around the manor. It was dark and not well kept, but it was also incredible. The tile in the foyer was exquisite. And the furniture, what wasn't hidden beneath drop cloths, was impressive. Heavy mahogany wood with scrolls and adornments that perfectly matched the attitude of the house.

When she stepped back from her suitcase, she saw the portrait of Samuel Loftus hanging above the mantle. The piercing eyes caught and held her. It was almost as if he were assessing her—and possibly finding her lacking. A very disconcerting sensation. She suddenly felt overwhelmed by her dream of creating an inn. She'd spent her late teens and early twenties learning to craft jewelry. She'd worked for some fine jewelry makers and had even developed her own style in creating rings, pendants, and bracelets. But working with precious stones and metals wasn't preparation for running an inn. Was she a fool to think she could manage this?

She wandered over to her uncle's portrait. He didn't look like a man who would kill himself in a moment of depression or loneliness. There was steel in his gaze, determination. And he'd been alone in the house for many years since the death of his wife, Rachel. The little bit of research Tommie had done, supplemented by what the lawyer was able to tell her, indicated that Samuel and Rachel had been childless.

The couple had taken up residence in the house in the 1970s, and while they'd entertained on holidays, they mostly lived quietly. As far as Tommie could tell, they'd never really developed close friendships in the town or region, though Samuel was a contributor to several charities centered around education. Rachel had financially supported some arts programs and donated to a literacy program at Draper State Prison in nearby Elmore. Other than that, the lawyer had little information for Tommie.

Tommie pulled some of the throw sheets off a beautiful brocade sofa, club chairs, and end tables built with grace and strength. She wondered if Rachel, who'd died in 1999, had decorated the house or if Samuel had hired someone.

Loftus Manor had some incredible details and beauty, but it was also an unwelcoming place. She'd have to change that if she intended to make a go of an inn, and she had some ideas.

She looked up at the portrait of her relative. "I'll do my best, Samuel. I'll have to change some things. I hope you don't mind."

She checked her watch. The Evanses would be at least another hour out. She could unpack her bag and haul her belongings, an armload at a time, up the stairs to one of the second-floor bedrooms or she could take a walk around the grounds. She admitted she was curious to see how well Harley Jones did his reputed job of groundskeeper.

Physically, he was an impressive guy. Tall, fit, confident, he'd had no trouble offering his advice or opinion. She wasn't normally a suspicious person, but she'd caught a hint of proprietary emotion in his behavior. She reluctantly accepted that it was also possible she was super sensitive because she felt like an outsider coming to town to benefit from the death of a man she'd never met.

Deciding to split the difference between unpacking and exploring, she hauled underwear and shirts up to her bedroom. When she'd lightened the suitcase some, she checked her watch. She still had time for a quick look at the Coosa and the beautiful October day was made for a person to be outside.

She grabbed some old jeans, a sweatshirt, and hiking boots, changed quickly, and slipped out the back door. Her cell phone had a compass, and she knew the general direction of the river, but as it turned out, she easily found a path that led in that direction. The going was a little hilly, but the trail was clear. She'd have plenty of time to scope out the river and get back.

When she made it to the edge of the woods, she turned back

for a glimpse of Loftus Manor. The stone edifice peeked through the trees, almost an image of a fairy tale castle. The house was beautifully proportioned, gracious and mysterious. She lingered a moment, drinking in the beauty of this place—her home now! It was almost too much to take in.

She shifted her weight back on to her heels, turned, and stopped. Someone stood in an upstairs window. Her heart pulsed, giving her a feeling of lightheadedness. The leaves on the tree branches danced in a light breeze right in front of her eyes, blocking the house. Stepping forward, out of the trees, she stared up at the window which now was empty and blank.

"I saw it." She spoke aloud to give herself confidence. "I saw someone up there."

Plans to visit the river disappeared. She started back toward the house at a jog. Whoever was in her house, she was going to find them and have them arrested for trespassing. She'd been warned by her uncle's lawyer that Harley Jones might somehow feel he had a grubstake in the groundskeeper's cottage, and that Nina Ahearn had been adamant that Samuel had intended to leave her the right to live in the manor as long as she wished. Legally, neither of those claims would ever hold up. But someone was in the house, and that someone had no right to be there.

She covered the wide expanse of lawn and used her key to open the front door, which was still locked, as she'd left it. Which meant the intruder had come in the back door. She rushed to the kitchen entrance to find it also locked, as were the double doors leading to the patio and garden and the back exit that had once been used by servants.

There was no sign of a forced entry. Which could only mean the intruder had come in through a window—or had a key. She had a choice. She could check the windows or go upstairs and search for whoever was in the house.

She picked up a poker from the fireplace and started up the stairs, moving as quietly as she could. She didn't want a real confrontation, only to scare the intruder out of the house and to possibly get a good look at him so she could describe them to the authorities.

When she made it to the top of the stairs, she paused to listen. The old house creaked and sighed in the October wind, but she didn't hear footsteps or anything that would indicate a human presence. Yet she'd seen someone in that window. A torso, arms, and a head—she'd seen that clearly.

Had the intruder had time to escape?

It was possible if he'd realized he'd been spotted. But Tommie knew she'd been almost hidden by the trees. She eased down the hallway trying to breathe deeply yet silently. She held the poker in one hand, raised and ready to swing if necessary.

All the bedroom doors were closed and though she listened at each one, she didn't hear anything. She made her way to the end of the hallway and stopped. This was her bedroom, the large suite at the end of the hall that included a small sitting room, a bedroom, a full bath, and a spacious closet. Because it was on the end of the hall, there were abundant windows and light. Why would someone be in her room? She'd only moved up a few of her personal clothes. The bulk of her belongings hadn't arrived from California yet, so there was nothing to plunder in her personal possessions.

She made it to the door and put her hand on the handle. To her utter horror, the doorknob began to turn, of its own volition, beneath her hand. She pushed the door open, leaped backwards, and tripped on a hall runner. As she fell, a wild scream tore from her throat.

Below her she heard the front door crash open and the sound of pounding feet on the stairs. She looked into the open bedroom and saw absolutely nothing. The sitting room was empty. As far as she could tell, so was the bedroom beyond.

Running footsteps vibrated behind her and she turned to see Harley Jones racing toward her, his face grim with tension.

"Are you okay?" He knelt beside her, feeling her arms and legs for broken bones. "What happened?"

"Someone was in my room. I reached for the doorknob and it twisted under my hand. Someone was on the other side of the door, turning it."

His worried eyes raked over her. "Are you hurt?"

She shook her head and slowly started to her feet. He grabbed her arm and gave her a lift, as if she weighed nothing. He was a powerful man.

"Stay here," he ordered before he headed into her rooms, leaving her to stand in the hallway as if she were a child.

The minute she got her muscles to respond to her command, she went right after him. She was grateful he'd arrived, but she didn't need a white knight to the rescue. She'd been looking after herself for a long time.

She found him at the very window where she'd seen movement. He was looking down at the ground below. When she stepped beside him, he eased over to give her room.

"Company's coming," he said, nodding down the driveway where a Mercedes sedan was passing the groundskeeper's cottage. He shook the curtain back into place.

"That's the renovation team," Tommie said. "They're coming to look at the manor to see about helping me make some repairs and change it into an inn."

"An inn? Like a place where people stay overnight?"

She gave him a curious look. "Exactly like that. I think it's a perfect property. We can do some kayaking on the river, build some nature trails through the woods, create a real destination place for people who love the outdoors."

"You can't do that." Harley was firm. "You can't turn this into a commercial business. Samuel would hate that."

At first, she was taken aback at the passion of his response, but then Tommie's temper hit high. "I am doing it. And you have no say-so at all in how I manage this property. In case you didn't get the word, I inherited. I have complete and total say-so."

"And you should respect the wishes of the man who left you this gift." Harley's gaze was unflinching.

"If Samuel had been so concerned about what happened to Loftus Manor, perhaps he should have left me a game plan and money to fund it. Right now, I own a huge old house that needs repairs and renovations. That's a liability. Unless I can turn it around and make a way to generate a living here, I'll have to sell it. Wonder what will happen then? Maybe a new subdivision for the elite?"

Her last remark hit home, and she saw Harley blanch. Good, she thought with satisfaction. How dare he tell her what she could and couldn't do with her inheritance. And he was acting like she intended to turn Loftus Manor into a brothel or some such unsavory establishment. The man had a real attitude, and she wondered if it was because she was a single woman. Some men had issues with women who took charge and made changes. She'd learned that hard lesson via experience. Obviously, Harley Jones thought he had some say in what happened to Loftus Manor. He was wrong!

Harley brushed past her, but then stopped, visibly collected himself, and turned back. He took a deep breath and blew it out before he spoke. "You're right. I apologize. I was thinking about what Samuel would want and not the practicality of what you might need to do. Loftus Manor does need a lot of work and unless you have a lot of money, the place will fall into ruin. I'm sorry I spoke out of turn."

Loud knocking on the front door made Harley turn away.

Before she could answer, Harley moved rapidly down the stairs and opened the front door to Tammy Lynn. A black cat that looked like the one she'd seen at the bookstore shot inside the manor and headed up the stairs. The cat darted past Tommie and disappeared in her room. Tommie shook her head as she trotted down the stairs to greet her guests. She didn't have time to search for the cat or even assimilate Harley's unexpected apology. She had to focus on one thing and one thing only. The success of her project relied on her ability to get the dynamic renovation duo on board with her remodeling concept.

"Welcome! Thank you for coming," she said.

"Harley, it's good to see you," Tammy said to the groundskeeper. "Let me introduce Katie and Hank Evans. They're with the renovation show on HGTV. I'm sure you've heard the commotion all over town. They're working on a number of Wetumpka historical home and business sites."

"The whole town is talking about the make-over TV show and how wonderful you two are," Harley said. "Your work speaks for itself." He glanced over at Tommie. "I'm a stick in the mud, but change is inevitable, I suppose. I'll leave you to your renovation plans and I'd better head back to the cottage. I've got some gardening to do. If you'd like to look around inside the cottage, I'll leave the door unlocked for you."

Tommie watched Harley walk down the driveway with a sense of relief. He'd been closer to her uncle than anyone else she knew, and for some reason it was important to her that he understand her circumstances and approve of her plans for the manor.

She realized her guests were waiting at the door. "Come in," Tommie said. "Why don't I give you a tour? In the process, maybe we'll find that cat that ran upstairs. If he gets lost in this house, we might not find him for weeks."

"That's my cat," Tammy said. "His name is Trouble. He's something of a detective." She smiled so that Tommie didn't know if she was teasing her or not.

"A detective cat?"

"It's a long story," Tammy said. "I think it's best to let Trouble show you what he can do. He's solved a number of crimes. And don't worry about him. He can take care of himself —and he may surprise you with some of the things he finds."

Tommie laughed. "Really?" Had she fallen down Alice's rabbit hole? Was the whole town of Wetumpka a little mad? First Harley, doing such a one-eighty, and now the bookstore owner with a black cat detective.

"Absolutely," Tammy said. "In fact, when we left the store to come here, Trouble insisted on coming with us. It was almost like he knew there was a crime to solve at the end of the journey. He has an uncanny sense about these things. And now," she shrugged, "he's off poking around the house. Is there a mystery here?"

The first thing that came to Tommie's mind was the shadowy figure she'd seen in her bedroom window, but she didn't want to go there, not when she so desperately needed the renovators to agree to the project. "The only mystery here is why my uncle left this beautiful place to me." Tommie was still a little shocked at her inheritance and all that it meant.

Tammy put a hand on her shoulder. "I don't know you at all, but the fact that you've already come up with a plan on how to keep Loftus Manor tells me exactly why Samuel left the property to you. He knew you'd love and take care of the estate. Even

Harley didn't kick up too much fuss," Tammy said with a knowing grin. "We all know Harley is a little gruff and abrasive, but I think he's a good guy. He cared a lot about Samuel. I guess living here for a while, he cares about this place too."

"I wouldn't want to do anything to displease my uncle, but I have to be able to make the property pay for the upkeep and care." Tommie wanted everyone to be clear about the future— Loftus Manor had to pay its own way.

"We understand," Tammy said, "and I'm sure Samuel does too. If his ghost is here, haunting the estate along with all the other ghosts he loved talking about, I'm sure he'll let you know if your plans displease him."

Tommie stepped back before she could stop herself. The one thing she really didn't want in her life was a disapproving ghost.

CHAPTER THREE

*W*atching Tommie's reaction to my mistress's teasing remark tells me that our host is a bit unnerved. Something is going on at Loftus Manor. I knew it! And I suspect that Harley Jones, our erstwhile groundskeeper, is aware of something too. That's why I've rushed to the windows on the south side of the house. He's walking into the woods right now, and he seems to have something on his mind. My Sherlockian sixth sense is tingling. The tosser is up to something, and I need to find out what.

He's poking around in some shrubbery as if he's looking for something. I wonder if he's dropped something or if he's looking for evidence like footprints.

I have to figure out a way to convince my humanoid to allow me to stay here in Loftus Manor for the night. Or maybe two. There's something going on that isn't quite right. There was tension between Tommie Sykes, who I shall dub the Lofton Lass, and the brawny groundskeeper. And not the good kind of tension between a man and a woman, but something more than that. She looks absolutely panicky, though she's covering it very well. If he was unchivalrous toward her, he will pay!

Now spying on him from my window perch, he seems as unsettled as

Tommie. He's examining some branches and scouring the ground. I believe he's looking for evidence of an intruder. Now that's an interesting thought. I'll snoop around later, but right now I want to listen to the conversation among the bipeds. I'll gather what facts I can.

HARLEY HELD the tattered leaves in his hand. The branches of the lilac were definitely snapped. Someone had gone that way, and it wasn't the heiress. She'd been on the trail to the river, not hidden in foliage. This was evidence of someone else. He thought back through the sequence of events.

He'd seen Tommie looking back at the house with concentration. Suddenly she was tearing across the lawn and she rushed inside. Curious, he'd walked up the drive and was standing at the front door, which was luckily open, when he heard her scream. That's when he'd hurried inside to help her. When he'd seen her stretched out on the hall runner, he'd been afraid she was injured. Thank goodness she'd only fallen backwards. He'd quickly scanned the bedroom and parlor and saw nothing out of order. If someone had been in there, they'd found a good hiding place. But how had they managed to twist the doorknob *and* then make an escape with the Sykes woman in the hall—which was the only means of exit.

It was impossible. How had a person managed to get out of the manor and into the edge of the woods so quickly? If this intruder was even real. Which made him wonder how long Tommie would stay in the manor alone if she was prone to spooks and fancies. Loftus Manor was big and old and there were plenty of tales about the house. It had been empty for years before Samuel and his wife Rachel had moved there and brought it back to life. Old, abandoned houses—or houses with a reclusive bachelor resident for that matter—often spawned ghost stories and legends, and Loftus House was very attractive to the teenagers of the area who loved to sneak onto the property, especially at Halloween, to search for ghost and ghoulies. If Tommie Sykes was scared, her life was going to be miserable, and that, more than any other reason, was why he'd softened his objection to any changes she might make on the property. She'd made a good point when she'd said the manor had to pay its own way.

Harley checked the ground for footprints, but it hadn't rained in several days and the soil was hard and dry. If someone had been there, watching the house, he couldn't tell for certain. Then why wouldn't the nagging sensation of danger go away? Harley walked deeper into the woods but found nothing else he could label as physical evidence. What he had discovered was too nebulous. The broken branches and tattered leaves could be as simple as an animal passing through the property.

The one thing he didn't want was a sense of responsibility for the new owner of Loftus Manor. Tommie Sykes was brave and foolish. She'd come across country with no idea how she'd live or manage. Women were often more trouble than anything else and this one clearly had a lot to learn about her inheritance, her family, and the Wetumpka area. Loftus Manor was one of the rare ancestral homes in the Southeastern portion of the United States. It had been built when Alabama was little more than a backwater. The floorplan of the house had been brought over with the Loftus settlers and reflected the grand design of Anglo-Saxon landholders. Samuel had been so proud of the house and of his family name. As far as Harley could tell, Tommie was unaware of all that Loftus Manor had symbolized for Samuel. Truthfully, now that Samuel was gone, maybe none of it mattered.

He walked back down the driveway, headed to his house.

When he turned around to stare at the regal old home, he stopped dead in his tracks. Someone was in the upstairs window —the very bedroom where Tommie Sykes was going to sleep.

He first assumed it was the renovators, the bookseller, or Tommie—until he saw Tommie and the group of visitors step outside on the patio. Each one was accounted for.

Samuel had told him all the ghost stories of the house, the hauntings, the strange bumps and rumblings that went on. Harley had written it off as Samuel's passion for a good tall tale or the settling of an old house. Now, though, the gooseflesh that moved down his arms told him otherwise.

Was there something to all the stories of ghosts wandering the premises? Had Samuel's death brought the shadows out? Or was there really someone in the house, and if so, what were their intentions?

As soon as the company cleared out and the heiress ran into town, he meant to search the premises from top to bottom. If someone—a real, physical someone—was slipping around Loftus Manor, he intended to put a stop to it.

Movement in a downstairs window caught his eye and he saw a black cat sitting there, staring directly at him, almost as if the cat were keeping an eye on him. Ridiculous. Cats were smart, but they were also vain. They were self-motivated, as far as he could tell. And he hoped to goodness the cat didn't belong to the heiress. Samuel had once had two very fine dogs, but no cats.

Harley was struck again by a swift stab of loss. He missed Samuel and couldn't understand why he'd killed himself. He'd been in fair health, mostly able to see after his own needs. What Samuel couldn't do for himself, the hired caretaker had seen to. Nina Ahearn. She was a pretty, young woman who volubly admitted to having a real tender heart for the elderly.

He brushed all his worries aside and entered the

groundskeeper's cottage, a place he normally called home. Now it was time to think about packing up and moving on. Where would he go? Anywhere and everywhere. He was beholden to no one, and that was just the way he liked it.

"THE COMMUNITY ROOMS on the main floor are in great shape," Katie Evans said after they'd explored a portion of Loftus Manor. "Hank says the house is structurally in excellent shape. And that library is incredible. It's almost like a museum to the past. I have some suggestions for dining areas if you intend to fill all ten of the bedrooms with guests. And the parlors are almost perfect as they stand. The fireplaces and chimneys will have to be checked for safety, but the furniture, the whole decor—I wouldn't change a thing."

"Except for the kitchen," everyone said in unison.

"That's a definite remodel," Katie said, looking at her husband for confirmation.

"We'll need to gut the room," Hank agreed. "Bring in some professional equipment like a range, refrigerator, and freezer. Expand the sink situation. There are a number of design choices these days that will be in keeping with a vintage look even though it's all new, highly efficient equipment." He waved his hands in the air as he talked. "In fact, I'm thinking we could take in a portion of the formal dining room to enlarge the kitchen and perhaps enclose the back patio with a glass sunroom to make more space for serving meals. *If* you want to include meals."

"I do," Tommie said. "I like to cook. It's a pleasure for me." She forced a smile. Just thinking about all the changes made her head ache. Could she really do this? Would she be able to make a go of it? Running an inn was a big, big job, and she didn't want to squander all of her inheritance on the renovations only to discover she didn't have the grit to make it work. But she wanted to live at Loftus Manor. She wanted to bring life back to it. Maybe because it had seen such sadness. She almost smiled at her fancy, as if she'd developed some kind of telepathic link to the old house.

"We'll work up an estimate," Hank said. "If you allow us to film the whole renovation process and feature our work on TV, it'll reduce the cost substantially."

"Sure," Tommie said. "I'd like to document the changes. I want to preserve this house, but I can't do it unless I can figure out a way to make it profitable."

Katie ran a hand over the elegant railing on the stairs. The wood was intricately carved with trailing ivy and hidden fairies. "It is a lovely place. Truly magical in some ways. Such history. But houses have to be modernized or no one wants to live in them. Imagine trying to live without an indoor bathroom. When this house was first built, there was no such thing. Changes were made to accommodate. You have every right to make the changes that will allow you to live—and thrive here."

"Thanks." Tommie realized she must have been wearing her heart on her sleeve for Katie to read her concerns so clearly. She turned to the bookseller. "I don't want to sound morbid, but could you show me where my great-great uncle died?"

"Are you sure?" Tammy asked. "It may not be the best thing to remember about the house."

"I'm sure. I never even spoke to Uncle Samuel. I don't know how he knew I was alive. But he did, and he took pains to see I got an inheritance. I'd like to know what happened."

"Okay." Tammy motioned them toward the back of the house where a small very masculine parlor was found. Two chairs were arranged in front of a fireplace with recent ashes. There was a chess board set up, a game in progress. On another table a backgammon game rested.

"He liked to play chess?" Tommie asked.

"That's what I heard. Harley spent a lot of time with him, passing the hours and talking." Tammy kept her tone level and matter-of-fact.

"And drinking." Tommie pointed to a full wet bar with two dirty glasses still there.

"Never begrudge a man a toddy in the evening," Hank said, giving a wink that made Tommie smile. She really liked the renovators.

"He was in here." Tammy led them to a small alcove where a beautiful old dresser stood, the top covered in family photos. "He hung himself from the lintel. It seems he just stepped off a chair."

"Could it have been an accident?" Katie asked as they all stood silently at the entrance to the little alcove.

"I don't think so," Tammy said, "but who knows?"

"Was my great-great uncle in poor health?" Tommie asked.

"He was eighty plus," Tammy said. "I didn't know Samuel all that well. He'd occasionally send Harley to pick up some books he'd ordered, but he had full time care here and no real need to come into town. He was something of a recluse, like Harley. I think that's why they got along so well. The only time Samuel really came out of his shell was when he was telling a story, and he was truly marvelous at that. And he helped people in the community, but all of that he kept under wraps. He was a kind man."

"Was he viewed as a weirdo?" Tommie asked.

Tammy smiled. "A little. Anyone who defies the herd mentality and lives alone is often viewed as different. That always breeds rumors. Like it does for Harley. Neither of them cared for parties or crowds or sometimes even conversation. But they liked each other, from all accounts. I believe Harley was very fond of Samuel. But you'd get better answers if you asked Harley."

"He doesn't seem to be a man much inclined to conversation," Tommie said.

Tammy laughed out loud. "An understatement. But you know, Tommie, it isn't a man's manners but his heart that truly matters."

"Let's check out the bedrooms upstairs and see what will need to be done, and then, maybe you can prepare an estimate for me," Tommie said to the Evans. "Now that we're talking about the work. I'm eager to see if this is doable."

"What about heat and cool?" Katie asked.

"We can install those ductless units for the most part," Hank said. "Work them into the design of the woodwork." He looked up. "I'd hate to do anything to the ceilings if we had to install ductwork."

"Good plan," Tommie said, smiling big. "I like the way you think. It's important to me to keep the house as original as possible while adding the things every guest would expect to find."

CHAPTER FOUR

*I*t was with some reluctance that Tommie watched as her guests prepared to leave. She hadn't even unpacked the rest of her suitcase. The house was so big. And so empty. And she would be alone there when the renovators and Tammy were gone.

The redheaded bookseller put a supportive hand on her shoulder. "You'll adjust, or perhaps you'll want to hire someone to live on the grounds to help you with all of this." She smiled. "Some company."

The black cat, who'd taken off exploring the house, was suddenly back at Tommie's feet. When the bookseller bent to pick up her pet, the cat scooted away. He stopped on the first step of the beautiful staircase and sat down.

"Meow."

"Oh, dear," Tammy said. "Trouble wants to stay here with you." Her kind eyes were deadly serious.

"The cat wants to stay here?" Tommie asked.

"Oh, not permanently. Just for a while. You might consider letting him. Trouble has a sixth sense about things."

"What kind of things?" Tommie asked. The creepy sensation of someone roaming around the house touched her again. She glanced over at the cat who blinked his huge green eyes three times, as if communicating in some kind of code.

"Oh, mysteries. He really is a cat detective. I wasn't making it up."

Tommie scoffed. "You're teasing me, right?"

"No, I'm not. I understand your reluctance to believe me. But Trouble has solved some pretty complicated mysteries, from stolen horses to art thefts."

Tommie glanced at the Evans, who looked as amused as she felt. "You're really serious?" she said to Trouble's owner.

"Deadly serious. Besides, he's good company and until you can find a human employee, he's a good friend to have on your side."

Tommie was about to refuse, but then she remembered the figure in the window. She'd seen it, no matter that it was impossible. "I've heard that cats have an ability to see ghosts. Is that true?"

Tammy shrugged. "I wouldn't doubt it. But just trust what he tries to tell you."

"Can he...talk?" Tommie felt like a fool for even asking.

"Not in human language but he has a way of getting his point across." Tammy shook her head. "And if there is anything untoward going on, he'll let you know."

"Untoward?" Tommie seized on the word. "Is there a reason I should be worried about that."

For the first time the bookseller looked concerned. "There's always talk about old houses. Nothing to it, but it can unsettle your nerves."

"What kind of talk?" Tommie didn't want to ask, but she had

to know if there was something more than the ghost stories Harley had already mentioned.

"That Loftus Manor is haunted."

Tommie tried not to react, but she couldn't help it. The image of someone standing in the window was too vivid. Too real. "Haunted by whom?"

"Oh, there are different stories. You should talk to Harley. He's been here for a few years. He'll know all the tales. Now we should get back to town. Would you like Trouble to stay?"

Tommie found herself nodding. "Please." She found the cat's steady stare directed at her yet again. He did seem...preternaturally smart, or at least focused.

"Call if you need us," Tammy said.

"Will do."

She closed the door and felt the emptiness of the house around her. It was a big place, and it seemed to echo. Because her imagination had been excited, she thought she heard someone shuffling about the second floor. She was about to laugh it off when the cat darted up the stairs as if he, too, heard something.

Loftus Manor is an elegant place. I can see where it would lend itself to a small inn and after listening to the talk about the nearness of the river, the potential for canoeing and kayaking, the development of the grounds with croquet and badminton, I can see this dream becoming a paying reality. But I have questions about Samuel Loftus's death. First, why has everyone seemingly accepted Samuel's suicide? Interesting. A man with no motive to kill himself, as far as we know. So why would a man hang himself? It's a question that begs an answer, and I'm just the cat to suss out some factoids.

Let's have a walkabout upstairs while Tommie busies herself moving her clothes from suitcase to bedroom dresser. Now would be a good time for that strong groundskeeper to show up. I need some time to read him. He's smart, and he's suspicious that all isn't right in this house, as am I. But is he the source of the disquiet? He's certainly had an opportunity to learn all about Loftus Manor, and this place has been his home for five years. Having a new owner show up with plans to change things must be very unpleasant. I wonder if Samuel left Harley the groundskeeper's cottage in the will. That's something I need to check into for sure.

Ah, the bedrooms are neat as pins. They need airing, and this is perfect weather to open the windows wide and let in the October sun and wind.

If I understood the living arrangements properly, there was also a caregiver dwelling here. One Nina Ahearn. Aha, I believe this must have been her bedroom. There is still the lingering scent of some perfume. The room is much more lived in, and the window air conditioner attests to a resident. I wonder if our Nancy Nurse left willingly or if she had some encouragement. I also wonder what she was doing the night Samuel allegedly took his own life. Yes, I say allegedly. I'm not at all convinced this was a suicide. I need to check medical records, see what drugs Samuel may have been taking, and determine the character of Harley Jones. My work is cut out for me. But first, I have need of a repast. It's been hours since I had breakfast, and my brain functions much better on a full stomach.

HARLEY WAS SPLITTING wood in the side yard of the manor when he felt someone watching him. It wasn't a sinister sensation—more of a tingle of alert that raced through his body. In Afghanistan he'd learned to listen to every signal his body gave. It was the only reason he'd come home alive when so many of his friends hadn't.

He put the ax down and turned around. Tommie stood with

her hand shielding her eyes from the bright afternoon sun. He'd wondered when she would make her way to him to ask about his residency at the manor. Would she push him to vacate the cottage? She had every right to, yet she'd failed to ask any questions about his arrangements or plans.

"Is there something I can do for you?" he asked.

"Yes. When you have time, I'd like to talk to you about the history of the house."

"I'm not connected to Loftus Manor in any way," Harley said, wiping the sweat from his forehead. "I just live here in the cottage and helped Samuel with the outside chores and gardening." He nodded to the wood. "I'm laying in a winter store of fuel for you."

"That's very thoughtful. Thank you."

"I promised Samuel I'd do what I could to help you settle in."

She blinked. "Uncle Samuel talked to you about me? I didn't think he knew anything. I was just the only relative he could locate."

Harley debated how to answer her question. Samuel had made it a point to know about Tommie Sykes—Harley believed he'd had her investigated—but was that something he really should share with her? Sometimes knowing too much did more harm than good.

"When he made his will, he tried to find out what he could," Harley said. "He wanted to be sure the person who took over Loftus Manor would love it like he did."

"So why didn't he just track me down and ask? I would have liked to know him. He was my great-great uncle, and I didn't know a thing about him. Not the first thing."

Her voice didn't hold bitterness, only regret, and Samuel realized she was missing that connection to family. She wanted to know Samuel, not just inherit from him.

"He only really completed his will recently. I was one of the witnesses, which is why I know the timing of it. He may have intended on inviting you here." He decided to fudge the truth just a little, for her feelings. "He talked about that."

"Was Uncle Samuel depressed?"

She was asking the right questions. Ones that Harley wanted answers to. "Not to me. He didn't seem to be distressed or depressed. I played a game of chess with him that evening, and he was just like normal. We had a glass of Scotch and talked. I built a fire for him. He said he was going to read a new novel and I left. I would never have left him alone if I'd thought he was...suicidal."

"Who found him?"

"His caregiver, Nina Ahearn. I heard her scream about seven o'clock that morning and I rushed inside. We managed to get him down, but it was too late. He was gone. Had been dead for a while, the coroner said."

"Nina lived in the house?"

Samuel nodded. "She seemed to take very good care of him, cooking the dishes he liked, laughing with him, spending time with him yet not crowding him."

"And where is Ms. Ahearn now?"

Again, he was impressed with her questions, her calm delivery, her desire to know the circumstances of her uncle's death—and the people who'd been around her uncle. Tommie Sykes was a pretty woman, but she was much more than looks. She had a brain and she used it. "She left shortly after your uncle's death and the reading of his will. He left her a small amount of money, and she said she needed to find a new client."

"I see."

"The coroner ruled suicide, Ms. Sykes. A few weeks later, the will was read, and what Nina said at the reading was that she wanted to be gone before the new owner arrived. That a chapter in her life had closed, and to stay at Loftus Manor would only make her sad." He hesitated before he added. "I could never get a good sense of what Nina was all about. She was a pretty woman, and living here, so isolated, must have been hard for her."

"And yet she did it willingly."

"True. And just so you know, I'm planning to leave too. I don't want you to feel you're going to have to push me out. My bond was with Samuel, not the cottage, though I love living here. You have plans and should have a clean slate to put them into action. I don't believe Samuel would approve of turning the manor into an inn, but as I understood the will, the place is yours and there are no restrictions on what you do with it and I really do understand financial necessity." He'd given it some thought. Some hard thought. "An inn is far better than a subdivision, which was his worst fear."

Tommie swallowed. "I wondered if perhaps he left the cottage to you. He seemed very fond of you."

"You've probably read the terms of the will, so you know I received some cash, but the property is yours without encumbrance." He forced a smile. "I wouldn't want to hamper you in any way."

"Please don't be in a rush to leave."

He was surprised by her request. He'd anticipated that she would be eager to see the backside of him.

"It's a very big house, and it's going to take some adjusting to. It's nice to know there's someone else on the property. We are a bit isolated."

"That's true."

"And I'd like to talk to you about Uncle Samuel and the house. I do have plans, but I want to always consider what he would have done. You're the only person who really spent any time with him. Maybe you can give me a glimpse of what he would think."

He nodded. "I can stay as long as you need me."

"Thank you." Her hands were balled into fists, and she squeezed and released them repeatedly. "Is Loftus Manor haunted?"

He couldn't help himself. He laughed out loud. "So you've heard the stories. You should know that your uncle was behind a lot of the stories about hauntings. He'd make up some fancy and then go to town to tell it to someone. He enjoyed that very much."

He was happy to see that Tommie laughed. "He sounds like so much fun."

Harley matched her smile with one of his own. "He could be. He was a real devil for pranks and mischief. Sometimes I thought he'd gone too far and Nina would quit, but he always talked her into forgiving him. He got me more than once, too, with some of his foolishness."

The sadness slipped over her features, and he was aware he'd told her something that made her miss a man she'd never known. He had some fun stories about her uncle he'd share with her, something to give her a sense of the man.

"Did you ever see a ghost here at Loftus Manor?" Tommie asked Harley.

"I have. I can't swear it was a ghost, but I've seen some strange things in the house and around the grounds here." He thought of the person—or the entity—he'd seen in the window. He'd been on the property for five years and he'd often had the sense someone was in the house or watching him, but he'd never really seen anyone. Until recently. Was the spirit of Samuel Loftus lingering in the manor?

Harley picked up the ax. "I'm happy to talk to you, but right now, I'm going to finish splitting this wood for you and taking it to the woodshed behind the house."

"I'll help," Tommie said. "I need to learn my way around."

Harley shrugged. He hadn't anticipated this move, but he found he didn't mind Tommie's company as much as he'd thought he would. When he loaded the farm wagon with the wood, she helped, working steadily beside him. As he began to pull the wagon around the back of the manor, he noticed the black cat sitting on the front steps watching them.

"You have a cat?" he asked.

"Temporarily. Tammy Lynn left Trouble here to watch over me." She laughed softly. "The cat is some kind of detective, or so she claims. To be honest, I'm glad he's staying a day or two. Until I get used to the house."

"Not a bad plan at all," Harley said. "I like cats. They're smart and independent and very clever. If I had to pick an animal to be a detective, it would be a cat. They see everything and owe their allegiance to no one."

"Are there mysteries to solve at Loftus Manor?"

Harley hesitated. "I don't know. I will tell you that I'm not completely sold on the idea that Samuel killed himself."

He felt her hand on his arm and he stopped to face her.

"Do you think my uncle was murdered?"

"I don't know what I think," he said. "But I wasn't satisfied that he harmed himself. Let me put it that way."

"The coroner's report said it was a self-inflicted injury."

"I know. If you don't mind, I'd like to see a copy of the report." He could see his request startled her, but she didn't balk.

"I'll ask the attorney for one. I'm meeting with Mr. Gordon

tomorrow. I was told that some real estate developer also wants to talk with me."

"Paul Rider?" Samuel was instantly on the alert.

"Yes, do you know him?" She walked beside him as he tugged the wood wagon. He glanced down at her—her head came only to his shoulder—and saw that her cheeks were red from exertion. She'd loaded her share of the wood. She wasn't a slacker. He realized that he had developed a tiny little grain of admiration for her, a woman coming to a rural area where she knew no one to start a new life.

"I've met Mr. Rider. He came out to talk to your uncle a couple of times, but Samuel ran him off. He didn't want to turn Loftus Manor into a private club with a housing development on the land."

They arrived at the woodshed before Tommie answered. "The lawyer, Mr. Gordon, set up the meeting. I'll hear him out, but I'm not interested in selling the manor. At least not right now."

Harley couldn't stop the grin that spread across his face. "I'm really glad to hear that. It's yours to do with as you please, but I know your uncle would be happy with your decision." Harley felt a sudden protectiveness, but he wasn't certain if it was for Tommie or for the old manor house. "I know you can't make any promises right now, but I'm glad to see you're going to try to keep the property intact."

"I am. I'm excited to see if I can make a go of it." She drew in a deep breath and straightened her shoulders. "It's intimidating, and I'm scared. But I'm going to try."

CHAPTER FIVE

Tommie dusted her hands together when they'd finished unloading the wood. She had a sense of satisfaction, though Harley had done all of the hard work gathering and splitting the oak. But the woodshed, which was spacious and well maintained, was nearly full now. She'd have plenty to burn through the winter, even if she had guests using fireplaces. Harley didn't halfway do a chore, he did it one hundred percent. He'd promised Samuel to fill the woodshed and full it would be.

The sun had dropped below the tree line, and the day was drawing to a close. Tommie looked up at Loftus Manor, an imposing stone building. She hadn't noticed the gargoyle water spouts near the roofline and she felt a shudder. Those gnarled and twisted creatures weren't her personal choice of décor, but she had some half-buried memories that the grotesques were supposed to be protectors of a place.

"Would you like me to start a fire for you?" Harley asked as they walked to the back door of the manor.

Tommie hesitated. "That would be helpful. It's been a while since I lived in a house with a fireplace."

Harley opened the backdoor and held it for her to enter. "Will you be staying in one of the parlors or the library or one of the bedrooms?" he asked.

"The little parlor that I think is called the morning room." It was the place that gave her the most comfort. The vastness of the library was too much, and Samuel's private study held memories, and she wasn't ready to go to bed.

"Samuel often worked in that room. The light in the morning is beautiful there."

"What did my uncle do for work?" Tommie really wanted to know more about Samuel. Each little tidbit was like a gift.

"He had some investments, and he corresponded with several people. He didn't have any use for computers and the internet. He did it the old-fashioned way and often asked me to take the letters to town to post."

They walked through the house and when they stepped into the morning room, Harley went to work lighting the fire. The logs were already set, indicating that this was a room her uncle used frequently. A store of wood was stacked in a brass rack beside the fireplace.

"Did he keep any of the letters he got as replies?" Tommie had a sudden image of curling up in front of the fire with her uncle's correspondence, learning about him through the letters he'd received. It would be like a step back in time, exploring a part of her family she knew little about.

Her mother had been her link to the Loftus name, but Florence Loftus Sykes had died when Tommie was only eight. She remembered her mother, but when her father remarried and Dee had become her stepmother, the Loftus connection had simply slipped away. There'd been no malevolent design or intention, it was just a natural progression. She'd grown up among her father's people, the Sykes, and Dee's family, the Hearndons.

There'd been no one to tell her the stories and history of the Loftus side.

"I don't know if he kept his correspondence or not," Harley said. "I mailed his letters, and I brought the mail up to the house from the box at the road. I don't really know what he did with any of it. He was a regular correspondent with several people, though."

"I hope I can find some letters. Just a glimpse into who my uncle was, what he cared about. What interested him." She sighed. "I must sound pathetic to you."

Harley's hand lifted for a moment but dropped back to his side. "Not at all. Family is everything. You learn that quickly enough when you've lost it. I hope you find things around here that will give you what you need. And don't forget the library. There may be some history of interest to you. I do know the Loftus name is Anglo-Saxon and it means a house with a loft or attic. It's a location name that dates back to the 7th Century. Samuel told me this, and he explained that when Loftus Manor was built, the architect had drawn the house with two floors. The Loftus in charge at the time, Rupert I believe, insisted on adding the attic, to honor the family name."

"Thank you for telling me that. I have a lot of study to do on my Loftus family connections, but I'm looking forward to it. I only wish I'd known about Samuel and had a chance to talk to him before he...." She looked away for a moment. "It's so sad that he was alone when he died."

She felt Harley's warm hand on her shoulder. "Samuel didn't strike me as a lonely man. His body was frail, but his mind was lively, and he followed a number of pursuits. I can't explain the hanging, but I'd like to look into some things, if you don't mind. I don't want to offend you or overstep your comfort zone."

Tommie was surprised at Harley's perceptive reading of her.

And she was also unprepared for the rush of gratitude she felt toward him. "I'd like to help you look into Samuel's death. Suicide is a choice some people make, and I can respect that. It's not that I want to invalidate his choice. I just want to be sure that's exactly what happened."

Harley extended his hand. "Deal?"

She put her palm against his, tightened her fingers, and shook. "Deal."

"Now I'll be going back to the cottage." He brought a business card from his pocket. "My number. Call me if you...see anything unusual." His clear gaze held hers for just a second longer than necessary.

"I will." She tucked the card in her jeans pocket.

"Cell phone reception isn't always great here," he warned her. "I don't know if the landline is still connected. If it isn't, you might look into getting one installed."

"Good advice." The last of the twilight was fleeing fast, a lavender overtone in the west. Full night was dropping around them like a curtain. She walked out on the porch with him to say goodnight and was struck by the beauty of the stars so much brighter than she'd seen in the big cities of California.

"I'll be off then." Harley went down the steps but turned back to face her.

"Tomorrow would you mind walking with me to the river?" she asked.

"I'd be glad to. I need to be sure the path is clear. Sometimes in the fall, dead limbs and things drop and I can point out to you some of the treacherous areas."

"At nine?"

"I'll meet you here on the porch." He turned and stepped into the night. She watched him for a moment before the darkness swallowed him.

Loftus Manor was isolated. There wasn't a light anywhere on the horizon. For a moment she felt as if she'd fallen into a void, but then she felt the pressure of the cat rubbing against her leg.

"Thank heavens you're here." She bent down and picked him up. She was really glad for the cat's company. As she was walking back to the parlor where the blazing fire had taken the chill off the room, she heard something on the second floor.

The cat stiffened in her arms and then leaped to the floor. Before she could do anything, he was sprinting up the stairs to the second floor. She only hesitated a second before she followed him.

THERE'S CLEARLY SOMEONE LOOSE in this house. I'm not imagining it, and neither is my Loftus Lass. My dad always made up nicknames for the damsels in distress he helped. I'll give it a try here, since the alliteration works so well.

I wish Tommie hadn't been so quick to dismiss the burly woodchopper. Wasn't it an ax-wielder who saved Little Red Riding Hood? And her grandmother? Honestly, I'd give a lot to have Harley and his ax sprinting up here beside me. To quote one of the wisest feline figures in literature, the Cowardly Lion, "I do believe in ghosts. I do believe in ghosts."

There's a scraping sound coming from the bedroom once used by Nina Ahearn. As if someone is pushing a piece of furniture. I see Tommie has followed me up here. She's scared, but she isn't going to duck out on me. That's good to know. I just don't know how effective she'd be in a fight. She's a little on the slender side. Then again, my very own Tammy Lynn is quite the scrapper though she doesn't look the part.

I move silently down the hallway toward the bedroom door. The Loftus Lass is following me, though she doesn't have the finely-honed skills of walking without making a sound that I have. I flick my tail at her to urge more caution.

When I get to the bedroom, I listen again. Now there is only silence from within the room. How is that possible?

Tommie slowly turns the doorknob and pushes the door. We step into the room, which is filled with velvety blackness. Tommie hits the light switch, and we step back in alarm. Someone has ransacked the room. Drawers are pulled from the dresser, the bed is torn apart, the knick-knacks set on the bedside table are on the floor.

"Who did this?" *Tommie asks.*

I don't have an answer for her, but I intend to find out. Of more importance, where did the intruder go? He, or she, was up here in this room. We both heard the noise. We were in the hallway almost instantaneously, so the intruder didn't leave by that exit. So how did he make his escape? The only possible answer is that our intruder is not of the flesh. Only a spirit could fade into stone walls and disappear. A little shiver runs down to the tip of my tail.

I check under the bed, in the closets, behind the drapes—nothing. I even jump on the mantle to see if I can trigger a secret panel. Tommie catches on to what I'm doing and moves beside me to press on the ornate woodwork of scrolls and carvings, hunting for a secret trigger. Nothing.

"Where the hell is the person who did this?" *Tommie said out loud.* "I won't be terrorized in my own home."

I notice the spots of red in her cheeks and the defiance in her eyes. She's a slip of a girl but she's more gristle than tenderloin. Good!

"Whoever was in here has to be around. I'm sick of this. Come on, Trouble. Let's find him."

But this isn't something she should tackle without a weapon. I snag the leg of her pants with my sharp claws and stop her from charging down the hallway. She's frankly amazed by my action, but she's smart enough to understand I want something.

I use my paw to pat the pocket of her jacket where she stashed Harley's phone number.

She reaches into the pocket, finds the card, and pulls it out. Doubt crosses her face, but I extend my claws just a little, to get her attention, then pat her other pocket where her phone is.

"You think I should call Harley Jones?"

That's right, little lassie. Dial that cell phone or knock him up or whatever it takes to get him down here to help search."

She's doing it. There she goes. And she's asking him to come back. Good plan. I can only hope that Harley will convince her to call the police. Super sleuth that I am, this needs to be reported.

CHAPTER SIX

*H*arley looked at the room and whistled. Someone had deliberately created havoc. "Looks like they were after something." He lifted the mattress that had been flung to the floor and put it back on the springs. "Or else it's someone who intends to upset you, make you afraid."

"I came to the same conclusion," Tommie said. She offered a wary smile. "The cat insisted I call you. Thank you for coming so quickly."

Harley's brows arched in surprise at her comment.

Tommie lifted her shoulders in an apologetic shrug.

He let his gaze drop to where the cat sat quietly studying him. "I'm happy to help, but as annoyed as I am by this mess, there's something more important. We have to find out how the intruder is getting in and out of the house. Is it possible there's an exit I don't know about? We were right near the back entrance while we unloaded the wood. We could have seen someone slipping in through the back entrance or the patio entrance. And the front was locked, right?"

"Yes. The house was locked tight when I went down to the

cottage to talk to you. I know people who live in the country don't always lock doors, but I spent too much time in San Francisco to be careless about something like that. I'm positive all of the doors were locked."

"I believe you. But if the person isn't going out through the front door or the back doors, how is he moving around the house so freely?" He knew the answer that was on Tommie's mind. He could see it, the fear and anxiety. Ghosts. That was the only answer that seemed possible—yet he was nowhere near ready to believe all the old creepy tales about Loftus Manor were real. Samuel had delighted in telling them—and, Harley had no doubt, making them up. But Harley wasn't a man who bought into unhappy spirits walking the halls.

Tommie took a deep breath. "There's a back entrance to the second floor through the servants' quarters but it's locked with a key and a dead bolt on the inside."

"Let me check the windows." Harley put action to his words.

He hadn't said anything to Tommie, but he was concerned for her. Someone was messing with her—or worse. He didn't know if it was an attempt to frighten her or something more sinister. His thoughts immediately turned to Paul Rider, the developer. The man had been relentless in his pursuit of buying Loftus Manor and the surrounding acreage. No matter how many times Samuel had told him no, he kept coming back with offers. He'd been pushy and aggressive, and Harley wouldn't put it past the man to try to frighten Tommie into selling, though how he could manage a disappearing act was beyond Harley.

He didn't have a much better opinion of Britt Gordon, the lawyer who'd handled Samuel's affairs. There was a long family connection between the Gordons and the Loftuses, but since Harley wasn't blood kin, he had a completely different take on the lawyer. One word summed it up: shyster. Harley didn't trust him as far as he could throw him.

He made his way around the entire first floor, finding all of the windows locked. So how was this mysterious intruder gaining access to and then exiting the house?

He realized the black cat was trailing after him, watching him as if he knew exactly what Harley was up to.

"Meow." The cat sat at his feet and looked up.

"Kitty, kitty." Harley bent down to stroke the sleek black fur. The animal was healthy and fit, and there was something about him that made Harley think he was above average in intelligence. When he finished his rounds, he picked up the cat and carried him to Tommie in the morning room where she offered him a drink. "Maybe you should get a watch dog." His suggestion was light-hearted, but he meant it.

Trouble jumped to the floor and Harley watched as the cat sauntered out of the room and disappeared in the hallway.

"Maybe when I'm settled I will. I'd actually love a dog, but for right now, Trouble is what I have. Tammy Lynn swears by him." She sipped the whiskey.

"I've never heard of a mystery-solving cat, but I'm not going to dispute the possibility." There was something about the cat that made Harley hesitate to mock him.

"Meow!" The cry came from the direction of the stairs.

Harley poked his head out of the little sitting room where Tommie had settled into a cozy club chair in front of the fire that blazed merrily. "You stay put. I'll see what Trouble wants."

"Probably food. Tammy said he's really finicky. Something of a gourmand." She smiled and Harley felt that at last she was loosening up around him, giving him a chance to be a friend. "She brought a container of food for him almost as if she knew he was going to stay with me."

Trouble meowed loudly again, and then hissed, a sound that echoed in the big old house.

"I'll be right back," Harley said.

But the sound of Trouble's hissing had Tommie out of her chair and following after Harley in search of the cat.

The knock that came at the front door startled them both.

"Expecting company?" Harley asked her.

"No." She stepped forward to accompany Harley to the door where Trouble waited, his back arched. "Whoever it is, Trouble doesn't like them."

"Something to keep in mind," Harley said as he stepped to the side so Tommie could answer the door.

THE WOMAN STANDING on the front porch was so unexpected that Tommie simply stared at her. She was blond and perfectly made up and dressed like a big city businesswoman. She even carried a small briefcase.

"May I come in?" the woman asked, not bothering to hide her curiosity about the house. She peeked around Tommie and Harley. When she saw the cat, a flicker of disgust crossed her features.

"Who are you?" Harley finally asked the pertinent question.

"Odell Rains."

The name meant nothing to Tommie, and she shrugged when Harley looked at her. "How can we help you, Ms. Rains?"

"You can give me my share of the inheritance. Samuel was my father."

Tommie's reaction was classic shock—she was momentarily stunned. She stepped back a half step and simply stared at the woman. Harley eased closer to her. When she didn't speak, he did. "Samuel and Rachel never had children." Tommie realized he was far better versed in Loftus family affairs than she was.

"That's your opinion, and your opinion doesn't concern me," the woman said. "My mother is Lucinda Rains. I'm Samuel's bastard child." Her smile was neither warm nor friendly. "I'm here to collect what's mine."

THE ONLY THING *we need now is some dramatic music and the director to shout, "Cut! Print that." Cruella de Vil has entered the building and she's going to kill every single puppy to get that coat she wants.*

This woman is physically quite attractive, but I smell menace all over her. She's come to cause trouble for the Loftus Lass, and she means to do it. The legal front will be her first attack. After that, I wouldn't put anything past her. Not even hiring someone to break into Loftus Manor in an attempt to drive Tommie out. And how strange that she appears just after we hear something in the house and find a room ransacked. This woman is bad news.

Let me see what I can deduce about her. My father, Familiar the black cat detective, and Benedict Cumberbatch as Sherlock Holmes always tout deduction. Rational thought and deduction. It's in the details that others fail to observe that we find our answers.

She is very poised and calm, coming to lay claim to something that isn't hers. Either she truly believes she's within her rights or she's as cold and calculating as they come. I don't care for her. Whoever she is, she has been left out of Samuel's will—and perhaps there's a good reason for it. I hope Mr. Brawny Man can shed some light on this. Did Samuel ever mention a daughter, and if he had a daughter, why didn't he leave Loftus House to her instead of to a niece far removed from him? Someone he'd never even met. And why has no one mentioned a daughter?

Looking her over, I catch a whiff of familiar cologne. Something expensive and popular among a certain type of woman. It's a scent that says she's one of those who love the finer things in life. I need to refine my olfactory sense when it comes to perfumes and colognes. They all stink the same to me. As a cat, I prefer au naturale. *The human odor, if clean and well maintained, is quite pleasant to a cat. Then again, we adore sardines.*

Her clothing is expensive. She's wearing a Rolex watch in a time when many have given up watches all together for the cell phone or smart watch. If she is a wrong side of the blanket baby, she's done well for herself. Not what one would expect from a shady chap.

But enough observation. It's time for some action. The Loftus Lass steps back and allows her to enter, though I hiss a warning at her. This woman reminds me of a black mamba snake. Once she's in, will we ever get her back out? She's certainly taking an inventory as she walks around the foyer.

I'm glad to see that Brawny Man is staying. Judging from the set of his chin, I don't think wild horses could drag him away from here now. I do believe he's feeling protective of Tommie. Now isn't that an interesting turn of events. I'm not sure I trust him completely, yet, but I trust him a lot more than the alleged bastard daughter who conveniently shows up the first day Tommie steps foot on the property. Whew, what a day this has been and it's far from over.

HARLEY SAW the expression of compassion in Tommie's eyes, and his red alarm bells began to ring. One look at the woman who presented herself as Odell Rains and he could clearly see she had the face of a practiced con-woman. She was expertly made up and dressed to the nines. Expensively turned out, projecting wealth and security. All very calculated as far as he could tell.

He stepped in front of the intruder. "Ms. Rains, is it?"

Her smile never touched her eyes. "That's correct. Samuel's

daughter from his illicit union. I'm a love child." She said it with venom. "I'm a Loftus but I go by Odell Rains."

"Forgive me, but Samuel never mentioned you."

"I'm not surprised. I'm sure he worked hard to forget me and my mother. Cheaters often try to run away from their past."

Harley felt his temper climb, but he kept a tight grip on it. "Samuel and I were very close. He would have mentioned a child, illegitimate or not."

"He wanted nothing to do with me or my mother. He would have been happy if we'd both died."

"That's not the man I knew that you're talking about." Harley stuck to his guns. He'd cared for Samuel and he wouldn't hear his friend talked about in that way. "Samuel was a kind man. He didn't run from life or anyone. How do we know you're who you claim to be?"

"Look," Odell raised the briefcase in her hand. "I have my birth certificate and pertinent documents in here. I'll take a DNA test. I only want what's mine, a portion of the Loftus estate." She waved a hand around the house. "This is a pretty swanky place. I'm sure there's some cash for the unwanted offspring. Enough to move me a long way down the road from here."

"If you had a claim to the estate, why didn't you show up at the reading of the will?" Harley asked her. He was watching Tommie out of the corner of his eye and he was growing more and more concerned. She looked like she was going to cry—or cave. Neither reaction would be helpful in this situation. She had to stand firm for her rights as owner of the manor or this woman would push her way in.

Odell looked at him. "Who are you? I don't think my business is with you. You should probably leave."

That was finally the spark that sent Trouble into an arched-back hiss.

"And take that cat with you. My father has some valuable furniture here. It's no place for a cat." She looked around the front parlor where Tommie had removed the heavy, protective sheets. "That sofa is worth at least ten grand. And those end tables at least five thousand each." Odell gave that tight, mean smile again. "I'm a furniture appraiser. I'll be able to calculate the value of things almost to the dollar. I only want my share."

"And what share would that be?" Tommie asked. "You weren't mentioned in Samuel's will. His attorney never mentioned any other living relatives. If Samuel even knew you existed, he chose not to leave you any part of his estate."

"Maybe, maybe not," she said. "Now may I tour the house?" She reached into her briefcase and brought out a pad and pen. "I want to document what's here before you have a chance to sell any of it off."

"Aside from the fact that your accusation is insulting, you have no right to do anything in this house. I'm the legal owner," Tommie said. "Now I'd like you to leave."

Odell jammed the legal pad back into her briefcase. "I was hoping we could accomplish this without animosity. But that's your choice."

Harley clenched his fists. He had plenty to say, but this was Tommie's fight. It would be best if he let her fight it. Odell, whoever she was, seemed like the kind of person who would give her trouble. Serious trouble. It was best Tommie learned to hold her own.

"My choice is for you to leave." Tommie motioned to the door. "Don't come back. Loftus Manor belongs to me." She stood tall to her full height. "I don't know if your claim of kinship is legitimate or not, but I do know that Samuel tracked me down. He found me to name me as his heir and he left this house to me. If he knew about you and wanted to find you, he would have. Now go." She pointed to the door again.

"I'll be back tomorrow with the law," Odell promised.

"You do that," Harley said. "Everyone in Wetumpka knows every detail of Samuel's will. That's the kind of town it is. Folks take an interest in each other. And everyone knows Samuel was childless. I'm sure the legal system will take all of that into account."

CHAPTER SEVEN

*H*arley realized Tommie was shaking after he closed the door on Odell Rains. Whether Odell was a Loftus or not, a simple swab would tell. But if her DNA revealed she was Samuel's child, her claim to part of Tommie's inheritance wouldn't be that easy to prove or disprove. Even if a court upheld the will and Tommie was declared to be the sole and rightful heir, it would still require lawyers and a trial. Looking at Tommie's haunted eyes, he felt certain she'd come to the same conclusion. And Tommie didn't strike him as a person with a lot of cash and time to fund an expensive, and probably lengthy, lawsuit.

"Come and sit down," Harley said as he took Tommie's elbow. "Let's go back to the morning room." He steered her down the hallway with the black cat at her side.

Tommie stopped dead still and turned to Harley. "Please tell me the truth. Did Samuel have an illegitimate child? He talked to you more than anyone. Did he indicate this might happen?" Tommie's hazel eyes were too wide, too stressed.

"He never mentioned a child or an illicit romance. He was

devoted to Rachel, even years after her death. He talked about her as if she'd stepped into the next room. As far as I know, he never dated another woman after her death. I can't imagine he would have cheated on her, and judging by Ms. Rains's appearance, I'd say she's old enough that Rachel was still alive when she was conceived."

"Sometimes people make mistakes." Tommie pushed her hair behind her ear, a gesture Harley was coming to realize indicated nervousness or worry.

He wanted to comfort her, but he wasn't sure it would be appreciated. And he didn't understand the impulse. He didn't get involved in people's lives. He'd learned not to the hard way. "Look, Samuel was the most deliberate man I've ever known. If he'd had an affair with a woman, it would have been because he had great feelings for her. And if that were the case, he wouldn't have slunk off into the night leaving her alone and pregnant. He wouldn't have."

"I don't know. If she is a rightful heir, I don't want to take something that should be hers."

Harley sighed. "Don't put the horse before the cart, Tommie. Let's see what proof she has and take it one step at a time." He cleared his throat. "My concern is that she isn't a legitimate heir but is up to some mischief. Someone is messing around in the manor. I don't know how they're doing it, but as soon as possible I want to check around more. Whoever is behind it, I worry they're either trying to scare you or they're desperate to find something."

"Find what?" Tommie asked.

"I don't know. Something they think Samuel had. Something they believe was hidden in the house. There were stories of jewels and riches from the 1800s hidden in the house, stories of Loftuses involved in gambling and land speculation, that a fortune was made before the stock market crash of 1929 and the money tucked away. Samuel laughed about all of those stories, but people are gullible fools. Someone could have the foolish idea that great wealth is here and now is the time to find it—before you do."

"And you think one of those fortune seekers could be this woman, Odell Rains?"

"I think it's possible."

"I should call Uncle Samuel's lawyer."

Harley didn't want to discourage her, but he didn't have a lot of faith that Britt Gordon wasn't involved. "Wait until tomorrow. That's plenty of time to decide your next move. Let's get some sleep and look at it fresh in the morning."

"I'm so sorry to involve you in this." She lifted her chin. "I want to do the right thing, but I don't want to be intimidated. Or played for a fool. I never expected this inheritance, and if it rightfully belongs to someone else, I'll leave. But if it's mine. Truly mine." Her mouth set. "I'm going to fight."

Harley felt relief. "That's the attitude." He checked the time. It was closing in on midnight. "I should go back to the cottage. Are you afraid to stay here alone? I've checked the house. There's no one here and all the doors and windows are locked."

"I can't be afraid. If I start being afraid, I'll never be able to stop." The cat rubbed against her legs and then reached up with both paws, asking to be picked up. She cradled him in her arms. "I have Trouble here. He'll keep me company."

Harley grinned. "Something tells me that cat can be a rough customer when he chooses. I can stay, though, if you want me to."

"You've done enough. You really have."

He didn't want to push into her personal space or presume to take on a role that wasn't his. And why was he even volunteering to babysit a woman he'd known for less than twelve hours? "Call me if you need me." He put another log on the fire. He had the idea Tommie would likely spend the night in the morning room rather than upstairs in a bedroom. He almost offered to help her make a place to sleep, but he didn't. He left by the front door, making sure it locked after him.

On the walk down to his cottage, he looked back at the house where lights were burning in the morning room on the first floor. The rest of the house was dark, the windows empty. Whatever was going on at Loftus Manor, he wanted a chance to figure it out.

AH, the Loftus Lass sleeps soundly on the sofa as the last log on the fire burns down to embers. She's had a restless sleep, but at last she seems to have found a safe nocturnal harbor. Catching a few nods is commendable, but first I need to see what's going on for food in the kitchen. Tommie forgot to eat, and she also forgot that I should eat. These modern women! They run on fumes. My da told me stories of the feasts he'd attend in D.C. when Eleanor and Peter entertained guests. That wasn't so long ago, but people had actual sit-down meals with courses. Now everyone eats on the fly. The biped civilization is going downhill fast with all this grab-a-bag dining. It's a fish and chips world--not for anyone with a hint of culture. But right about now, a hamburger from a drive-through would be delicious. I'm starving.

Loftus Manor is very quiet as I make my way to the kitchen. I know Tammy left some food here for me. She warned the Loftus Lass that I was finicky and needed plenty of sustenance—a warning that has gone unheeded. But even though I don't have thumbs, I can open a refrigerator door.

And there, on the shelf, is the container of chicken livers sautéed in butter with a handful of cooked rice that Tammy left for me. I'll have to eat it cold. A price will be extracted for this tomorrow, when my hostess is well rested. Now, though, it's a matter of getting the lid off the bowl.

There, it's coming now. Almost off!

What is that noise? The fur all over my body is standing on end. Someone is moving around upstairs.

To be honest, I've had enough of this foolishness. And despite my best efforts, I can't twig onto what exactly is happening. I'm not certain I believe in ghosts, but I absolutely believe someone is trying to make Tommie believe the manor is haunted. These appearances and disappearances are designed to spook her, not really harm her. But that doesn't mean harm isn't on the agenda.

The arrival of Odell Rains tonight clued me in to the tenuous nature of the claim Tommie has—if there is a more direct blood heir like a child. Samuel left a will, but how valid is that if there's a close blood relative alive? I've seen cases where a judge made some surprising rulings.

I took a good look at Ms. Rains, and while I didn't see a family resemblance to Samuel, at least the Samuel in the portrait, what does that mean? Nothing. Tomorrow will tell that tale.

And there's that noise again.

The racket is coming from upstairs. By the sounds of it, from the bedroom of the former caretaker, where earlier someone wreaked havoc. Now without the humans stomping after me, I'm going to slither up the stairs and find out what's going on in this house.

The October chill has seeped into the unheated upstairs. I'm padding down the hallway, listening. The sounds have stopped, but I find myself in front of the door to Nina Ahearn's old quarters. There's only silence. Did I imagine someone walking about? I'm not a feline prone to fancy, but the house is quiet as a tomb, if you'll pardon the expression.

When I reach up with my paw to try the doorknob, it fails to turn. It could be stuck—impossible for me to tell since it's hard for me to grasp the round knob. If I were president, I'd ordain that only the lever type handles could be used on doors. Those I can open in a flash.

Peering under the door gives me nothing—except for the distinctive scent of perfume. Musky. Otherwise, the room is still. My sense is that it's empty, but I can't be certain. The secrets of that room will have to remain until Tommie or Harley open the door for me. What I can be certain of is that any person inside won't leave. I'm going to park myself right here in front of the door until morning. If they try to escape, they'll have to step over me.

My hunger pangs will make me that much more alert. The things I do for the people in my trust.

CHAPTER EIGHT

ommie opened her eyes and had a jolt rush through her. Where was she? She looked around and didn't recognize a thing. When she sat up, she remembered the intruder and the strange woman who insisted she was Samuel's daughter. She put her head in her hands. "What I wouldn't give to hide in bed all day today. Uncle Samuel might have been one to stare his actions in the face; I'd prefer not to deal with confrontation."

She realized the black cat was missing, so she stood up, stretched, and headed barefoot to look for the cat. The floors were cold, though the morning room was still toasty. She dropped another log on the fire to keep it going before she peeked into the hallway. No cat was in sight. When she passed the staircase, she heard the cat yowl from the second floor, but he didn't come down.

"Be there in a minute," she said, as if he could understand her. "I'm going to make some coffee."

She hoped she had coffee. She wouldn't, unless Samuel had left supplies and a coffeemaker in the kitchen. She hadn't noticed while she'd been showing the renovators around. When she turned on the light in the kitchen, she saw the container of Trouble's food on the floor, the lid half-pried off. She stopped and studied the situation. It seemed pretty clear Trouble had come into the kitchen for a snack and been interrupted. But why? Why had he gone upstairs and abandoned his food?

She picked up the livers, which were still chilled, put a few on a plate and put them in the microwave. While they heated, she filled a kettle to boil water. An old dripolater sat on top of the ancient stove. Thank goodness it was gas. She turned on a burner and a small blue flame popped up and she centered the kettle over the fire.

She searched the old cabinets and found a container of gourmet coffee. Caramel pecan. She sniffed it and smiled. She liked Samuel's taste. Looking at the other supplies, she realized a trip to town needed to happen before too much time elapsed. Funny how she'd failed to think about food or supplies. Her jewelry making tools, gems, and precious metals were due to arrive soon. That would give her a little sense of stability, normalcy, and of belonging. Once she had her shop set up, she could notify her customer list and maybe even find a retail outlet in Wetumpka.

"Meow!" Trouble's call was insistent.

"Coming your way," she called out to him. Whatever he was up to, he seemed determined that she would go to him.

As the hot water heated, she took the dish of chicken livers up the stairs, calling for the cat. She felt a twinge of guilt that she'd forgotten to feed him. No doubt, he would be hungry. She found him stretched out in front of the door to the old caretaker's suite of rooms. Almost as if he were guarding it.

"What's going on?" she asked the cat as she put his food in front of him.

He gave a half-purr, half-yowl as he daintily began to eat.

Tommie stroked his sleek fur. He was a very handsome cat. She'd love to keep him, but Tammy appeared to be quite attached. "You could scare the ghosts out of Loftus Manor," she told him. The cat stopped eating and stared directly into her eyes.

He walked away from the food and patted his paw on the door.

"You want me to open the door?" She suddenly felt a wave of fear. Ridiculous. There was no boogeyman lurking inside, waiting to grab her. The cat was acting so strange, though. As if there really was someone inside.

Trouble patted the door again. "Meow."

It was clearly a command to open the door.

Tommie grasped the knob and twisted. The door opened easily. She walked into the room with the cat beside her. The smell of expensive cologne rushed at Tommie. Trouble even wrinkled his whiskers.

Tommie felt her stomach drop. Someone had been in that room. Trouble was clearly guarding the door, but where had the person gone? The room was empty.

Trouble jumped up on the bed and walked around, sniffing. Movement out on the lawn caught Tommie's attention and she slipped to the window to get a better view. What she saw made her gasp and step back

A woman wearing a dark floor-length cloak was standing in front of a tall bank of flowers. The hood covered her hair and shadowed her features so that Tommie couldn't get a good look at her. She was staring up at the house—seemingly at the very window where Tommie stood.

Trouble jumped to the windowsill, gave a low growl, and then ran out of the room. Tommie knew all of the doors and windows were locked, so she ran as fast as she could behind him. She was sorry she hadn't bothered to put on some clothes and shoes, but she didn't have time now. She raced barefoot in her shirt and underwear down the stairs and to the back door, which was the closest exit to the person in her yard.

The cat was already waiting for her at the door. When she opened it, he rushed out and she was hot on his heels. Panting, she found herself beside the giant gardenia shrub. Alone. Even the cat was gone. There was no evidence of the woman at all, and when she looked around on the ground for any tracks, there was nothing. Not a single bit of evidence.

The cat poked into the bushes, growling and yowling softly. Tommie picked him up in her arms. She was freezing, standing out in the cold in her underwear. She turned back to the house and stopped. Harley stood not ten feet away, his gaze rivetted on her bare legs. He instantly turned his back, but not before Tommie caught the grin that crept over his face and revealed a dimple in his right cheek.

"So sorry," Harley said. "I didn't realize you were up and outside."

Tommie no longer felt the cold—heat rushed up her neck and into her face. She was half-dressed, outside. "I saw someone down here," she said, edging away from Harley and toward the back door. "The cat was chasing this woman in a dark cloak. I didn't have time to...put on pants."

"I'll look around," he offered. "Go inside before you catch your death."

She didn't need a second invitation. She ran toward the back door and didn't stop until she was in her room. How would she ever face that man again?"

. . .

HARLEY ATTENDED the serious issue of searching for evidence of an intruder. No matter how thoroughly he examined the ground and shrubbery, he found nothing. Just like when he hunted for evidence of someone in Loftus Manor. He'd seen someone in the window, but he could find no trace of them.

And it didn't matter that his mind kept drifting back to the image of Tommie in that oxford button-down shirt and little else. She had lovely legs—and even though he didn't want to think of that, he couldn't stop. He regretted catching her by surprise, but they'd both been caught off guard.

He was worried that Tommie's embarrassment would make her reluctant to allow him to help. To that end, he stood up. Better to get this discussion out of the way before she had time to stew about it. Best to meet this situation head-on.

When he started to leave, he saw the cat in the bushes, digging away at something. He thought at first it might be a cat tending to feline business, but he decided it would be wise to investigate. Trouble meowed at him and scratched some more. Harley knelt down and began to look at the mulch the cat was disturbing. He'd put it down only a few weeks before in preparation for the coming winter. It took a moment but then he saw it. A button. A large, blue-black button crafted with a shiny black stone that seemed to have a star in the center. The button itself seemed made of bone rather than plastic. It could have come off either a man's or woman's clothing.

He bent down and picked it up and the cat brushed against his hand purring. "Is this button a clue?" he asked.

The cat blinked at him twice and then gave a low rumble—not a growl or a meow. Harley could have sworn the cat said, "Top that." He smiled at his fancy. Now he was not only seeing phantoms in the windows of Loftus Manor, he was hearing talking cats. A tenure in the state mental hospital couldn't be far behind. The saving grace was the unique button he held in his hand. This proved that someone had been in the yard. Tommie had seen some*one*, not some apparition.

AT LAST WE'VE found solid evidence that the figure in the black cloak was real and not some revenant. The perfume is another clue, but one only I've noticed. I suspect the scent was deliberately left behind to tease the Lass into believing a ghost is in the house. Strange bumps and smells are tropes of a haunting. But who is going to so much trouble to plant seeds of doubt—and how are they moving about so freely? Brawny Man said he wanted to investigate the house and I think that's a fine idea. I'm generally sensitive to the smell of a strange biped, but I've sniffed all around the caregiver's room, and nothing. There's nothing I can detect behind the walls. But there has to be, unless there's a real ghost in the manor. If I could swing a sledge hammer, I'd have some answers by lunchtime.

I have to convince the Lass that now is the time to knock in some walls. The renovation crew is here in Wetumpka and there will never be a better time to do it. And I haven't had a chance to explore the attic—a task I'm not looking forward to and will attempt to relegate to someone else.

Even if I am the Sherlock of black cats, I'm reluctant to chase down leads in attics. Or basements for that matter. Bad things happen in attics and basements. I've watched too many horror movies with Tammy and her significant other Aiden not to realize that those who creep into the attic to check things become part of the body count.

I see Mr. Brawny has worked up the courage to knock on the door. And there's the Lass, dressed in jeans, a turtleneck, and a thick sweater, as well as boots. A little over-compensation for her earlier bare legs, if you ask me. She's also sporting a blush that goes all the way to her hair roots. It's a little old-fashioned and a lot very appealing. Even Harley sees it, and when he turns back to look for me, I see that elusive dimple in his cheek. Call me foolish, but I think the man is developing a crush. Perhaps the inheritance of Loftus Manor will prove bountiful in more than one area for Tommie. He's got the look of a man who'd like a little snogging.

Now isn't the time, though, to encourage what he fancies. Let me slide in the door and scamper down to the library. Surely there are some family genealogy records. I'd like to peruse them for a bit. And then I'll need a lift to town. I want to investigate that lawyer's reputation. Britt Gordon. I can tell Harley doesn't think much of him, and I'm beginning to trust Brawny Man's judgement. He may be reclusive and lack skills at fluffing up the birds, but he's got a level head on his shoulders.

Now to the library. I wish the humanoids would come in there to work so Harley could build a fire. This October morning is nippy, and there's much to be done. And truth be told, I feel a strong inclination to nap. I shan't, but I really want to. Time is limited to figure out what's happening with Loftus Manor. I definitely intend to be in on the meeting with the lawyer.

CHAPTER NINE

ommie held the unusual button up to the light. It was exquisite, for a lot of reasons. She avoided looking directly at Harley—she was still humiliated by being caught running outside half dressed. He was pretending it had never happened, and she was good with that. It would suit her just fine if no one ever mentioned her *faux paus.*

The button was an interesting find. And the black cat had actually discovered it. "The stone, as you noted, Harley, is a black star sapphire. They vary in price. This one would be expensive for a button because it's so big. But it would give a garment a very distinctive and sophisticated look." She moved closer to the window in the morning room so she could examine the button in the light. "Look at this. The base is bone, not plastic."

"Does that mean it's old?" Harley asked.

Tommie knew he was thinking about the woman she'd seen in the full-length cloak. She'd had a chance to give him more details, and he'd agreed that she sounded like a historical figure, not someone from modern times. "It could be old or new. I can't tell by looking at it. The stone is firmly glued to the bone plat-form. The glue might date it more accurately. The catch in the back of the button allows it to be sewn to the garment, generally an outer garment I'd guess. I wouldn't think a washing machine would be a good idea for this type of button." She finally looked Harley in the eye. "Bone and horn were popular with button makers for many years. This could be antique or it could be retro. I can't tell. The figure I saw out in the garden looked to come from a different time, though. It would make sense if she drop..." She hesitated. "Do you think the button is proof that someone was there, or perhaps that a ghost left it for me?"

"I'd never believe it was a ghost until we prove it wasn't a human," Harley said. "I'm willing to believe in ghosts, but only after all reasonable explanations have been exhausted."

She blew out her breath. "That's the right approach." Still, she couldn't shake the feeling that something supernatural was happening in the house. If she didn't figure out what was really going on, she wouldn't be able to make her home in Loftus House. She'd lived without lots of amenities, but she couldn't live in a house that made her afraid.

Harley seemed to sense her worry and hesitation. "Trouble, on the other hand, seems to be quite capable of finding clues. Until I met him, I would never have believed that a cat would engage in solving a mystery." Harley smiled to show he was gently teasing her.

His point was well made. At least Trouble was doing some-thing proactive. The black cat prowled the library shelves. He was lithe and agile and able to move along the ledges with great skill. It was almost as if he were cataloguing the books there. Crazy thought.

"Trouble is up to something," Harley said. "I've been watching him. He's looking for something."

She liked that Harley could almost read her mind. Their thoughts traveled in the same direction. "Look, he's sniffing and rubbing against a book." She went to the cat and drew the volume off the shelf. "It's a history of Loftus Manor by Farthwright Loftus, a second-generation resident of the manor." She flipped through the table of contents. "Here's some interesting tidbits. Farthwright Loftus landscaped the original property and built the stables, which were down the hill from here toward the Coosa River. He also put in the docks on the river that allowed timber and cotton to be transported to the Port of Mobile for sale. He was a busy man, able to see the potential for new inventions like the cotton gin and the paddleboat."

She flipped through a few more pages and then felt a smile creep over her face. "He married a Native woman much to the consternation of his neighbors. That's the point where Loftus Manor began to be looked upon with a degree of suspicion by the community. Farthwright and his bride Onnalee were perfectly happy together and didn't care that the community shunned them. Their children were later accepted into polite society and the Loftus name was once again honored."

"Samuel told me that the Loftus tribe was never one to bow down to the rule of others, whether it was a king or a merchant." Harley spoke with pride of his friend. "He was a fine man, Tommie. I'm sorry you didn't get to know him. He stood up for what he believed in, which is why you have to fight for this house. He chose you. He wanted you to have it and he went to the trouble of tracking you down and finding out about you."

Tommie felt her spirits rise. "Thank you. I have such big plans for this place."

"Are you sure you can't keep it a private residence?" Harley asked, worry in his voice.

"I would if I could. Economically it's impossible, but other than enlarging and modernizing the kitchen, I swear I'll keep it as true as I can. And with the renovation team in town and the chance to do this on television, which will offset the cost, I have to make my decision now." She had a glimmer of what was troubling Harley. He was a man who valued his privacy. He knew that if guests flocked to Loftus Manor, the quiet of the grounds would never be the same. And he wanted to stay there. Even stranger—she was beginning to want him to stay.

"I understand." He walked to the windows and looked out at the backyard and grounds that sloped into the woods. "It's hard to see change. Even though this is your home now and you have total say." He turned back to her. "All things change. I know this. Loftus Manor became my home after some hard times and it's been a wonderful refuge for me."

"Tell me about those hard times." Tommie was aware that before long she needed to head into town to see the lawyer. Right now, though, Harley was opening up to her, and she realized how rare that might actually be.

"After Afghanistan, I came back to the States and kicked around for a while. My folks tried to move me in with them, but it just didn't work. I was haunted. So many of my friends in Afghanistan, mostly locals who were brave enough to support the American troops, had been killed in the three years I was there. I came home and it was such division. Watching Nazis parade in city streets, it was like all I'd fought for meant nothing."

Tommie felt a pang for what he'd been through. "I'm so sorry."

He shrugged again. "This is where the world is at right now. I couldn't take it, though. I withdrew into my shell. I read an ad that Samuel was looking for a groundskeeper and that a house was supplied with the job. It was everything I could ask for—

hard physical labor, isolation, and a place to hide out. Samuel himself was the huge bonus. We played chess and backgammon and talked. If you haven't noticed, there's not a single TV in the place. Samuel didn't watch TV. He read books and journals and periodicals. In fact, I have a stack of them for you. You'll need to cancel his subscriptions."

For the first time, Tommie considered how much Harley had lost with her uncle's death. Samuel's suicide had taken away his place to live, his friend, his companion, his way of life. And yet he hadn't complained about anything and had made it clear he was ready to vacate the premises on her word.

"Please don't be in any rush to leave." She said the words before she could lose her nerve. "Having you here has been a real help to me."

Harley's crooked grin revealed the dimple. "Thank you. I'm glad to help you. Samuel would want me to. Let's just see what's happening here in the house and once this is all settled with the intruder and the unexpected, alleged daughter, we'll figure out the rest of it."

The beep of a horn interrupted their conversation and they both hurried to the front door where a moving van was parked in the drive.

"It's my belongings from California." Tommie felt flustered. She hadn't really thought about where to put anything. Her possessions consisted mostly of her jewelry-making tools and supplies and a few items of sentimental value, along with some clothes.

"Where should I unload?" the driver asked.

Tommie directed him to the building behind the house which she'd decided to make her workshop. In only an hour they had the van unloaded and the belongings and boxes set up in the building. She noticed the black cat was snooping around, sniffing everywhere in the workshop. It was likely that wild animals might have found their way into the building since no one seemed to use it.

"Why didn't you have your workshop in the house?" Harley asked her.

"I do some welding and soldering. I'd just rather have those tools out here. If something should go wrong—"

"You wouldn't burn down the house," Harley finished for her. "Good, practical thinking."

For Harley, that was a high compliment. She shook her head at him. "Thanks."

"Are you ready to head into town to talk to Samuel's lawyer? If you don't mind, I'd like to come along. And maybe you could ask for that copy of the coroner's report while we're in town?"

"You really don't think Samuel killed himself?" She felt a spark of hope and fear. If Samuel was murdered, that put the intruder in her home in a completely different light.

"I don't know. But I'll bring this button. There's a woman in town I want to ask about it. If we don't have time to see her today, I can talk to her tomorrow. We have a lot to do, and I'm starving. We can stop for something to eat first." He lifted his chin toward where Trouble sat complaining in a low but steady meowing. "Your cat is hungry."

"Let me get my coat and purse. Then I'm ready."

CHAPTER TEN

I can't believe the blokes were going to try to leave me behind —and I thought we'd bonded over the discovery of the strange button. I guess the humanoids still don't value my skills properly. Had I not been alert and aware of the foibles of the human intellect, I would have been left behind. Not happening. To their credit, once I shot up into the front seat of Tommie's car, they accepted the inevitable. If only some Einstein would invent a car that cats could drive, I wouldn't have to rely on the bipeds for transport.

The perfect October day reminds me how much I love Wetumpka and the surrounding area. My very first case as a feline detective happened right here. Well, actually nearer the crater caused by the meteorite strike some eighty-three million years ago. A vile serial killer was using the crater as a dump site for the bodies of his victims. There were a few harrowing developments for me and my beloved Tammy Lynn, but that case also introduced her to her main squeeze, Aiden Rivers. And true love was born—once I nudged them into giving it a try. Ah, the work of a black cat is never done!

We've made it into town, and Harley and Tommie seem content in each other's company. They steal a look at each other too often for me to ignore it. Feelings are growing, it would seem. And I'm not adverse to that at all. Humans just complicate romance too much. As Sherlock would say, just throw a leg over and get on with it.

First stop is a diner for breakfast. At last! Someone will attend to my gastric needs. And this is a place where I'm well known and will be served without question. Mr. Brawny actually holds the door for me so I'm assuming he's learned his lesson about trying to leave me behind. I go where I want to go. And yes, coddled eggs with a bit of smoked salmon sounds perfectly delicious. At last, these two are getting on board with egress and ingress demands and my dietary needs. Why is it so hard to train humans?

At any rate, the waitress gives me the side eye because I'm not with Tammy. I charm her with a tail curl and a sweet meow. Bella takes us to a table in the corner where I can sit up on the booth seat without drawing attention. She's a smart cookie, our Bella is. She is also a friend of Tammy Lynn's and so she knows me and has served me often.

I point to my menu selections. Harley looks a little surprised, but he rolls with the flow. Good for him. And in two shakes of a lamb's tail, our food is hot and in front of us. Ah, this will greatly improve my outlook on the day. Bella even remembered to bring just a dollop of fresh cream for me. I don't often indulge in it, but why not today?

Someone entering the restaurant has caught Harley's eye. He leans forward to Tommie and whispers, "That's Nina Ahearn, your uncle's caregiver."

I do a double-take as the buxom blonde walks past us with a definite hitch in her get-along. She works the magic of the badonkadonk, just like the Trace Adkins' song says. I have to admit, she's not what I pictured as a caregiver. She looks more the...center stage type of woman.

"That's who took care of Samuel?" *Tommie is as shocked as I.*

"She really was very good to your uncle," *Harley says.*

No matter what conclusion the humanoids come to, I have to say that

Uncle Samuel's stock has risen in my eyes. If you have to have a caregiver, why not have one that makes you feel like Hugh Hefner?

Ms. Ahearn is dining alone. And Harley is getting up to speak with her. A brief exchange. Harley motions to Tommie, but Nina Ahearn shakes her head, negating an introduction, I would assume. Well, it's the Bombshell's loss. But Tommie isn't one to be left sitting on the front porch. She's getting up and walking over. She's holding out her hand, obviously introducing herself.

Ah, Nina doesn't take her hand. I need to get over there so I can hear this.

Nina pastes a smile on her face, but it doesn't reach her eyes. "Nice to meet you, Ms. Sykes. I have to say, your uncle never mentioned you. Not one single time. Your uncle was a very wonderful man, but there are things you don't know about him. Things that will shock you."

Nina is laying the groundwork for something. Just what exactly, I'm not sure at all. It's my personal opinion that Nina is stacking it on a little too thick. Tommie is young, but she isn't as easily shocked as one might think.

Tommie is not one to be pushed into the shade. "I regret I didn't get to know Uncle Samuel. I've learned he was an intelligent and interesting man who went to a lot of trouble to track me down so I could inherit Loftus Manor. I have big plans for the estate, and I believe Uncle Samuel would support them."

"Big plans? Do tell?" *Nina can't seem to hide her sarcasm. I wonder what she's got cooking on her back burner, because she's up to something.*

In this little verbal dance, Tommie ignores her question and parries with one of her own. "When you were living in the house, did you notice anything odd in your room?"

Ah, I see now, the Loftus Lass is sleuthing, not making a social contact. Good for her. I like a woman who knows how to keep an investigation on track.

For a moment—a long moment—Nina considers her answer. "Loftus Manor is old and there are always creaks and groans, the sound of someone moving about. It's probably raccoons in the attic. Have you checked? Or are you too afraid to poke around?"

"Not afraid, and not yet, but I will. I only arrived yesterday."

Nina turns to Harley. "When are you leaving, Harley? I'll bet your bags are packed and the car loaded."

"I'm helping Ms. Sykes settle in."

Harley tells only as much as he has to. So he is somewhat suspicious of Nina Ahearn. I wonder why. I can't wait to ferret that information from him.

"Oh, I'm sure you are. Funny, I don't recall you helping me to settle in," *Nina responds.*

Harley only laughs. He doesn't answer at all. Sparks smolder in Nina Ahearn's blue eyes. There is definitely something between these two. This will bear additional investigation, when I have time.

Thank heavens Bella appears with Nina's breakfast and Harley and Tommie excuse themselves. They're eager to go, and since I've finished my repast, I'm feeling much friskier and I'm ready too. I'm sure I haven't seen the last of Nina, but for now, it's on the road again.

TOMMIE SAT in the leather chair in front of the lawyer's desk, Harley at her side and the cat at her feet. She carefully studied Britt Gordon. He was a man who perfectly fit his physical surroundings of heavy mahogany furniture, plush modern throw rugs of primary colors, expensive art on the walls, and a few well-tended potted plants. His desktop was cluttered, and he was digging around in his files looking for her uncle's will. Tommie felt a flash of annoyance. She'd had an appointment with Gordon and yet he acted as if he hadn't anticipated seeing her. For all of the trappings of success in his office, he seemed disorganized.

"It's a shame you missed the reading of the will," he said as he thumbed through file tabs. "I have it right here, somewhere, if I can just lay hands on it. I must confess, filing isn't my greatest talent. Now why weren't you here for the reading of the will?"

Tommie tried not to show her aggravation. "I wanted to be here, but I had to load up some things to ship."

"Then you won't be going back to California?" He looked up at her over his glasses. "I'm surprised. A young woman leaving the excitement of California for a crumbling old house in the woods of Alabama?"

"Actually, the house is in pretty good repair. Loftus Manor is...a dream come true."

The lawyer turned to her. "Oh?"

"The renovation team, Hank and Katie Evans, looked it over yesterday. Structurally sound. There are some modifications we'll be doing, but the house is in great shape."

The lawyer laughed. "Excellent. I guess all the ghost stories are just so much foolishness. That Samuel. He was always going on about how the house was haunted and how he smelled strange perfumes."

"What kind of perfume?" Tommie could have sworn the cat's interest picked up also.

"I don't know." Gordon waved his hands. "Samuel only said it smelled nice and feminine. Anyway, as I was saying, when I realized how young you are, and single, I assumed you wouldn't want to stay in Wetumpka." He looked at Harley. "But it seems you've already made a friend."

Trouble jumped into Harley's lap, stared at the lawyer, and hissed.

Tommie looked down to hide her smile. She didn't like Britt Gordan and neither did Trouble. The cat was a wicked judge of character!

"I don't allow animals in my office," Gordon said. "Some of my clients may be allergic."

"So sorry." Tommie motioned Trouble into her lap. When he obeyed and jumped over to her, the lawyer arched his eyebrows.

"He's very clever. He's not a movie cat, is he?"

"Indeed, he is clever, but so far no starring movie roles. I'm just glad to have him with me at the manor. And I'm happy that Harley is there, too." She waited until the lawyer looked away and then she winked at Harley, letting him know that she was going to mess with the lawyer. "Yes, it's wonderful to have a ready-made support group. Now if you'll give me a copy of the will, Trouble, Harley, and I will be leaving." The lawyer was going through files again. "And oh, did you realize Uncle Samuel had a child?"

Britt Gordon slowly lifted his head. Something shifted in his eyes. She couldn't pinpoint it, but it was enough to make her suspicious. "A child? You don't say."

"She claims to be his daughter. Did Samuel mention anything about a child to you?"

"Not a word."

"Then I'm assuming that she has no claim to Loftus Manor? I just want to be clear about this. She seems to think she's owed part of the property."

"She does?" Gordon frowned. "Does she have proof that she's truly Samuel's daughter?"

"She says she does. You didn't know anything about her?"

"Samuel was always a very private man. Rachel died years

ago, and as far as I knew, he remained alone. It would be normal, though, if he had a relationship with someone. That doesn't shock me. But he never said anything about a child."

"If she has no legal claim to his estate, that's all I need to know. Just assure me of that."

The lawyer cleared his throat. "She wasn't included in the will. Unless she has grounds to prove her blood ties and that she was left out of the will by accident..."

Tommie felt the skin tighten on the top of her head. "Then she may have cause?"

"This is very unusual. If Samuel was aware of her, he would have included her or he would at least have given me a head's up. He's just that kind of man. If he wasn't aware, how does that impact her standing as an heir?"

"That's exactly what she's asking you," Harley said, a bit of snap in his voice.

"It depends." The lawyer shook his head. "I'd have to talk with her. See what proof she has."

"It doesn't matter what she may or may not have. Samuel left the manor to Tommie," Harley pressed.

"Inheritance laws are complicated. Especially when an illegitimate child shows up. And a lot depends on why Samuel didn't know about her, what she wants..." The lawyer dusted his hands together. "It can be complicated."

"But you wrote Samuel's will so you're certain it's airtight," Harley said. "That was, after all, what he paid you for."

"Yes, of course. But there are extenuating circumstances."

Harley stood up. "Either you did a proper job of the will or you didn't. There are no extenuating circumstances. Now please give us a copy of the will and we'll be on our way. And I'll recommend to Tommie that she hire her own lawyer in this situation."

Tommie stood up with the cat in her arms. The top of her head was buzzing with anger, a very bad sign.

The lawyer stood too and pushed his glasses up his nose. He looked first at Harley, then the cat, then Tommie. "Ms. Sykes, I assure you I'm not trying to make life difficult for you. I'm not your lawyer. I'm the lawyer for Samuel and the estate. My job is to be sure that Samuel's wishes are fulfilled. If he didn't know he had a daughter...this might require the intervention of a judge. As Mr. Jones recommends, you might want to get your own representation in this matter."

"If Ms. Rains pursues this claim, I will," Tommie said. "But until then, I'm going forward with my plans. I am the legal heir until proven otherwise."

"I can't stop you, though I would suggest you use caution with any permanent changes to the structure."

Harley stepped forward. "Samuel left the house to her. I don't see how that can be disputed. It's in black and white." He picked up the copy of the will the lawyer had put on the desk. "It says it right here."

"I agree—" Before the lawyer could complete the sentence, the door burst open.

"You can't go in there." The lawyer's receptionist was doing all she could do to stop the leggy blonde from entering the room.

"Nina?" Gordon said. "What are you doing here?"

"I've come to claim my rightful share of the Loftus estate. I'm Samuel's wife."

CHAPTER ELEVEN

*T*his goes beyond the pale. We have an alleged daughter and an alleged wife claiming part of Samuel Loftus's estate. And all within twenty-four hours of Tommie setting foot on the property. It's like the vultures were just circling and waiting for Samuel to die.

And that caregiver! I was right when I met her in the diner and thought she was someone to be wary of. Now she claims she's Samuel's wife. Funny how she didn't stake her claim at the will reading, even though she was there.

There is one solid clue here, though. One the humans haven't detected. The scent Ms. Nina Ahearn, allegedly Loftus, wears is very heavy. I've smelled it before. In her room when no one was supposed to be there. Is this an effort to make Tommie think her home is haunted? And how is that scent being disseminated throughout the house? I wish I could convey this tidbit to Tommie or Harley, but as much as it humbles me to admit it, I don't know how.

All three of the bipeds look as if they've been hit in the head with a baseball bat. Stunned. Oh, and the Lass is getting angry. I see the heat rise in her face. Uh-oh. I'm going to hunker down by the desk because I feel an explosion coming on.

. . .

HARLEY SPOKE BEFORE HE THOUGHT. "Nina, you aren't Samuel's widow any more than I'm Mahatma Gandhi. That's a ridiculous claim. You forget, I was with Samuel almost every evening, talking into the wee hours. He had no romantic relationship with you. He valued what you did for him, but there was nothing indicating love."

"That shows what you know, Harley Jones. And it may be ridiculous to you, but Samuel and I were in love." Nina waved a paper about like it was a handkerchief of victory. "And we're married now. I'm Nina Loftus. Legally."

"This can't be happening." Britt Gordon looked confused. He turned to Nina. "The bank said you cashed your check last week. That was your settlement from the estate. You were at the reading of the will. You know that was your share."

"Oh, I took that paltry amount of cash and now I've come for the rest of it."

"There is no rest of it," Gordon said. "That's what Samuel left you."

"Too bad he didn't tell you the truth. We're married." She held out her left hand where a golden band sparkled. "I'm his wife. I get an elective share of the estate, I do believe."

"This is unbelievable," Tommie said. "My uncle didn't have a wife or a daughter that no one knew about. This is bull."

Nina smirked at Tommie. "I'll be by the house this evening. I'd like to move back into my old rooms."

"That isn't going to happen." Harley moved beside Tommie. "Ms. Sykes is the rightful owner, according to Samuel's will. This last-minute marriage won't work."

"I have the marriage application forms." She reached into her bag and pulled out a piece of paper. "Signed and witnessed. I just have to file it with the proper people."

Harley took the paper and handed it to Tommie. She studied it for a moment. "Who is this Reverend Krystal Child?"

Britt Gordon sat heavily in his chair. "Oh dear Lord, she's an internet preacher from Knoxville, Tennessee. She's on one of the television channels."

"This isn't worth the paper it's on," Tommie said, tossing it on the lawyer's desk.

"Reverend Child is licensed to perform marriages, and that's what she did. She came to the manor and performed the ceremony. And Samuel signed on the dotted line. Right there."

"You'll have to take me to court," Tommie said. "That's the only way you'll get in the manor. Unless you know a secret entrance."

Harley saw the shock pass over Nina's face though she did her best to cover it up. The woman knew something. He filed that away until he had a chance to pursue it. The black cat, too, was watching her with suspicion.

"Harley, we should go," Tommie said. She clutched the copy of the will and reached over to the desk and picked up the marriage documents too.

Harley lifted Trouble into his arm. As he walked by Nina, the cat hissed in her face. She gave a startled little cry and stepped back. Harley held his laughter, but he did enjoy the cat's spunk. Whatever else Trouble might be, he was smart about humans. He knew who to like and who to dislike. When they were clear of the office, Trouble jumped to the floor.

TOMMIE MULLED over the startling turn of events as she walked beside Harley, the black cat trailing behind them. At the parking lot, Trouble scampered over to a black SUV with Elmore County tags on it.

"Trouble, come on." She had accepted the cat understood her. "We have a few more things to do."

Instead of obeying, the cat hopped on the hood of the car and began scratching the front windshield with his paw.

"Grab the cat," Harley said as he opened the driver's door of the car. "He's going to get in trouble."

"Like his name," Tommie responded as she went to gather him in her arms. Instead, he darted to the top of the SUV and began patting the driver's window. "He really wants in this vehicle."

"Not a good idea," Harley said. "Not everyone is fond of cats."

Trouble gave him a look and a low hiss.

"But they should be," Harley added.

Tommie laughed at the big, muscular man intimidated by a fifteen-pound cat. "I'll grab him." She reached up for him and he jumped back to the hood. Peering into the SUV, she stopped in her tracks. "Harley, this is Nina Ahearn's car. There's some paperwork on the passenger seat."

"Her brand new car," Harley said as he joined her. "She was driving an old Escort the last time I saw her."

"Money from Samuel's estate." Tommie couldn't help the hint of bitterness in her voice. "It seems like everyone only cared about my uncle for his money or what he could do for them. It makes me sad to think his last years were spent surrounded by people waiting for him to die."

"He had friends, Tommie. I was one of them. I don't care for Britt Gordon, but I think the man viewed Samuel as a friend. And just to be clear, I never expected to benefit from Samuel except in the pleasure of his company."

Tommie felt a wave of remorse sweep over her. "I wasn't including you in my statement, Harley. I really wasn't. I'm sorry if I sounded like I was."

He put a hand on her shoulder. "It's okay. Let's grab the cat before Nina comes out and catches him up there on her new ride. She'll file some kind of damage claim against him and you."

Tommie chuckled, but Harley was right. "Trouble, come down here now."

The cat only batted the window again.

"The car isn't locked." Tommie gave in to an impulse and pulled the door open. Instantly the cat jumped into the driver's seat and Tommie was hit with a wall of heavy perfume. She thought Nina had likely taken a bath in it.

And then she realized that it was the very same scent she'd smelled in Nina's old room. The perfume had wafted around the enclosure on the night she'd heard an intruder. "We have to get to the bottom of what's going on at Loftus Manor," she said. To that end, she picked up the sheaf of paperwork on the passenger seat. Trouble leaped out of the car to the ground as if his work was done.

She went through the papers quickly, glancing up to be sure Nina wasn't coming out of the lawyer's office. "It's information about that internet preacher and also about inheritance laws of Alabama for a wife left out of a will. She's done her research. She is due a share of the estate."

"If she is legally married," Harley reminded her. "Your uncle would have told me if he married."

She dropped the papers on the seat and backed out of the car, closing the door. "Are you sure?" She wanted to believe him. More than anything.

"I'm positive," Harley said. "Samuel was in a good mental

condition. His health was holding steady. I don't believe he married Nina and I don't believe he killed himself."

"This haunting business. So far it's been more annoyance and intimidation, but there's a lot at stake here. If something happened to me, who would inherit?"

Harley's eyebrows drew close together. "I don't know. The daughter might, but since she's no relation to you, maybe not. If Samuel's marriage to Nina is legal, Nina might also have a claim. If you died."

"Then we have to make sure I stay alive," Tommie said. "And we have to find out how someone is slipping around the manor. Once we resolve that, I think we can put the ghosts to bed."

CHAPTER TWELVE

*H*arley had finally managed to contain Trouble in the vehicle—the day was cool and there was plenty of ventilation—before he and Tommie stepped into the coroner's office. It was a tiny closet in the courthouse with barely enough room for a desk, the young woman behind it, and five filing cabinets. The receptionist brightened at the sight of Harley, and he gave her a smile and a nod. He'd spoken to her in town on occasion and he knew her first name.

"Can I help you?" the receptionist asked.

"I'd like an official copy of the autopsy report on Samuel Loftus," Tommie said.

"Are you a relative?"

"Yes, his only living relative. I'm his niece."

Harley hadn't realized how much Odell Rains and Nina Ahearn had gotten under Tommie's skin until those words popped out of her mouth. She was defending her claim to Loftus Manor to a total stranger. Forcing her into that corner was wrong. She was a good person, not a money grubber. "Nancy, this is Tommie Sykes, Samuel's great-great-niece. She inherited Loftus Manor." He gave Tommie an encouraging smile.

"Nice to meet you," Nancy said, extending a hand for a shake. "I'm Nancy Smith. We thought a lot of Mr. Samuel here in Wetumpka. And it's good to see Harley is showing you the lay of the land."

"Yes, he's been very kind." Tommie stepped back from Nancy's desk.

"I understand the coroner here called in the state medical examiner for a more...professional opinion," Harley said helpfully, hoping to initiate a conversation.

"That's true," the receptionist said. "Mr. Loftus's death was ruled a suicide, but the coroner wanted to be sure there was no indication of foul play. The state medical examiner did the autopsy and ruled the death a suicide. Mr. Moore, the coroner, was very thorough and particular so calling in the medical examiner is no reflection on him."

"I'm so glad he did everything by the book," Tommie said.

The woman picked up a file on top of her desk and leafed through before she snapped out three pages, stapled them together, and handed them to Tommie. "Glad this was right at my fingertips."

"Yeah. Thanks for your help." Tommie frowned. "Why was the file on your desk?"

"Another person was in here earlier. She said she was Samuel's daughter and needed the report for insurance claims." Nancy kept her expression perfectly blank, but she smiled at Harley. "I didn't give her a copy."

"Thanks. That was smart," he said.

Nancy's smile widened at his praise. "Sure thing. I just thought you'd like to know. Will you be staying on at Loftus Manor, Harley?"

"For the time being," he said, "until Ms. Sykes here gets settled in and has all the loose ends tied up."

Nancy looked at Tommie. "That woman that showed up here with her fancy clothes, I didn't much care for the way she acted." She watched Tommie. "But I'd say the sudden appearance of a daughter would be a mighty big loose end."

Harley was surprised when Tommie started to laugh. Her laughter was rich and musical.

"You're right, Nancy, and that's a heckuva understatement. An unexpected daughter is a huge loose end. You can't imagine."

"Then perhaps you'd like to know that Ms. Rains was also in the bank this morning. I had to stop by to take care of a deposit for the sheriff. When I'm out and about in town I run errands for a lot of the courthouse offices." She waved a hand. "Anyway, that woman was trying to get a list of your uncle's accounts. The bank wouldn't give them to her, and she was hotter than a firecracker."

"She's really pushing her luck," Tommie said, her laughter fading. A hint of pink touched her cheeks.

"No one in town is going to help her," Nancy said. "They know that Mr. Samuel left his estate to you. And they have a great deal of skepticism that Mr. Samuel had a child he didn't claim. He wasn't that kind of man."

"Thanks, Nancy." Harley gave her a warm smile. "You've been a real help."

"Yes, thank you a lot," Tommie said. "I'm still trying to figure out exactly what I think of Odell's claim."

"She was making noises too that Mr. Samuel might have been murdered." Nancy bit her bottom lip. "The idea of that is so... repugnant. Mr. Loftus was a nice man. He was always nice to me, to everyone. And he knew Mr. Rider in the real estate office didn't treat me very well. That's why he helped me get this job here with the coroner."

Tommie was intrigued. "You worked for the real estate developer, Mr. Rider."

"For nearly ten years." She shook her head. "He was so nice at first, but the bigger he got in the business, the harder he became to work for. It was to the point he thought I should work seven days a week because *he* wanted to work that much. But he was the one making all the money and I was getting minimum wage. He didn't believe anyone should have a personal life."

"I've heard a few rumors about Paul Rider," Harley said. "Money seems to be his prime motivation in life."

"I'm glad Uncle Samuel helped you," Tommie said. "I know Uncle Samuel preferred to stay at the manor but it seems he touched a lot of people."

"He was a wonderful man," Nancy said. "He could have made a fortune developing the manor and the property around it, but he didn't want that. He said he had enough money. More than he could spend. So few people recognize when they have enough, you know."

"What exactly did Ms. Rains say about my uncle's death?" Tommie asked.

"Did she have any specifics?" Harley was curious what trouble the alleged daughter was trying to stir up.

"Just that it was a very convenient death. For you, Ms. Sykes. She implied that you'd run up on hard times in California and the gift of the manor house rescued you."

"Did she say how I'd learned about my uncle, the manor, or how I managed to manipulate him into a noose from fourteen hundred miles away?"

Nancy looked stricken. "I didn't mean to imply..."

Tommie palmed her own forehead. "Sorry, Nancy. I didn't mean to sound like I was jumping on you. It's just such an unfair accusation and she's obviously going all over town spreading lies. Thanks for telling us. I'm just frustrated with these alleged relatives popping out of the woodwork."

"Is there another one?"

Harley caught Tommie's eye and she could read his thought clearly. She nodded. It was best for them to tell Nancy because in another hour the gossip would be all over town anyway.

"Yes, there is another relative. Nina Ahearn is now claiming that she was married to Samuel."

"What?" Nancy stood up so fast she bumped her chair backward into the wall. "That's insane."

Harley felt a pinch of gratification. At least Nancy saw how preposterous all these fake relatives were. It was a type of insanity. Nina and Odell were way over the top. "It's okay. We'll prove both claims are false."

Nancy settled back into her chair. "That Nina. She was really good to Samuel, but everyone in town figured she had some kind of agenda. In the last few months, she made such a point of driving him around when he had to go somewhere and Harley was busy. Cooing and oohing over the little errands she ran for him. That kind of thing." Nancy's face brightened. "Maybe she was the one with an agenda to see him dead. I wouldn't put it past her."

"Is she that...cutthroat?" Tommie asked.

"I shouldn't have said that because I don't really know. But looking back on things in hindsight, it seems she was building her case. You know, showing up in public with Mr. Samuel. Making it look like they were together."

"Thanks for the paperwork, and the information," Harley said. He took Tommie's elbow and edged her toward the door.

"If I hear anything else, do you want me to let you know?" Nancy said before Harley shut the door.

"That would be great." Tommie went back to her desk and wrote her number on a slip of paper. "Call me here. And thank you, Nancy."

"No problem."

TOMMIE AND HARLEY walked across the courthouse grounds and back to Tommie's car. She realized instantly that Trouble was missing. "Where could he have gone?" she asked, turning in all directions. It was a beautiful fall day and the sound of saws and construction could be heard about two blocks away.

"I don't see how a cat that...healthy could squeeze out the open window," Harley said.

"I was warned he was smart. And determined. Now we need to find him."

"He belongs to the bookstore owner. Maybe he went back there," Harley suggested. "Wherever he is, the cat is smart and most likely doing exactly what he wants to do."

"Or maybe he's at the construction site. Let's check there first. I need to talk to Hank and Katie Evans anyway."

"The construction is on the way to the bookstore so that's a plan."

As they were walking companionably down the sidewalk, Tommie cut a look over at Harley. "Nancy is a little sweet on you."

"You think?" He looked honestly surprised.

"Definitely."

"She's a nice enough woman."

"She thinks you're a bit more than nice." Tommie couldn't believe she was teasing Harley. When she'd first met him, he'd seemed so somber and formidable. Now she was causing his ears to turn red. "If I had to guess, I think she's hoping you'll ask her out. That's why she was being so helpful."

"I don't want to disappoint her, or anyone, but that's a false hope."

Tommie unexpectedly felt a little thrill. She liked that Harley wasn't interested in the receptionist.

As they approached the construction area, the sounds grew louder. A big saw kicked in and it was impossible to talk more. Tommie saw the petite Katie in a hard hat, steel-toe boots, and a tool belt. She was working right along with the men as they began taking a front porch off an old house. When the saw stopped, Tommie called out. She didn't want to enter the work area because of liability issues for the renovation crew.

Katie waved, called to Hank, who came out from under the porch, and they walked over. "We've got an estimate for you," Hank said. "It's low because we really want to do that work. It would give our TV show a little extra juice." He handed her a folded sheet of paper from his pocket.

Tommie read over the figures and grinned. It was so much less than she'd anticipated. "When can you start work?"

"In a day or so. I'll have to order supplies and have them delivered. We'll work as quickly as possible, but you'll be without a kitchen for a little while."

"Not a problem," Tommie said. She wanted to dance a jig in the street. This was better than she'd ever dreamed. "How long do you think?"

Hank chuckled. "Well, if you wanted to, you could open the inn by Christmas I would think."

"Christmas!" Tommie couldn't help herself. She saw the manor all decorated in Christmas finery and the windows ablaze.

The front parlor would be perfect with a giant fir tree trimmed with colored lights and ornaments.

"Tommie, honey," Katie touched her shoulder. "Are you okay? You kind of left us."

Tommie shook her head to hide her embarrassment. "I was just seeing the manor all decorated for Christmas. You know, a little time-forward fantasy."

"You're giving the approval to move on this project?" Hank asked.

"You bet I do." She saw that even Harley was smiling. He might not care for the idea of the manor being an inn, but he seemed genuinely happy for her.

"Me-ow!" The adamant cry of a cat made them all turn and look across the street where Trouble sat on top of the same black SUV that had been at the lawyer's office. Nina Ahearn's car. And he was swatting at the window again. Tommie's heart jumped into her throat. Trouble was going to get himself killed on such a busy road.

"I'll get him." Tommie dashed across the street with the intention of scooping the cat into her arms. "You little beggar, you're going to be a pancake in the road if you keep taking such risks. Now stay with me or I'm going to take you to the book-store and leave you where you're safe."

She heard Harley calling her name in an agitated voice and she stopped as she was reaching up for the cat. She heard a woman scream and Hank Evans call out, "Stop! Stop!"

The next thing she knew she was smacked hard by a heavy body and she was flying through the air. She landed against the curb with a bone-jarring thud. There was the sound of squealing tires and a red sports car sped away.

She looked over to see Harley also sprawled in the asphalt. He slowly sat up, blood coming from the palm of one hand where he'd scraped it on the roadway. A heavy silence had fallen over the work crews as they gathered at the edge of the road to gawk.

"Are you hurt?" Tommie asked him while she was still moving her arms and legs to make certain nothing was broken on her.

"I'm fine. Just scraped up a little." Harley pushed his hair out of his face as he sat up taller.

"What happened?" Tommie was still stunned. She hadn't hit her head, but nothing made sense.

"Odell Rains almost ran you down," Harley said as he stood up, dusted off his hands, and pulled her to her feet.

"You knocked me out of the way." She was still trying to process what had occurred.

"Odell either wasn't looking or she meant to harm you. We need to call the police."

"No!" Tommie realized she wasn't hurt. "No, I don't want to involve the police. Not until we get to the bottom of what's going on here."

"Are you sure?" Harley asked her, lowering his voice as Hank and Katie started running toward them.

"I'm sure. For the moment. It could have been an accident." But she didn't believe that for a minute. There were far too many accidents associated with Loftus Manor and the people there for Odell's near vehicular homicide to be mere coincidence. She reached up and grabbed Trouble from the top of the car. The cat was uncharacteristically docile, as if he felt guilty for what had happened.

Tommie forced a smile for Hank and Katie as they rushed up. Katie was extremely pale. "Are you hurt? Harley, what about you? That was some flying tackle you performed. You literally flew ten feet through the air! It was amazing."

"We're both okay," Harley said, but the look he shot at

Tommie was less confident. She knew he really wanted to call the police and he didn't understand her reluctance.

"Where did Odell come from?" Tommie asked.

Hank cleared his throat. "I saw the whole thing while Harley was perfecting his flying tackle to help Tommie. That woman was parked down by the bookstore in the city lot. She tore out of the parking area like the devil was after her."

"Do you think she was trying to injure you?" Katie asked Tommie.

"I don't know," Tommie answered truthfully. She didn't know anything for certain, and she didn't want to level any accusations she couldn't back up.

Harley brushed at some dirt on her shoulder. "Odell, the woman in the car, has made a claim against Samuel's estate. It's possible she didn't mean to cut it that close to hitting Tommie. Maybe the sun was in her eyes. Maybe it was...deliberate. A warning or a real attempt to harm Tommie."

Hank snorted. "There was no sun blinding her. What kind of claim is she laying?"

"That she's Samuel's illegitimate child," Tommie said quietly.

"Then you need to watch your step, Tommie," Hank said. "You could have been killed. I agree with Harley. Let's call the police."

"No." Tommie wasn't ready to do that, even though both men had voiced the exact same sentiment. Judging from Katie's face, the renovator was also thinking that it was time to involve law officers. "My step-mom used to always tell me to give a person enough rope and they'd hang themselves. I want her to show her hand, and that's going to take some time." Tommie picked up the list of proposed changes that Hank had written up. "This is an incredible list and price. I'm so excited. Let's get started on the renovations as soon as you can," she said.

"I'll have some supplies delivered as soon as possible, maybe tomorrow even. I'll be there with a work crew to start tearing out the old kitchen as soon as the goods are delivered. And you need to have in mind the type of professional cooking gear you'll need. The range and refrigerators will be key to your success."

"I can't believe this is really happening," Tommie said. She was a little stunned, from the speed of the renovations and the near brush with death.

"It won't all go this fast," Hank warned her. "Keep in mind that we may run into plumbing or electrical work that needs to be done also. That could slow us way down."

Tommie nodded. "I understand. But at least we're getting started."

CHAPTER THIRTEEN

*T*he Coosa River was fast flowing, as evidenced by the white water where it rumbled over rocks and boulders. Tommie sat on a blanket on the bank of the river with Trouble in her lap and Harley beside her. The near car accident had taken the wind out of her sails, and even though she needed to clear up some legal issues and dig deeper into Odell and Nina, she simply couldn't confront it. Not yet.

Harley had suggested a walk to the river when they'd returned to Loftus Manor. He'd brought a bottle of wine. She'd finished one glass and sipped at a second, letting the tight spring in her gut uncoil.

The area around her—the woods and bluff that fronted the water—was more beautiful than she'd expected. The South wasn't known for colorful fall foliage, but there were touches of red and yellow in the trees that surrounded them. The solitude was fabulous. She couldn't hear a car or any human-made noise, just the calls of various birds, the chatter of a squirrel in a walnut tree, and the rustle of the leaves in a breeze.

The black cat stretched on the blanket beside her leg. While he was relaxed, he was also vigilant. The ability to be both simultaneously was a feline talent, and one she envied. She had so much to do, but she longed to stay here, in this safe little paradise, a bit longer.

"You mentioned that the docks are dangerous," she said to Harley, who sat quietly beside her. "Why?"

"Getting down the bluff here can be a challenge for even someone skilled in hiking rough terrain. If it's raining, it's very dangerous. The banks are clay and they get really slick when wet. Your feet will fly out from under you, and you could end up falling all the way to the river."

The prospect of a twenty or thirty-foot drop wasn't appealing. "And the water? Is it okay to swim in it?"

"The Coosa has been clean and a wonderful recreational river —so far. But the currents are treacherous. The docks were once an important part of life at Loftus Manor when supplies and goods came and went by water. Now it's just for pleasure craft. I don't know when the last time the docks were checked for safety and stability, so please stay away from them until an expert has assessed them."

It was the *please* that made her smile. "Okay."

He poured another dollop of wine in her glass. "All of this will come together in good time, Tommie. You've been here less than forty-eight hours. Give yourself some time."

"Do you think Odell really meant to hit me?" she asked. It was a tough thing to ponder. She'd never had enemies in her life. Sure, there were people she disliked, but no one who would deliberately do her harm.

"I don't know," Harley said. He met her gaze. "I really think we should report the incident to the police. I can call the bookseller's boyfriend, Aiden. He'll look into it and be discreet."

Tommie shook her head. "I don't want to escalate this. If

Odell truly is Samuel's child, I'd like to be able to work this out with her. If we bring the law into it, then it's out of my hands. An officer may charge her. He would have to, in fact, if he thought she'd tried to harm me."

"Which would be the smart thing to do," Harley pointed out. "She could have killed you."

"But she didn't. Thanks to you." Tommie was still a little in awe of Harley's bravery to leap in front of a speeding car to push her to safety. "Thank heavens you weren't hurt."

"We were both lucky, but if that woman is gunning for you, you might not escape unscathed the next time."

He was right about that. She knew it. She also knew she was latching onto a foolish notion that if Odell was really a Loftus, then they were related. If part of the Loftus estate belonged to Odell, Tommie wanted her to have it. That was a really big if, though. The matter needed to be settled quickly before she got so involved in turning the manor into an inn that she got her heart broken in the process.

"Give me a chance to talk to her again."

Harley only sighed, and the black cat bumped her chin with the top of his head. She stroked his sleek fur. From the pocket of her jeans she pulled up the coroner's report. "We should look at this." She shifted closer to Harley so they could read together.

The report was brief with the basic facts of Samuel's life and a bit of medical language—and the ruling of death by suicide, hanging.

Harley read it through and got to his feet. "I still don't believe it. They can rule anything they want, you know. And it isn't signed by the medical examiner, only the coroner here in Wetumpka."

"Do you know this Leo Moore?" Tommie asked. She'd begun

to understand that in a town the size of Wetumpka, most people knew everyone else. It was both charming and horrifying.

"I don't know Leo well. Never had an occasion to be around him."

"Is he honest?"

Harley didn't answer right away, and Tommie sat up taller as she waited for his answer.

"He has no training. Coroner and sheriff are elected here. Sometimes the people elect professional office holders, and sometimes popular ones. Leo is a real glad-hander. Folks like him because he puts them at ease. I'm pretty sure he just went along with what the medical examiner in Montgomery had to say."

"Britt Gordon, Uncle Samuel's lawyer, said they'd done an examination of the body in Montgomery and the ruling was without doubt." She faced Harley. "But I have doubts. And so do you."

"People make mistakes." Harley offered his hand to pull her to her feet. "Let's see if we can find any information on Odell Rains."

"How can we do that?" Tommie asked.

"I have internet and a computer in the cottage. We can start there. Samuel was deeply involved in the Loftus history. He was always researching and writing letters to people. He was obsessive about the Loftus line, which is how he knew about you. I have to believe if there was a chance he'd had a child, he would have noted it. I believe he would have claimed Odell as his child. If he knew. *If* it's real and not some elaborate scheme made up to cheat you."

"Odell is one problem, what about Nina Ahearn?"

Harley laughed softly. "She was good to your uncle. Never doubt that. If I'd had any idea she was trying to pull off a scam like this, I would have intervened. She always seemed to enjoy being Samuel's personal assistant, managing the house and meals, driving him to doctor's appointments. He didn't require care, as in skilled nursing care. It was always my impression that Samuel gave her a place to live and a job so he could pay her because she didn't have a lot of options."

That sounded a lot more like what she'd come to expect of her uncle. "You didn't think it odd that someone so...young and attractive would be happy so isolated in an old house with an older man?"

Harley hesitated before he answered. He seemed to be thinking her question through. "The first time I saw Nina, I was shocked. I admit that. It seemed incongruous. She does look like a woman who'd be out to marry into a more permanent...situation where her future was assured. Watching her interact with Samuel, though, I completely bought the story she told—that she enjoyed caring for him and living in the manor was the solution to a lot of her problems."

"But..." She appreciated Harley's careful wording. He wasn't a man who wanted to blacken or malign anyone in a slap-dash manner.

"I was suspicious at first, but after the first few months, Nina became a part of the manor. She stayed busy and seemed content with her life. Samuel and I just drifted into the rhythm. She made it easy for us with home-cooked meals and always a laugh. And she wasn't intrusive. Sometimes she'd eat with us but just as often not. When the meal was done, she'd clean the kitchen and then disappear in her room."

"How long has she been here?"

"I have to think," Harley said. "Over a year."

"How did Samuel find her?"

Harley's eyes widened. "I don't know. I don't believe he ever said. One day I was working in the side garden and saw her old car go down the drive. When I walked up to the big house to see if Samuel wanted to play a game of chess, Nina was here moving the last of her things from her trunk up to her bedroom. Then she was simply here. She fell into place."

Tommie didn't want to ask the next question, but she had to. "You never got a hint of anything romantic between Nina and Uncle Samuel?"

"Not the first whisper," Harley said with conviction. "They were friendly, but there was never an indication that they felt anything for each other."

"She's a pretty woman." Tommie found it hard to drop the subject.

"She is, but Samuel was devotedly in love with his wife. Rachel was gone, but not from his heart. He said it and he meant it."

Tommie smiled at the quaint sentiment Harley expressed. So few people seemed to believe in true love forever. "How can we prove this so-called marriage is a fraud?"

"The place to start is the internet." He gathered up the blanket and wine bottle while she grabbed the glasses. Trouble, who'd been asleep in the sun, yawned and gave them a friendly meow as he started on the trail home.

"He knows where we're going," Harley said, amused and amazed. "He is uncanny."

"Too bad he can't get us a DNA sample of Odell Rains."

Trouble stopped and looked back at them. He gave a loud meow.

"I wouldn't be so sure he can't," Harley said. "Maybe you should invite Odell over for a chat."

"That's exactly what I was thinking of doing," Tommie said.

. . .

I THINK a sit down with the alleged daughter is an excellent idea. Perhaps she'll reveal far more than she intends. A DNA sample is easily within my abilities. Never underestimate a black cat trained by the inimitable Sherlock Holmes. Cumberbatch, in his portrayal of the master detective, is brilliant. Think how much easier it would be to help the bipeds if I could have those pop-up little thought bubbles that Benedict has at his disposal on film. They'd be able to follow my brilliant deductions. The Loftus Lass and Mr. Brawny seem bright for all that they're human, but if they could truly comprehend my thoughts, it would surely speed things up.

I'm eager for the renovation team to arrive. I'll have to insist that Hank examine the walls of the upstairs bedrooms for hidden rooms or passages. Someone is slipping around the house—of that I have no doubt. The perfume is a hint, but it seems almost too deliberate. Two women show up claiming that they're rightful heirs. Both women wear strong scents. Nina Ahearn's old bedroom also contains a strong perfume at times. Call me a skeptic, but this is too coincidental to be an accident. The problem is that I don't see how perfume could play into false claims on property. The clues haven't revealed themselves, but I am alert and watching.

I trust that Harley will keep a close eye on Tommie. She truly has no one else but me to safeguard her. Now the riddle of what's happening in this old pile must be resolved and soon. I can't be certain that the noises and smells and movement of objects are not part of the alleged daughter/wife scam that is currently underway. It's like a loose thread—pull it a little and all may unravel.

Now I'll saunter along with Tommie and Harley to the lodge to see the marvels of the internet. Yes, as we approach, I see a satellite dish. A communication link to the outside world, as it were. Time to poke into the true story of Loftus Manor.

CHAPTER FOURTEEN

*H*arley installed Tommie at the kitchen table in his cottage. In a minute he had coffee going and his laptop powering up. He kept glancing at her, drinking in the way the sunlight filtered through the kitchen window to ignite the highlights in her hair. She was a beautiful woman, but better than that she was a good person. She had values and a sense of right and wrong, and to Harley that was important. After the harsh experience of war, when the only thing standing between him and death was the honor and bravery of his comrades, he'd come to understand how important a person's moral code was.

The group of Rangers he'd gone into Afghanistan with had been a tight, cohesive unit of soldiers who lived by a code. He'd watched too many of them die. One of his buddies, Stephen, had died protecting Harley from a sniper's bullet. It was a moment in time that haunted him in the dark hours of the morning. And when he'd come home, he'd learned that few civilians understood the meaning of living by a code. He'd been disillusioned with his country and the citizens who lived there. That's when he'd lucked into the job of groundskeeper at Loftus Manor.

"Harley, thank you for being with me today." Tommie turned in her chair and put a hand on his lower arm. "I don't know why you're so determined to help me, but I appreciate it. It means a lot to me to have your support."

"I want you to have a fair shake. Samuel left the manor to you. I want to see his wishes carried out."

"Even if I have to turn the manor into an inn? I know you don't really want it changed."

He sat down across from her while the coffee brewed. "I don't want it changed, because I think Samuel would want it to stay as is. And I have a personal aversion to change." His smile was sad. "I've grown comfortable here, Tommie. But that isn't your problem. You have to make this arrangement work for you, and I understand economic needs. The bottom line is what happens to Loftus Manor isn't up to me. That's for you to decide and I believe Samuel left it to you without any restrictions. It's one last thing I can do for my old friend and now my new friend."

Tommie pondered his words. "You're a good man, Harley. My uncle was lucky to call you friend, and so am I." His hand covered hers and he gave a little squeeze. And he held on a little longer than was necessary. It was only a fraction of a second, but Tommie felt it all the way through her body. "I think the coffee's ready." She had to break the connection.

Harley withdrew his hand and turned to the range to pour them two cups of strong black coffee. When she took her cup, Tommie's gaze met his. She saw an openness that she'd never expected to see. Harley Jones was slowly lowering his guard with her. And she could feel the same happening with her.

"How do you have internet but the manor doesn't?" she finally asked.

"There's a satellite behind the lodge. I offered to help Samuel set up an internet connection, but he never wanted internet or cell phones or any of the newfangled devices." Harley grinned. "When he needed anything ordered, I could do it for him or Nina would drive him to town where the store owners obliged him. The truth is, too, that reception is spotty. And sometimes slow. Reliable rural broadband is still a dream for folks like us."

"I understand. Once I get my jewelry business back up and running, I'll need the internet to sell," she explained. "And also to advertise the inn." She felt her stomach flutter with nervousness at the idea of what lay before her. If she worked twenty hours a day, she'd still be behind.

"When will the Evans start work on the manor?" Harley asked.

"Very soon. Which is why I'm going to contact Odell Rains right now. I want to sit down with her and feel her out. If there's a way to settle this amicably, I'll definitely consider it."

"You'd buy her out?" Harley asked.

"I would. If I had the money, which I don't." Tommie was aware that her attempted smile was a failure. "Money is nice to have, but what I have here at Loftus House is a dream, a lifestyle. I want to make it a reality, if I can afford it."

"I don't know if trying to compromise with Ms. Rains or Nina is the right path." He held up a hand to stop her from a passionate reply. "I'm just saying think long and hard. Don't make any offers today if we can find Ms. Rains."

"You're right." This time her smile won out.

"Then let's get busy and see what we can uncover."

THE NAGGING WORRY that Tommie was too kind and accommodating chewed at Harley as he went through the process of researching Odell Rains. While he searched for facts, what he mostly found was an absence of facts. Odell had no criminal record that he could find, not even unpaid parking tickets.

"She was born in Tennessee," Tommie said. "Did Samuel ever go to Knoxville?"

Harley put his coffee cup down. "He made some trips there when I first moved in. He was stronger then. He said he was meeting a genealogist there for some help with the Loftus family tree."

"You're sure it was Knoxville?"

The problem was that Harley remembered the conversation perfectly now that his memory had been jogged. "It was Knoxville. But look, if that's the case, Odell would have been at least eighteen, judging by her looks now, which I'd put at maybe twenty-three or so. He might have known Odell and her mother, but there's no indication Odell is his child."

"Thank you." Tommie put her hand on his.

His impulse was to grasp her fingers and hold on, but he didn't. Romantic gestures could be fraught with danger. Harley had fallen into the trap of caring for someone once. Caring deeply and believing in that woman. The truth of how wrong he'd been about Lyda, on top of his war experience, had almost driven him to desperation. He removed his hand and pointed to the computer screen. "Looks like Odell lived in Knoxville with her mother and sister."

"I know it's a long shot, but do you remember the name of the genealogist Samuel was visiting with?"

"No, but that's where the records in his office might come in handy."

Tommie looked around the kitchen. "Where's Trouble?"

Harley realized the cat had followed them into the lodge, but he hadn't seen the feline for quite some time. He did a quick examination of the compact building but there was no cat. "Maybe he went back to the manor."

Tommie looked longingly at the computer. "I want to stay and research Odell more, but I should go look for Trouble. He isn't my cat, and if something happened to him, I would feel terrible."

Harley wasn't about to let her go back to the manor by herself. "We can research later. Let's find the cat." He closed the computer and picked up his jacket. The day had been beautiful —perfect weather—but when the sun began to set, the chill would return.

When he held the door for her, she brushed against him going out and he again resisted the impulse to pick up her hand and hold it, to simply keep the physical connection. And that told him it was time for him to move on. Things were getting complicated here at Loftus Manor, and complications generally meant trouble. He'd help Tommie settle this business with the two grifters. He'd make sure she was safe and whoever was slipping into the house was caught and appropriately punished. He'd stay until the renovators were involved in the necessary changes. And then he would go—before he discovered he wanted to stay more than he should.

As they walked up the driveway to the manor, their shoes scrunching in the white oyster shells, Harley thought of the hard physical labor required to create the fine homes of the landed gentry. The oyster shells had been brought from Mobile Bay up the Alabama River and finally on the Coosa River. The shells were the first hard-packed "paving" available, and every big house had an oyster shell driveway.

The afternoon shadows of the trees slanted across their path, and Harley thought of the many times he'd walked up to the manor about this time of day to check on Samuel, to be sure he had his prescriptions or the necessary food for supper. Often, he'd find Nina in the kitchen, pots bubbling and the delicious aroma of a homecooked meal wafting through the manor. Samuel always invited him to stay for dinner, a drink, and a game of chess.

Tommie stopped so suddenly that he almost bumped into her. "What—" He saw it then. The front door was standing wide open. Trouble sat in the doorway licking a paw.

"What the hell?" Tommie said as she started running. "I know I locked the door."

"I know you did too," Harley said. He'd watched her lock it. He sprinted past her with raw determination to find whoever was in the house and make them pay. This had gone on long enough.

CHAPTER FIFTEEN

The cavalry arrives. At warp speed. Humans, standing upright and using only two legs, are not the best runners on the planet. They try, bless their hearts. They have none of the grace and agility of a feline who can emulate the wind. We're also rather more stealthy. But comparisons aside, I'm happy to see these two.

I thought I might patrol the manor while Tommie and Harley were engaged in their computer work. A good thing, too, since I found the house open but empty of any other human. Someone has been here though, and they were in Samuel's study. Were they looking for something or leaving something behind? There are elements of this case that make no sense at all. Take Nina's marriage to Samuel. If it were real, why not make it evident before he died? She had to know that every person with half a brain would question the timing of her revelation. Indeed, if she was Samuel's wife, why didn't she say so and handle the funeral arrangements? As I understand it, Harley took care of the details for the service and burial, per Samuel's instructions. But that is clearly the purview of a wife. Yet not a peep out of her.

I'm convinced this marriage is hog-wash, as we Southerners say. Benedict would be more erudite and call it illogical. In this instance, deep-fried hog wash works best. The question is, how to prove it or even better, push Nina into a confession. I know the bipeds are working on background information about the "instant" daughter and wife. Perhaps they will extract a lead that puts us on the path to disproving their claims.

Tommie and Harley are at the front steps. Let me lead the way to Samuel's small study so they can assess if anything is missing. Harley will know more than the Loftus Lass, but it's good for all of us to examine the circumstances.

They are both following me—as they should. The Loftus Lass and Mr. Brawny are more easily trained than most humanoids. Now as I jump on top of the built-in desk, I see some books that have been knocked askew. Good news that Harley is checking out the rest of the house to be sure our intruder has really gone. I've already had a look about, and there's no one here, unless they're hiding in the walls, which is not as far-fetched as it sounds.

Tommie is walking around the room, snapping photos with her cell phone. Grand idea. Document, document everything!

Harley returns with an all-clear. He found exactly what I found— nothing. He's practically bubbling with aggravation. He's scanned the room, and he hasn't yet noticed what they need to see. I yowl to call atten- tion to the bookcase above Samuel's desk. When Tommie doesn't act fast enough, I daintily use a claw to pull down an over-large edition. The book is old, the pages yellowed. Tommie carefully catches it before it can splat on the floor. She gives me a look of consternation, but her attention is instantly drawn to the pages of the book while Harley examines the room to see what else has been disturbed.

My work here is done—for the moment at least. I'm going upstairs to see if anything has been disturbed in the bedrooms. I gave a cursory exam- ination, but now I have more time to truly inspect the upstairs area. And yes, the attic. I know, I know. Never go into the attic or the basement. But this isn't a horror story. At least I hope not. I have much to explore.

And to once again see if I can deduce how our unwanted visitor is departing.

Tommie sat down in the chair by the chess game and opened the book Trouble had pulled from the shelf. It was the size of a photo album, and the pages were handstitched into the spine. The craftsmanship was beautiful. Handwritten penmanship flowed elegantly across the pages. There was no title on the cover of the volume, but the first page read, "The Loftus Family of Hawick, a story of ill deeds and hauntings."

She felt a hand on her shoulder and looked up into Harley's clear eyes. "I'm going to track down the cat and check out the rest of the house. I get the idea the cat knows more than we do. What's that you have?"

She showed him the cover of the book. "A ghost story. It's dated from the early 1800s."

"A ghost didn't open the front door and leave it open."

"I know, but it couldn't hurt to know a little about the house. Besides, Trouble wanted me to examine this book. It was slightly pulled out of order."

"Good idea since nothing else in this room seems to be disturbed. I don't know why anyone would slip into the house to read a two-hundred-year-old ghost story, but not a lot makes sense about what's going on here. As soon as we have a chance, I'm changing all the door locks for you."

"Thanks, Harley. I mean it. You've been a godsend. I wouldn't be able to stay here without you." That was hard for her to admit, even to herself. She'd grown up feeling like an outsider even though her stepmother had been nothing but kind. But it wasn't the same as having her real mother, no matter how hard they both worked at it. When she'd hit eighteen, she'd gotten a job in a veterinary clinic and that's where she met Jonathan. She'd fallen hard and fast, and because she was on her own and desperately needing a connection, she'd put one hundred percent into the relationship. When he'd betrayed her, two years and fifty thousand dollars in debt for his law degree, she'd been crushed. She'd convinced herself she'd never allow herself to need another person ever again. Now, with all of the strange things happening at Loftus Manor, she needed Harley to be there. Just to be there for the time being.

"You okay?" Harley brushed his fingers lightly against her cheek.

"Yes." She sat up taller. "I'm fine. Just troubled by whatever is happening in this house. It defies reason."

"I'll be back shortly. I want to take another look around."

Tommie discovered she was holding her breath until Harley left the room. She filled her lungs and closed her eyes for a second. Harley was working on her. There was a chemistry between them that they'd pretty much been able to ignore, but it was becoming harder and harder to continue pretending they both weren't aware.

She forced her attention back to the book she held and began to read. "The actions of Reynard Loftus brought the curse down upon the bloodline. Few will dispute that fact. Reynard was not a just man or a fair man, but he was a powerful man in the Village of Hawick and even more powerful when he moved to America."

Tommie found herself pulled into the story of the Loftus Curse—something neither her uncle nor Harley had told her about. As she read, she felt the hair at the nape of her neck starting to rise. The tale from the 1800s, when Loftus Manor was newly constructed, dealt with a widowed Loftus, Reynard, who lived alone with a female caregiver in the house—one who obviously had ulterior motives.

"Leeanne was a beautiful woman who used the artifices of lip paint and kohl with all the expertise of the harlots of King Louie's palace."

She skimmed the pages, listening for Harley's return, but she was soon again absorbed in the story. It turned out that Reynard and his wife had one child, a son, Pritchett. After the death of Reynard's wife, Pritchett went to school in England, then returned to earn his law degree in the Northeast. He was working in a firm in Boston when Reynard took ill. Pritchett returned to Wetumpka to settle his father's will and estate, and that's when he met the beautiful and very young Leeanne, who claimed that she and Reynard had been married in the last months of his life.

Tommie stopped reading. The house was so quiet, and she was struck by the scent of heavy perfume that seemed to come out of nowhere. Her pulse quickened and she lowered the book to her lap and looked all around the room. No one had entered. The perfume had to be an olfactory illusion of some type. As much as she wanted to call out for Harley, she didn't.

The sound of footsteps behind her made her shift suddenly and the book slipped from her lap to the floor. When she was certain no one was behind her, she bent to pick up the book but froze. It had fallen open to a drawing. Right on the page was a beautiful woman in a hooded cloak with three unusual buttons on one shoulder. The exact same image she'd seen outside Loftus Manor that early morning when she'd run out to chase the phantom. A flush of fear slipped through her body, but she inhaled and picked up the book. Was this a rendering of Leeanne? It was the easy conclusion to jump to. But the drawing wasn't labeled or marked in anyway. The haunting image had no real explanation.

She flipped back to her place in the narrative, knowing that Harley would be equally as intrigued—and concerned—as she was.

She read through the entire story, feeling more disturbed with each paragraph. Pritchett refused to believe Leeanne's claim. He forced her from the manor on a bitter night. A sense of impending doom permeated the tale.

Tommie abruptly stood up. She had to tell Harley. It was like the events portrayed in the book were happening again, as if history had been caught in some time loop. "Harley!" She called his name because she had to talk to someone before she popped. He came through the door and she felt relief.

"What is it?" he asked.

"The Loftus Curse."

"What?"

"Samuel didn't tell you that the bloodline was cursed?"

"He told me ghost stories and things like that but nothing about a curse on this house."

"Not on the house, but on those with Loftus blood."

"Maybe you'd better explain what you're talking about." He came into the room, the cat in lockstep with him. When he took the book, which she clutched to her chest, the cat jumped up on the desk and rubbed against her empty hands. "What is this curse?" he asked.

"First, take a look at this." She flipped to the back of the book where the drawing of the cloaked woman seemed even sadder and more sinister.

"What the—" Harley bent closer to examine the drawing. "The woman in the cloak. This is her!"

"I know."

"I wonder if Samuel knew this old legend and perhaps

worked it into some of the stories he told. Maybe our cloaked phantom is a local who knows about this supposed curse."

"*If* any of this is true." Tommie pointed at the book. "This could just be a story someone made up. We don't know. Perhaps Samuel wasn't the only storyteller in the Loftus clan."

"I wouldn't be shocked or surprised, but it still doesn't explain why someone is haunting the manor dressed from a drawing supposedly from long ago." Harley rubbed his chin.

"Someone, or something," Tommie muttered. She pointed to the book. "It's too much to believe what's happening at Loftus Manor now is merely coincidence, Harley. It's all happened before. And Samuel had to know this because the book was kind of pulled out on the shelf over his desk as if someone had been reading it."

"You have to slow down and tell me what you found." Harley grasped her shoulders gently. "Take a breath and just tell me the tale."

"Reynard Loftus had a beautiful caregiver named Leeanne after his wife died."

"Reynard?" Harley's brows drew together. "An ancestor of yours?"

"Yes, 1800s. According to this story, Reynard died and the caregiver, a woman named Leeanne, claimed she and Reynard were married. But Reynard had a son who was a lawyer, and Pritchett Loftus denied Leeanne's marriage claim and fought it."

"This *is* sounding a little too familiar."

She could tell that Harley was connecting the dots, just as she'd done. "Pritchett had the woman evicted from the manor on a bitter winter night. The next day, Pritchett shut the house up, intending to put it on the market and sell it. He had a wealthy buyer who was willing to pay cash and he was eager to get back to the Northeast. It was said Pritchett hated Loftus

House and the Alabama territory. He was more than eager to leave Loftus Manor and Alabama behind."

"He obviously didn't sell the manor or it wouldn't still be in the Loftus family," Harley concluded.

"You're correct. Pritchett forced Leeanne, the caregiver, out of the house before he locked the doors. He was getting ready to board a stage and return to Boston, thinking the sale was all but done. But it never happened, because Leeanne got back into the house and hung herself in the exact spot where Uncle Samuel hung himself."

"Well damn," Harley said softly. "That's horrible." He frowned. "I don't understand why Samuel didn't tell me this if he knew about it." He flipped a few pages of the book. "What's the curse?"

"Before Leeanne died, she cursed Pritchett Loftus and all of his heirs. She left a handwritten note with the curse on it. 'Deny the truth, and death shall come for you. Deny justice, and I shall return to call you to the grave where your bones will molder beside mine. In the end, I will have my revenge against a bloodline consumed with greed.'"

"What happened to the property?" Harley asked. "After Pritchett died?"

"After Leeanne's suicide no one would buy the property and Pritchett discovered that Reynard had unsettled debts. Big debts. Pritchett was forced to stay in Loftus House and run a law practice from here. He married a local girl and had children, but his dream of living in Boston was destroyed. He was a bitter and angry man without a single friend. It's said that before he died, he told his wife that none would ever be happy living in Loftus Manor. That they would meet a death worthy of their sins, just as he did. He was also a suicide."

Harley chafed her ice-cold hands. "Well, this is certainly a story that Samuel never bothered to tell me. I doubt he even knew about it."

"I think he knew. The book was there, on the shelf just above his desk. It was halfway sticking out when Trouble pulled at it. The question is, who else knew about this legend and was it someone who might have set Samuel's murder up to mimic this tale?"

TOMMIE FOUND comfort in the cup of hot tea that Harley made for her. She had to put the shock of the drawing of the cloaked woman and the possible sordid past of the manor out of her mind. Loftus Manor was not haunted by the ghost of Leeanne or anyone else. Loftus Manor was the focus of a very sophisticated grift by two women who would stoop to anything to run her off. Tommie knew she had to keep her thoughts focused in that direction or she'd run screaming out of the manor and never return. To that end, she smiled at Harley, who hovered over her.

"I'm okay. I swear it. The drawing did startle me, but don't you see? It's evidence that Nina and Odell knew about this and they're using it for their own ends." She didn't wait for him to agree or disagree. "Did you find anything upstairs?"

"Nothing. The doors and windows are all locked from the inside. There's no way someone could get out of here. At the lawyer's request, I changed all of the locks and you have all the keys. No one should be able to open the door."

"Except the front door was open," Tommie reminded him. "Maybe the intruder was inside for a time and left the open door."

"That's a possibility." Harley's concession was half-hearted. "Tommie, let's get those renovators out here tomorrow and measure these rooms. There's something going on behind the walls. I'm serious. It has to be stopped. If you're going to live here in peace, we have to end this."

Tommie nodded. What he said was true. There was just one little thing—money. She had enough of a nest egg saved to renovate the kitchen in Loftus Manor. She could do that and still survive if she was actually up and running by Christmas and had some guests. Knocking out walls looking for secret passages would be expensive and time consuming.

Trouble let out a low meow.

"What's wrong?" Tommie asked him.

The cat shuffled some papers around on the desk, knocking several things to the floor. At last he uncovered a mahogany box at the back of the desk almost covered in papers.

Tommie picked it up. It was not heavy. She opened it up and stopped. Game cameras were tucked in the box. She bent down and kissed the cat's head with a little squee of joy. "Perfect. The perfect solution. Game cameras! We can set them up outside and record where our intruder is coming and going from."

Harley's grin was ear to ear. "That's one smart cat."

"Why did Uncle Samuel have these cameras?" Tommie asked. "He didn't hunt, did he?"

"Oh, heavens no. Samuel wouldn't harm a fly. And I sure don't hunt. In fact, the land here is posted against hunting. Samuel enjoyed the wildlife, and I suspect that's why he had the cameras. He probably was intending to put them out so he could watch the wild creatures. He was proud of the fact they had a safe haven here at Loftus Manor."

"Well, they can serve a dual purpose. We can enjoy the wildlife and possibly catch an intruder." The drawing of the cloaked woman and the old family history—true or tall tale— only made Tommie more determined to get to the bottom of what was happening at the manor.

CHAPTER SIXTEEN

*B*y the time Harley had finished installing the game cameras outside the lodge, Tommie had gone through a handwritten account of the Loftus Manor history. Leeanne was not mentioned.

Together, she and Harley continued to look through the library shelves. She found a few more interesting tidbits, but it was the drawing that she went back to again and again.

Leanne Prestwood. Tommie studied her face. She was a compelling woman with dark eyes and lips painted red. "What's your story?" Tommie asked her, not expecting an answer but feeling the need to vocalize her question.

"Meow." Trouble rubbed against her wrist.

She stroked the cat. He was pretty darn perceptive—even though it was hard to admit it.

"Meow." Trouble lifted his front paws to the shelf where the book had been stored. He began to claw at the wood.

"Hey, don't do that." She stood up, but the cat clawed and dug. Before she could stop him, he pulled something down onto the desktop. She picked up the tiny notebook that had been crammed in the back, behind several other books. It contained a list of dates with numbers written beside them. They began in June of the current year and stopped the day before Samuel died.

"Harley!" She called him over from where he was searching a cabinet on the other side of the room. "What's this?"

He took the booklet looking a little sheepish. "Samuel and I sometimes played chess or backgammon for money. Samuel had a habit of claiming he won when he didn't. It was more of a joke than anything serious, but the dates look like he was keeping a record of his 'debt.' Money never really changed hands, but it looks like he was actually keeping track of it."

Tommie almost laughed—in some ways Harley and her uncle seemed like young boys. It was delightful. She checked her watch. The dinner hour had passed, but it wasn't too late to take action on solving the mysteries of the manor. "The lawyer mentioned Odell was staying at the Hilton. I'll call her and ask her to meet us for drinks this evening."

"Good idea. Your uncle kept a fully stocked bar, and I can mix a mean drink, if you want me to be here."

"Please. I really want you here." She wasn't pretending, and even though it scared her to be so open, she was determined to explore the feelings Harley aroused.

"I'll run down to the cottage for some lemons and limes. Anything you want me to check on the computer while I'm down there?"

She handed him the drawing of the young woman in the cloak. "Could you see if there are any likenesses of this woman or this cloak on the internet? Something isn't right about this."

"I don't have the image recognition software to really do that, but I'll see what I can find. If push comes to shove, there's a lovely woman in Wetumpka, Patricia Murphy. She was a runway model back in the 1970s and she studied fashion and design. The cloak is distinctive. Maybe she can offer some clues."

THE LOFTUS LASS *found the drawing, a shockingly good clue. If I were a biped with opposable thumbs and had a car, I'd drive to the nearest art studio and learn what I could about that picture. The woman is beautiful. Was she married to Reynard Loftus and then cheated of her rightful inheritance? Did she have his child? Is all of this some foolishness Samuel cooked up? He was known to love a good yarn, and he was deeply into the bloodlines of the Loftus family. It's possible he could have managed to find old paper and ink—the volume is hand-stitched so he could have added pages or composed the entire thing. It's only thirty pages or so. There's so much to consider, and I hope my fellow detectives use their noggins to work through the multitude of clues I've now provided for them. But why would he do this to Tommie? He went to a great deal of effort to find her so she could inherit it. Why would he pull a prank that might jeopardize her inheritance?*

There was no one else in the house but Nina Ahearn and, on occasion, Harley. Did Samuel suspect Nina of plotting against him? And if he did, why wouldn't he send her packing? The picture Harley paints of Samuel is certainly not a helpless man, someone who would be a victim of a caregiver.

There are answers here at Loftus Manor, but there are other sources that must be properly investigated. Tommie is following the bloodlines of Loftus relatives to see how an event from the 1800s has suddenly happened again, while the button of a cloak has also appeared. As if by magic—that's the part that has me befuddled. I'm into Harry Potter as much as the next black cat, but I have to say, something is rotten in Denmark here. It will just take persistence to figure it out.

On the plus side of this situation, I detected a certain spark ignite between the two bipeds. They are so cautious, so caught up in their

*patterns from the past. They have much to learn from the Sherlock of cat
detectives. In sleuthing and the heart department.*

HARLEY WASN'T PARTICULARLY FOND of modern technology, but
he used it when necessary, and now was the time. He scanned in
the drawing of the woman in the cloak. It didn't take long. He
was anxious about leaving Tommie alone in the manor. He kept
telling himself it wasn't his place to worry, but that didn't stop
him. The things that he liked about Tommie—her desire to do
the right thing—were the very things that also made her vulnerable to scam artists, and that's exactly what he'd come to view
Nina as, with her ridiculously timed marriage. The magical
appearance of the illegitimate daughter, Odell, was equally suspicious. Both were opportunists. Had either of them had a legitimate claim they would have spoken out about it long
before now.

He pulled the drawing of the woman in the cloak up on his
computer and tried for a search that would find similar images.
There was software that might have done it, but he didn't own
it. He'd look into it in the morning in town. There were several
computer whizzes in Wetumpka who would know exactly the
program that would do the trick.

He searched for cloaks, and though he found hundreds of
images, none looked like the one in the photograph. He hoped
his friend the fashion designer, Patricia Murphy, would know
something about the cut and fabric.

Before he left, he found the online portal to check for a
marriage license in Elmore County. There was no record of
Samuel and Nina marrying—and interestingly enough, a
marriage certificate was no longer required, merely notarized
forms of the marriage. While he was there, he searched to see if

the marriage was legal if it hadn't been filed with the proper authorities.

There he struck gold. If the notarized application for marriage had not been filed, then the marriage was not legal, no matter who performed the ceremony. He searched for information on an unfiled marriage form and a deceased partner. No luck there. He'd have to talk to a lawyer about that one, but he felt more hopeful than he had. That still left trouble from Odell, who'd clearly shown she was a dangerous person. Tommie hadn't wanted to prosecute Odell for a near assault with a car, but Harley wasn't that compassionate. He'd be more than happy to put the imposter in jail if he could.

Still stewing about Nina and Odell, Harley did a simple google search on Odell Loftus and Odell Rains and came up with three people, none of which were the Odell in Wetumpka. He picked up his cell phone to call Aiden Rivers—as a law officer Aiden had all the equipment necessary to check out Odell and see who she really was and where she came from. But Tommie had been adamant about not contacting the authorities. He put the cell phone back on his desk. Maybe he could convince Tommie to talk to Aiden, but right now she would only get angry if Harley stepped over her request.

Next he checked Nina Ahearn's background. He wasn't surprised to find that she had a Facebook page—something he hadn't thought of because he didn't use social media. But he joined Facebook so he could explore her posts. Nothing exciting popped up, but there were a number of photos of Loftus Manor, going back months, that she called "her home." The clear implication was that she owned Loftus Manor.

"So, Nina, you've been working toward this for some time," Harley mumbled as he continued. He was deep in his tracking when he saw the black cat at the window. The cat was obviously crying, and he opened the window to let him in. Trouble had other plans. He rushed back to the driveway and cried again.

Harley shut down the computer, picked up the drawing, and started out the door. He didn't question for a minute that Trouble had come to get him. He couldn't help the nagging worry that something had happened to Tommie in the manor. He simply had a creepy sensation that she wasn't safe, and he'd learned to honor those gut instincts.

CHAPTER SEVENTEEN

ommie gripped the telephone tightly. "Odell, I do think we should talk about your claim."

"I'm not interested in proving anything to you or that freeloader living in the groundskeeper's lodge. You can tell him for me that as soon as I prove my relationship to Samuel, he'll be gone."

Tommie sighed. This was harder than she'd thought. In a way, she didn't blame Odell for being angry and aggressive—if she was indeed Samuel's legitimate daughter. She was like a piece of luggage that had been left at the airport terminal. Battered and unclaimed. But that still didn't give her the right to try to run over a person. "Look, let's just talk. Come over for a drink. If you want to explore the house, you can."

There was a slight hesitation. "I can look around? Without a keeper?"

"Keeper?" Tommie asked.

"I can look around on my own without someone following me like I'm going to steal something."

"Yes." It might be a foolhardy ploy, but Tommie wanted to

see Odell in the house, to see what she reacted to. Did she have any lingering love for Samuel as her father, or had she been raised to hate him and believe that he deliberately abandoned her—despite what the real truth might be? Or was the whole thing just a made-up attempt to get money?

"Come over at eight," Tommie said. "We'll talk for a while and then you can explore the manor. It's best to do it tonight. I'm going to start some renovations tomorrow or the next day."

"You can't change the manor. It isn't yours!" Odell was hostile.

"At this moment, it is completely mine. And if I want to open Loftus Manor to guests by Christmas, I have to start now. I'm sorry. This was all decided before you arrived on the scene. You should have pressed your case when Samuel died."

"Maybe I didn't know." Odell spoke angrily. "Maybe no one told me that my deadbeat old man had croaked."

"Maybe he didn't know about you."

Her statement was met with a cold silence. At last Odell spoke. "I'll be there at eight. Don't try to sandbag me or trick me."

Tommie thought of the car speeding toward her and the way Harley had saved her from serious injuries. If anyone was capable of pulling a fast one, it was Odell. "I wouldn't dream of it," she said sweetly. "See you in a bit."

She hung up and turned abruptly toward the door of the library. Someone was in the hall of the house. She heard footsteps. Her first instinct was to look around for Trouble, but the cat was nowhere to be seen. He'd vanished while she was on the telephone.

The sound of footsteps on the hardwood floors was distinctive. One person walking. She heard it clearly. She picked up her phone to text Harley but didn't. By the time he could get there, the person would be gone or she'd be dead—if killing her was the intention. After the car incident with Odell, she couldn't discount that someone would hurt her. Odell or one of Odell's supporters. Heck, she was a stranger in Wetumpka. She had no idea where allegiances might lie or what ant bed she might have unknowingly stepped into.

She grabbed a poker from the fireplace set and tiptoed to the library door. Fear made her breathing shallow, but she wasn't about to cower in the library and wait to be attacked. And whoever was sneaking around the manor—it was time to confront them. If it was someone trying to make her leave her inheritance, they were not going to be successful.

Her grip on the poker tightened as she held it up and slowly turned the doorknob. The heavy mahogany door opened without a sound and she stepped into the empty hallway. There was no evidence of anyone in either direction. The footsteps had stopped, and for a long minute she stood still and listened. Where was that cat? She could use his company right about now.

She was beginning to relax when she heard what sounded like furniture being dragged across the second floor. Her heartbeat tripled as she walked silently toward the stairs. A stab of terror went through her when she realized a stranger in the house could move about silently—if they chose to. Whoever was in the house didn't care that she knew they were there. Perhaps they even wanted her to know. It was a chilling thought.

Carefully she went up the stairs, her ears straining for any sound out of the ordinary. The old house had a soft sighing, whispering music of its own, and she was growing accustomed to it. An intruder was another matter.

When she got to the second floor, she looked down the hall-way. The doorway to the bedroom suite where Nina Ahearn had lived was open. She started down the hallway and caught the scent of a musky perfume. She'd smelled it before—in the lawyer's office. When Nina had made her appearance to report her alleged marriage to Samuel.

If Nina was in the bedroom, Tommie vowed to physically throw her from the house. Without a court order, Nina had no business in the house for any reason and she certainly had no business sneaking around and scaring people.

Tommie advanced on the open doorway, listening, hardly breathing, poker lifted above her head. She stepped through the door and had a clear view across a small sitting room to the bed. She knew before she investigated further that the room was empty. The room was quiet, undisturbed except for the lingering perfume. Tommie knew that whoever had been there—and someone had been in the room—was gone.

She lowered the poker and caught a strong whiff of the cologne. She tried to follow it, but it seemed to emanate from the walls. And from one particular corner of the room. She pressed the beautiful wallpaper that covered the walls, running her finger along the places where sheets overlapped looking for a split or crack or something that would indicate there was a false panel behind the floral print of violets. It all seemed to be of one piece. There was no indication the wall concealed anything.

Moving across the room, she went to the fireplace. She'd read enough books and seen enough movies where something sinister was concealed behind a fireplace or bookcase. She pulled and tugged at the decorative design in the wooden mantle, hopping that she'd trigger a lever to open to a secret passage. There was no other possible excuse for what was happening in the house.

She heard something behind her and turned to watch a book on the bedside table move slowly to the edge. Mesmerized, she couldn't look away. The book moved incrementally, a fraction at a time. But it was moving. And there was no one nearby to account for it. At last the book crashed to the floor and Tommie snapped out of the trance she'd fallen into. She rushed to the book and picked it up. "No Rest for the Wicked" was the title, a ghost story. Her heart was pounding and her hand shaking as she held the book.

The crash of the front door and footsteps in the foyer brought her completely back to herself.

"Tommie! Where are you?" Harley called out to her. And with his voice came the cry of the cat.

"I'm up here, in Nina's old bedroom." She quelled the tremble in her voice. She would not be afraid. She would not. Or at least she wouldn't admit it. "Someone's been in here. I heard them and followed them up here, but they're gone."

Harley and Trouble burst into the room. Harley looked positively wild-eyed, and Trouble wasn't in a much better state. The cat leaped up, bumping into her chest, and she caught him. In a split second, they were both enveloped in Harley's arms. Tommie felt such a sense of comfort that she never wanted to move, but she did. She eased back from Harley and released Trouble to the floor. The cat took off, prowling the room. Putting her hand on Harley's chest, she felt the rapid beating of his heart.

"What's wrong?" she asked, aware that Harley was equally as upset as she was.

"Have you been down to your room?" Harley asked.

"No. I've been here. Why?"

"There was someone standing in your window as I approached the house. I saw her as clear as day. She was a dark-haired woman and she was wearing a cloak with a hood. Her face was almost obscured, but she had on red lipstick. I caught a glimpse of that. Trouble saw her too." He added the last sentence as if she wouldn't believe him.

"What's going on here, Harley. In Loftus Manor." She held the book out to him. "This was on the bedside stand. I watched it creep across the bedtable and fall to the floor, as if it meant to get my attention."

"A ghost story?" He held the book with distaste.

"It's time we truly found out the truth about Samuel and the history of this house." She took the book back. "Until we do, Harley, would you mind staying in the manor at night? Just to be on the safe side." She was not afraid, she told herself. She was merely cautious.

CHAPTER EIGHTEEN

I am at my wit's end with this phantom figure that haunts the halls of Loftus Manor. If I were a superstitious kind of cat, which I am not, I would be believing in ghosts right about now. There's nothing else to explain how the figure both Harley and I saw moves around the manor so freely. I've searched for passages and come up empty handed. My skills of deduction—and scent—are acute, and if there was a secret entrance, I believe I would detect it. My logical side tells me there is no such thing as a ghost, but my detective side tells me that the only thing that explains what is happening in Loftus Manor indicates a ghost at work.

While some may view my internal monologue as foolish, I would point out to them that one man is dead. Hanged by his own hand, or so the local authorities would have us believe. The longer I'm at Loftus House, the less I believe that Samuel Loftus took his own life. From all indications, there was no preparation for suicide. No cause for it, either.

Something happened in Loftus Manor the night Samuel Loftus died, and until we resolve this, no one is going to rest easy in this old pile. Now I'm going to saunter down to Tommie's room and see what my becloaked phantom has wrought. I swear, if old E. A. Poe, one of my literary idols, could have spent a week in this house he could have added a dozen stories and poems to his backlist.

As logical as I am, walking down this hallway gives me a shiver. I catch the whiff of perfume, which was also in the bedroom the Ahearn woman used. A strong scent. Musky, expensive, and the type of perfume I associate with both Odell Rains and Nina Ahearn.

Luckily Tommie's door isn't locked, and while I'm waiting for Mr. Brawny and the Loftus Lass to get their act together, I can get inside the room without their help. I have to hand it to Tommie. She's a neat-nik without being overbearing about it. She's already put away her clothes, the bed is made, the room is orderly, which makes it so much easier to see if anything is disturbed.

A quick perusal and I find nothing out of order except one thing. A woman's handkerchief soaked in perfume with the initials L.P. stitched in the corner. The hanky has been wadded up and left behind the dresser. I'm not an authority on the fabrics humans value, but this appears to be fine linen with the elegant stitching. And the perfume. Very old. And who would L.P. be but Leeanne Prestwood.

A definite clue. And perhaps one that is a little too convenient and easy. Someone is trying to lead us to a specific conclusion. Now I must decide if the wiser choice is to allow them to draw us down that certain path and pretend we're unaware of the machinations, or to balk and put an end to this now.

To quote an old showman of high merit, "The show must go on." Most think this phrase stems from theatrical endeavors, but a cat with a sophisticated education knows that it comes from the world of the circus. I have to admit that the humanoids have created a language rich in history and variation. Nothing to compare to what cats have contributed, but that's a story for a different time.

HARLEY PULLED and tugged at the mantel above the fireplace to no avail. Nothing moved or shifted. No creaking panels or sliding doorways. He turned to Tommie. "If there's a passage here, I can't find it."

"Whoever was in this room...I guess she could have gotten past me and gone down to my bedroom. But why?" Tommie pushed her hair out of her left eye.

"Why the perfume? Why are they sneaking around and moving a book? None of this makes sense," Harley said with some frustration. "What's to be gained by playing this silly game."

"Unless there really is a spirit here." Tommie bit her bottom lip, as if she thought he would laugh at her.

"I don't blame you for thinking that after watching the book creep across that table." He'd examined the table to be sure there wasn't some device that had moved the book, or even some principle of physics that could explain it. As far as he could tell there was no reason for the book to have moved. Unless a ghost had pushed it.

"I was willing to believe that whoever was sneaking in and out of the manor intended to frighten me out of my inheritance. That they'd found a secret way in and out of the house where they could shake me up, make me afraid. I've believed that all along, and therefore I haven't taken the events seriously. That was until Odell tried to run me down in the street and I saw a book move on its own. Now, it's serious."

Harley didn't blame her. This had gone on far too long. He should have been able to catch the intruder—because he sure didn't believe it was a ghost. Someone, a very devious someone, was at work in Loftus Manor and he had no doubt their intention was to drive Tommie from the premises. That wasn't going to happen.

Walking beside Tommie in the hallway, Harley had an

impulse to put his arm around her shoulders, a gesture of support and comfort, as well as something more. That more was the emotion he didn't want to evaluate. His time at Loftus Manor had allowed him to remain isolated from people, especially women. The one thing he didn't need right now was a romantic complication. Life was hard enough. But he couldn't deny that he felt something for Tommie. She was smart and beautiful, a deadly combination. On top of that, she seemed to operate on a code of values, much as he did. Were they the same values? Only time would tell. For the moment, he intended to make sure Tommie stayed in Loftus Manor at least long enough to show him who she truly was.

"Kitty, kitty, kitty!" Tommie called for Trouble as she entered her bedroom. "Where did that cat go?"

The black cat leaped to the bed and curled up, ignoring both humans. Harley couldn't help chuckling. The cat was running circles around all of them. And he had something in his mouth. It took him a moment before he realized it was a lacy women's handkerchief, the kind his grandmother had carried in her sweater sleeve when she attended church.

Tommie picked up the hanky and sniffed it. "It reeks of perfume. Like the scent in my room." She examined the hanky, taking in the delicately embroidered flowers and the L.P. initials. "Leeanne Prestwood. It seems a little too convenient," she said.

"It does," he agreed, and promptly sneezed. "It's a heavy scent."

"Does it remind you of anyone?" Tommie asked.

"Both Odell and Nina. I'm not sure it's the same scent. I can't tell. All I know is that it's a heavy perfume."

"Expensive," Tommie confirmed. "The handkerchief proves someone was in this room, though."

"Tommie, I don't mean to scare you, but maybe you and

Trouble should come stay in the cottage. There's a guest room." He made the offer before he could talk himself out of it. "Or I'll definitely take you up on the suggestion that I camp out in the manor with you."

Before Tommie could answer, he heard a knock at the front door. Tommie checked her watch. "That must be Odell. It's eight o'clock."

Together they hurried down the stairs to open the front door.

CHAPTER NINETEEN

Odell stood in the doorway, hands on her hips, as if she was ready for an argument.

"Come in," Tommie said, stepping back. "Why don't we go to the library for a drink?"

"You said I could tour the house."

"Yes," Tommie said evenly. The young woman was like a balky mule. "After we talk."

"I don't have anything to say to you," Odell said. "Or let me rephrase. What I have to say will be said in a courtroom when I claim my inheritance."

"You came very close to hitting me with your car," Tommie said to the young woman. "Perhaps we'll speak about that in a courtroom too." She saw the surprise and approval on Harley's face and the worry that appeared fleetingly on Odell's face. The black cat stood up on his back legs and danced, as if he too approved of her.

"I didn't see you," Odell said, though Tommie noted she didn't deny the accusation.

"If I hadn't knocked Tommie out of the way, she would have been badly injured." Harley stepped closer to Tommie. "It looked to me as if you meant to strike her."

"I didn't see her. The sun was in my eyes. But thank heavens for the cavalry," Odell said smartly. "What would you do, Ms. Sykes, without a man to save you?"

Trouble hunkered down, poised for the kill. Tommie scooped him into her arms. "Let's get settled. What would you like to drink, Odell?" She forced herself to keep it civil, but she turned her back and started to walk away. Odell could follow or not.

"You're not going to trick me into saying something I'll regret."

Tommie turned back to her. "I'm sorry for whatever life you've led that makes you so unhappy. I really just want to talk with you. I don't want to take anything that belongs to someone else, but I do want what's mine."

"And that's exactly what I want," Odell said, her words heated.

Tommie glanced at Harley, who shook his head slightly, as if to say—she's not going to be reasonable. That was likely true, but Odell was there now, and it was best to see the thing through.

When the drink order was settled and Harley had stoked up the fire, he went to play bartender and returned with vodka tonics for all. Except for the tinkle of ice in the glasses, silence settled over the room. Trouble prowled the bookshelves, but he didn't make a sound.

"That cat is going to ruin those books, which are probably valuable," Odell finally said. "You shouldn't let him have the run of the house."

"I doubt he'll ruin anything," Tommie responded, "but as of

right this minute, the manor and everything in it is mine to destroy if I choose to. This is a fact. The best road forward for all of us is to try to determine what, if anything, is owed to you. I don't want your inheritance, Odell. But we need to see some DNA paperwork, and we need to speak with your mother, Lucinda."

"Why?" Odell looked truly confused. "She's an old bag that wouldn't tell the truth if her life depended on it. She'd lie about me just to keep me from having anything, just like she's lied to me all of my life." She glared at Tommie. "Just like she lied to my father about my existence, I suppose."

"Nonetheless, I need to speak with her." Tommie caught the slight nod of approval Harley gave her. His support bolstered her confidence.

"What if she won't talk?" Odell remained belligerent.

"Then I'm afraid she'll have to be hauled into court to help prove your claim. We need dates and times of her meetings with Samuel. We need testimony, under oath, that proves their relationship was real. We need to see your birth certificate."

"Documentation. That's all that matters to you."

"Put yourself in my shoes, Odell. What would matter to you? I'm not trying to cheat you, but I also won't allow myself to be cheated. Did your mother tell you that Samuel was your father when you were a small girl?"

Odell's creamy complexion flushed. "She used me as a tool against men. She'd make me find them in a public place and call them daddy, using public humiliation for a pay day. She milked money out of me. But she always said my real father was Samuel Loftus, owner of Loftus Manor, but that he'd never acknowledge me because he had too many lawyers and too much money to protect him."

"She never confronted Samuel with her claims?" Harley broke his silence.

"As far as I know, never. She only went after men who could hand over a couple thousand dollars to pay her to keep silent. That's how she made the rent or a car note. She said Samuel was the big fish she was no match to land. But I'm his daughter, not someone he slept with and forgot as quickly as he could. I won't go away."

"Why didn't you ever contact Samuel?" Tommie had to fight the impulse to feel sorry for Odell. She had to keep in mind the woman may have tried to kill her, though looking at Odell, fidgeting in the wingchair in the library, she looked pretty toothless and sad.

"My mother always made me feel like I was something he would be ashamed of."

"And yet here you are," Harley said.

"He's dead. He can't look at me like I'm some kind of grifter or cause me humiliation."

Tommie caught Harley's eye. It made perfect sense. A child who'd been rejected and used her entire life wouldn't want to risk that final rejection by the man she thought was her father.

"I promise to treat you fairly, Odell, if your claim is legitimate." Tommie could do no less. If Odell was truly Samuel's child, she could not deny her part of the estate.

"What does that even mean?" Odell asked, the sadness disappearing and the fire returning to her eyes.

"It means I'll share what I've inherited."

"How much of a share?" Odell leaned forward.

"We can discuss all of that once your claim is proven," Harley said. "It's premature until then."

Odell's gaze almost shot fire at Harley. On the shelf, Trouble knocked a book to the floor, reminding Tommie of the volume that had shifted off the bedside table. Another ghost story, one she hadn't had an opportunity to even look at. She had a sudden idea. "Odell, I know you wanted to tour the house, so please whenever you wish."

Tommie saw the look of alarm in Harley's eyes and Trouble's sudden leap to the floor with his tail straight in the air. Neither approved of what she'd done. She winked at Harley. She had a plan, after all.

Odell drained her glass and set it on a coaster. "I'm ready."

"No doubt you've heard the stories about Loftus Manor," Tommie said, her eyes wide with innocence.

"Stories?"

"We have a ghost," Tommie said with excitement. "I've seen her myself. So has Harley. In fact, she's legendary in the town of Wetumpka. Been here for decades and some believe she may have played a role in Samuel's death."

Harley was clearly horrified by what she was saying, but judging from Odell's expression, Tommie knew she was on to something.

"I don't know why you think I'm stupid," Odell said. "I don't believe in ghosts. No sane people do."

"Okay," Tommie said. "I just wanted to alert you while you're poking around the house. Just give a yell if you see something that upsets you. Harley and I will be right here, enjoying the fire."

As soon as Odell was gone, Harley closed the door to the library and rounded on Tommie. "Do you think it was smart to just let her snoop around Loftus Manor? The very fact that she wanted to go alone is suspicious."

"I know, but she isn't alone."

"The ghost is with her?" Harley was incredulous.

"No, the cat, which is almost equally unbelievable, but I'm beginning to comprehend that Trouble is everything Tammy said he was." She'd watched the cat slip out the door undetected by Odell.

"And we're just going to wait here until she's finished poking through all of Samuel's things, and possibly yours too?" Harley was finding it difficult to believe Tommie's foolhardiness. He'd grown to view her as measured and thoughtful.

Tommie held up a key. "I locked my door, but I'm curious if she'll explore Nina's room."

"Why would she be interested in Nina's old room?"

"It's the source of the ghost activity. I know I sound a little crazy," she held up a hand, "but my brain has been in a whirl ever since I found the perfume-soaked handkerchief." She pulled it from the sleeve of her shirt. "If Odell is part of this conspiracy to scare me out of Loftus Manor, it will be interesting to see what areas of the house interest her."

"You think Odell is the ghost?" Harley asked, his voice a harsh whisper.

"Maybe. Or maybe someone is setting her up," Tommie said.

"You're absolutely right," Harley said. "So you're hoping Odell will do what?"

"Trouble will be able to show us whatever Odell shows an interest in," Tommie said. "Then we'll know whether she's part of the intruder business or not."

Harley picked up his glass and Tommie's and mixed two fresh drinks. "So we wait here?" he said as he handed her a glass.

"No, I think it's time we go looking for Odell," Tommie said. "I'll bet we find her in Samuel's study."

Harley knew she was right. They left the library, feet silent on the thick Turkish carpets that adorned the first floor of the manor. The parlors were dark and empty, and they passed several closed doors. Harley trusted Tommie's hunch that Odell had gone into Samuel's little study. He wondered if Odell knew a lot more about Samuel and Loftus Manor than she'd let on and was possibly hunting for something specific.

When they arrived at the little study, the door was closed. Tommie turned the knob gently.

The door opened on well-oiled hinges, and Harley stepped ahead of Tommie into the room. He didn't mind being second fiddle most of the time, but he had to make sure she was safe. He quickly scanned the room and found Odell at the cold fireplace, pushing and tugging at the trim, as if she, too, were looking for some kind of secret passage or hiding place. Trouble sat at her feet, watching every move she made.

Harley glanced at Tommie, who nodded. There was a tiny glint in her eyes. "Do you need some help, Odell?"

Odell literally jumped into the air and let out a little shriek. "You aren't supposed to be here."

"We thought you might need some help," Tommie said, barely able to hold back her smile. "Sorry if we startled you, but if you tell us what you're searching for, maybe we could help."

Harley stepped forcefully into the center of the room. "Give it up now, Odell, or whatever your name is. You aren't Samuel's daughter, but you have some connection to Samuel and Loftus Manor and you're looking for something specific. Now tell us who you are, what you're looking for and who sent you to do this, and we won't press charges."

Harley realized his abrupt and aggressive change was working. Odell looked scared. "Are you going to press charges?"

"You almost killed Tommie on the Main Street of Wetumpka. Half a dozen people saw you." Harley let his anger show. "You really could have injured her severely. Now, we find you trying to rip a mantel off a wall searching for what? A passage or room or hidey hole? We know you aren't Samuel's daughter, and we know you're trying to defraud Tommie. Those are serious charges. You better prepare to spend the next twenty years in prison, because I swear to you, we'll push this prosecution hard. Samuel left Tommie enough money that she can hire all the experts she needs to prove you're a con woman and a grifter."

Harley was satisfied to see how Odell blanched.

"Tell us what you were searching for," Tommie followed up. "Obviously you thought something was in this room, but what?"

"I...I'm not searching for anything."

"Why did you try to run over Tommie?" Harley asked, changing the subject to throw her off balance.

"I wasn't trying to hit her. I drove fast by Tommie because she was messing with Nina's car. I saw that and I panicked, but I only meant to discourage her away from the car. That cat!" She pointed to Trouble. "He was on the roof of the car and he was going to start something. I know all about him and his detective business. Everyone in Wetumpka knows that once he starts messing around with someone, they get arrested."

"And why would you care if Nina Ahearn was arrested?" Tommie asked. "And you'd better tell the truth this time. Harley and I are willing to speak on your behalf—if you tell us the truth right now."

"I haven't done anything wrong!" Odell insisted. "I haven't."

"Why should you care what happens to Nina Ahearn's car?" Tommie pressed.

Odell shook her head and began to cry. "Nina's my cousin," Odell said. "She pulled me into this plan. I wish I'd never listened to her. Are you really going to press charges? Nina said, even if we got caught, no one would do anything to us but run us out of town, and I don't live here anyway." Odell looked at Harley but shifted her focus to Tommie. "She was lying, wasn't she? Please don't call the police."

Tommie' smile held victory. "That depends on how cooperative you are."

CHAPTER TWENTY

I do believe the quaint American phrase for what Odell Rains is doing is called "spilling her guts." All I know is that Odell is not the arch-criminal. She's a pawn. And while that job description may still include some grave punishment, she isn't the mastermind behind the strange events happening here.

Tommie has put on a pot of tea and the bipeds are gathered at the kitchen table as poor, poor Odell attempts to save herself from criminal charges. I don't know if that's even possible, but it won't hurt for her to have Tommie and Harley on her side if she goes before a judge.

When Harley grilled her, she claimed not to be involved in Nina's alleged marriage. She says her only involvement was that her cousin called her in to play the role of the bastard daughter.

Odell says she doesn't know if Samuel and Nina were truly married, but from listening to Mr. Brawny explain how the marriage laws in Alabama work, it's clear to me that the marriage isn't legal. It was never filed with the State Department of Health, therefore not legal. Interesting laws the bipeds have for consummating a mating season. Felines are not bound by the frazzling intricacies of documents, filing, ceremonies, witnesses, and so forth. And what's the point? Especially when so many of these legally enacted partnerships end in divorce, which only requires more paperwork, more documentation, more lawyers, and more expense. The antics of the humanoid are difficult to comprehend.

But enough ruminating on the unfathomable. The mystery at hand is what I need to focus on. Odell insists that she has not been inside Loftus Manor and she knows nothing about Nina or anyone associated with her visiting the house. I'm not sure that I believe her, but she is consistent with her denials and Mr. Brawny pressed her hard.

She claims she was in the study looking for a hidden safe where Samuel was supposed to have kept some cash, jewelry, and other assets. She admitted she would have stolen them and left town, despite the fact Nina would have been seriously chuffed with her.

"I never wanted to do anything mean to anyone," Odell insists. "I was only doing Nina's bidding. It was her plan, and we just wanted some of the money. Nina said there was so much money that what we got wouldn't even be missed. I was just a diversion, someone to make you focus on while she tried to get all she could. We both knew that the DNA would prove I wasn't a Loftus."

Yes, the chickens have come home to roost here, and Nina Ahearn has a lot of things to answer for. I daresay Harley and Tommie will be talking to her soon—perhaps through prison bars.

But what hasn't been settled is who has been slipping in and out of Loftus Manor. Odell swears it wasn't her, that she only knew to examine the "little study room" because Nina told her that was the most likely place Samuel would have hidden some of the money everyone said he had hoarded through his life. Odell swears she hasn't been on the property since she stopped by the other evening. And she also says Nina has not been back. Perhaps she's telling the truth. Perhaps not. But if Nina and Odell haven't been snooping around the manor, who has? That's the question that troubles me.

Now Odell is preparing to leave. Tommie and Harley are allowing *her to do that without calling the law on her. Is this wise? I honestly don't know. But Odell has agreed to help them in the future. I guess this negates the need for a sample of her DNA. Too bad, I was looking forward to notching out a piece of her hide with my claws. But it is never a misstep to avoid violence, as my mentor Sherlock would say.*

I'll follow her out—to be sure she actually leaves. You can say I have trust issues, but if you'd seen the things I've seen...the heart of man can beat with foul intent.

A SINGLE NIGHT had never dragged on so long—or at least that's how it felt. Harley heard the front door close behind Odell and he watched as Tommie sank into a chair in the parlor. He'd never expected Odell to confess, but it seemed the young woman simply wanted out of the plot to steal part of the inheritance. She'd given Tommie her home address in Greenville, Alabama, and she'd promised to come back and testify, if necessary, but in the meantime, she was getting the heck out of Dodge.

Harley sank down into a wingchair opposite Tommie, and she asked him, "Did Uncle Samuel really keep money hidden here at Loftus Manor?"

Harley flexed his fingers several times before he answered. "I honestly don't know. It doesn't sound like Samuel. He was so traditional in his views of money and banks. I can't think that he would hide money under pillows or in holes in the yard."

"Were you aware of the rumor of hidden riches? Something maybe he promoted in some of his foolishness?"

"You may have hit the nail on the head. Samuel loved to stir a reaction. Ghost stories, eccentricities, things like having Nina live here. Yes, some of it was done for effect. He never talked to me about hidden treasures, probably because he knew I would disapprove. Some things you can mark up to good fun, but it's not wise to dangle bait in front of a hungry cat." He glanced over at Trouble. "Sorry, change that to dog."

Tommie had left the ghost story novel she'd found in Nina's room on the staircase when Odell knocked. She went there and picked it up. She read the flap aloud to Harley. "Does that sound familiar?"

"It does," Harley said. "Samuel told that story." Harley had always viewed Samuel's hijinks and fondness for a good yarn to be harmless. Maybe not, though, if he'd been telling everyone in town about hidden treasure.

"Tonight didn't go as I'd planned, but it all worked out okay," Tommie said. "I have the goods on Nina now, thanks to Odell."

"You do, up to a point." It occurred to Harley they should have called the police and at least had Odell charged with something. On further consideration, it didn't seem likely she'd appear to testify against Nina or anyone else. Chances were she was gone from the area. "What are you going to do about it?" Harley's hope was that Tommie would take it to the police and let them deal with the attempted fraud.

"I'm going to talk to Nina."

He didn't object, because this was exactly what he'd expected her to do. Tommie always gave people a second chance. It had worked out well with Odell. Nina Ahearn, though, was a different kettle of fish. She'd masterminded a complex scheme to steal and extort. She wouldn't break the way Odell had done. Putting this in the hands of the law seemed the wisest decision.

"Let's sleep on it," he said. "And either you're coming down to the cottage or I'm staying here. Take your pick. There are a dozen bedrooms available."

Tommie held up a hand. "No argument from me. Thank you, Harley. I don't know why you've chosen to spend all this time helping me out, but I do appreciate it."

"Me-ow!" Trouble threw in.

"I'll set up whatever room you'd like." She stood up holding the book.

Together they walked up the stairs with Trouble right at their heels.

TOMMIE SLIPPED between the cold sheets, too tired to start a fire in her bedroom. All she wanted to do was sleep. As she settled into the bed, she realized her brain was still spinning with thoughts and worries. Harley had taken the room next to hers for the night, and she spent a few minutes thinking about him, settling into a strange room when he could have easily been at his home. He'd stayed in the manor for her. That wasn't a small thing.

She closed her eyes and tried to sleep, but she couldn't drift off. Trouble seemed to sense her unrest, and he curled up beside her hip and purred loudly. At any other time the delicious purr would have sent her to visit the Sandman, but the events of the last two days had her keyed up. She shifted in the bed and tried to focus on an image of the Pacific Ocean crashing against some rocks. Nothing relaxed her.

She picked up the book she'd brought into her room and turned on the bedside light. If she couldn't sleep, at least she could read.

Sam Willis was the author and she noted it was published in 1975. To her surprise, the book was copywritten to Samuel Loftus. She'd had no idea he was an author. The pen name Sam Willis—she would never have assumed it was her uncle.

She dug into the first pages, instantly caught up in the story. To her amazement, it was almost as if she could hear her uncle's voice, or at least his voice as she imagined it, reading the story to her. He had a clear, distinct presentation, and the book was crafted toward the young adult age, as best she could tell. From what little she knew, it was the perfect age for a good, creepy ghost story.

The story followed Ada Carter, a young girl who lived in a big manor house in the middle of nowhere. Her fondest dream was to have a friend, another girl her age. One night very late, Ada was in her bed sleeping when she heard someone sobbing outside her door. Little Ada, braver than she was smart, put on her slippers and crept to the door.

When she jerked it open, a child was sitting on the carpet runner just outside her door.

"Hello," the girl said. "I've come to be your friend. My name is Jacquelyn but you can call me Jix. I've been so lonely without a friend. Now you're here." And thus a friendship was born.

Jix never appeared when there were other people about, but as time passed, Ada accepted her friend's strange behavior. Jix wasn't like other young girls. She wasn't like other people. Ada knew she was different, but she never questioned how or why.

The two young girls developed a bond and friendship as the summer months passed. When it came time for school, Ada went, but Jix did not. As Ada grew older, so did Jix. But inside she was still the lonely little girl who'd first appeared outside Ada's bedroom door. And in the way of life and growth and change, Ada found many friends at school. The pull of the outside world became stronger than the pull of Jix and the manor.

In her teens, Ada developed a special relationship with a young boy named Mark. Ada had less and less time to daydream, talk, and play with Jix.

High school graduation came and Ada was accepted into a university. Mark would be going to the same university and they were so excited, planning their classes, their future. Now, after school, Ada stayed in town to be with her friends. Jix was left behind.

The day Ada accepted the keys to her spanking new car, a high school graduation gift, Jix waited for her in the woods behind the gardens. When she called to Ada to join her, the teen reluctantly came. Ada wanted to drive to town, to show off her car. She was ready for a new adventure, a new life, and Jix made her feel guilty. Ada had come to realize that Jix was bound to Loftus Manor. That she would never leave the premises. Would never have a real life with boys and college and a future. The childhood friend of summer days and fall walks in the woods was too limited for a flesh and blood girl. The manor was no longer Ada's whole world.

For Jix, her role at the big house was the past, the present, and the future. It was all she had now or could even remember. She would never leave. Never have another friend, if Ada left. After Ada died, Jix would still be there. All alone.

All alone.

All alone.

All alone.

The words repeated down the page, and Tommie heard them as they echoed around the room.

Tommie paused in her reading, aware that something was off. Her watch showed two a.m. The bedside lamp spilled light around her, and in the glow she could see the cat standing on the footboard of the bed, back arched, tail fluffed. A low growl came from his throat.

She sensed it then, someone else in the room. She couldn't see anyone or hear anything odd, but there was someone watching in the shadows. She knew it.

She exhaled a deep breath, and to her horror she saw that the air around her was so cold it condensed. Classic sign of a ghostly presence. She felt paralyzed, as if she couldn't move though she wanted to get up, to scream, to call for Harley who was, after all, only forty feet away, just on the other side of her bedroom wall. But nothing came out of her mouth, not even a whisper, and her arms and legs were too heavy to lift.

The cat leaped up to the hand-carved foot of the bed, faced the sitting room that was part of the suite and the door to the hallway and hissed again, an angry sound that promised violence.

Then she heard it, a voice so lonely it penetrated her heart. "I'm so lonely. Will you be my friend?"

The child's voice came from the shadows in a corner of the room.

Tommie couldn't believe it. She didn't want to believe it. She couldn't speak or move. She was trapped.

"All you have to do is say you'll be my friend. I won't hurt you. You know that, don't you?"

Tommie struggled against the fear, reaching for courage and her voice. If this was the ghost, the prankster who was haunting Loftus Manor, this was her chance to solve that mystery once and for all.

"Who are you?" she asked. Saying the words took all her strength.

"You know who I am. You found my book. You know the secret Samuel kept."

"You're Jix." She said it flatly. "You're the ghost of Loftus Manor."

"I knew you were smart. And you'll stay with me. You won't leave me alone. I've been so alone."

"I intend to stay here and make Loftus Manor my home," Tommie said. "Perhaps we can be friends." The idea was terrifying, but she couldn't help but feel pity for the lonely child, ghost or not.

"I need a good friend. They always leave me, but you won't leave me, will you?"

"Not by choice," Tommie said. She was aware of Trouble pacing on the footboard, growling. The cat was very unhappy, but the ghostly child seemed so desperate. Lonely and harmless. She'd begun to relax and see the intruder as someone she might be able to help. The cat was over-reacting.

She reached for Trouble to comfort him, but the cat swatted her hand, claws extended, and jumped to the floor, hissing at her.

"Trouble?" She'd never seen the feline behave in such an aggressive way. "Trouble?"

"Don't leave me," the little ghost voice said again.

"Come into the light," Tommie said. She swung her feet to the floor. She wanted Harley to see this. He'd never believe her unless he saw it with his own eyes. "Come here."

"No."

"Oh, come on. How can we be friends if I can't see you?"

"No."

Tommie felt another whisper of apprehension. Something wasn't right. "Jix, please, I want to see you. I want you to tell me about this house. There're so many secrets here."

"So many secrets," Jix repeated. "And I'll tell you all of them!" She rushed toward the bed, and when the light fell on her, she was hideous. There was little human left of her. She was mostly bones in the clothes of a nineteenth century female child. She snapped the air with her teeth.

Tommie screamed and fell back in the bed. She felt the thud of the cat beside her, and she screamed again and again. There was the sound of her bedroom door crashing open and Harley was at the bedside, grabbing her shoulders to keep her from thrashing.

"Tommie! Tommie! Wake up." He held her tightly and pulled her against him so he could hold and simultaneously restrain her as she struggled. "Tommie, you're having a nightmare, wake up!"

At last his voice penetrated the terror and she stopped fighting him. Trouble headbutted her, giving his own version of comfort. When she finally looked around, the room was flooded with light—Harley had flipped on the overhead in the bedroom and the parlor as he came in. There was nothing else in the room. Nothing at all.

"She was here," Tommie said. "She wanted to be my friend. It's the ghost from Uncle Samuel's book. Jix. She was here." Her voice lost assertiveness the more she talked, and she knew she'd suffered one of the most real nightmares she'd ever had.

"Uncle Samuel's book?" Harley was puzzled.

"Samuel wrote the book, back in 1975. A young adult ghost story." She handed him the book. "He was quite the storyteller," she said. "It certainly provoked a nightmare for me." She glanced into the corners of the room. The idea that she'd been visited by a ghost was still with her, even though rationally she knew it was a dream.

"He never mentioned being an author," Harley said. "But that doesn't surprise me. Samuel loved telling his stories."

"This one scared me senseless," Tommie said, remembering with panic the sense of helplessness and paralysis.

"You're okay now," Harley said. He held her in his arms. "You're okay. It was just a bad dream."

"It's a good thing Uncle Samuel is dead or I'd be tempted to kill him," Tommie said, taking a stab at humor. Safe against Harley, she felt the cobwebs of the dream slip away from her.

She wasn't normally prone to being such a fraidy-cat, but the ghost story had really worked on her.

"Think you can sleep?" Harley asked.

Incredibly, she felt her body relaxing. "I think so."

"I'll stay until I'm sure you won't have another nightmare."

She didn't argue. Harley's presence was comforting. She reached for the cat to bring him to snuggle against her. "Thank you."

CHAPTER TWENTY-ONE

*H*arley watched Tommie sleep for a long time. He wanted to be there in case she had another nightmare. The weeks of stress—from the notification of Samuel's death and her inheritance to loading up her old life, moving to a new one, and then confronting imposters and ghosts—it had been a hard journey for her. No wonder she was having nightmares.

As he sat with her, he leafed through Samuel's book. It was a classic ghost story and one he'd heard Samuel tell in various forms. When he felt his own eyelids drooping, he got a blanket from his room and settled into a chair beside Tommie's bed. Tomorrow they'd deal with ghosts and grifters and everything else.

He awoke before Tommie and folded his blanket and returned it to the guest room. Then he went downstairs to make coffee. The manor was chilly—not nearly as snug as the cottage where he lived. While he was waiting for the coffee to brew, he stepped into Samuel's small office. Odell had talked about hidden money, a stash of some kind. If Harley had ever foreseen the troubles that would come from Samuel's love of telling stories, he would have warned him not to list Loftus Manor as a site for hidden treasures. How many other people suffered under the delusion that great wealth could be found in the manor? One more would be too many. While Tommie was sleeping, he'd take a quick look around the room. And he'd mention it to the renovators when they arrived. Hank would have a lot better idea if there were hidden spaces for some special use of the room.

He sat down at Samuel's desk, his fingers running lightly over the burnished wood, and had a sudden wave of loss. He missed the old codger. Samuel could be a devil with his stories and pranks, but he had been Harley's closest friend for the past five years. Harley realized things had begun to happen so fast that he'd failed to even grieve his loss. Now, Samuel's death was all too real. Whatever happened in the future, whether Loftus Manor became a successful inn or simply Tommie's home, Samuel was gone from the premises. He was just a memory now, but Harley vowed to share how special Samuel had been with Tommie so she could know her great-great-uncle, at least a little.

He was deep in melancholy thoughts when the black cat jumped to the desk and began digging and pawing at the center desk drawer. Harley obligingly opened it and the cat demanded that he open it wider, until the drawer slipped out of the desk.

Trouble gave a cry of delight and began pawing at the back side of the drawer. Harley knew before he even looked that he would find something. And he did. A key taped to the back of the drawer. But a key to what?

He pulled it free and put it on the desk. "What now?" he asked Trouble.

Before he or the cat could formulate a plan of action, Harley heard the sound of Tommie stirring, and as he got up to pour them both coffee, he saw the coroner's report of Samuel's death on the floor. The form was simple enough, a few places to check and some handwritten notes. He picked it up and stopped as the morning sun coming through a window highlighted an oddity. The coroner had written, "Death by hanging by his own hand. Suicide." Harley squinted. It was a copy of the official report, which was probably in the coroner's office in Montgomery. He studied it closely. Something else had been written and changed. He turned on the desk lamp and bent over the paper. Something had been whited out on the original, and the verdict of suicide put in. Because it was a copy, the change was easy to overlook, He sat back from the paper. It might be nothing—or it could be something very significant.

"Harley? Are you still here?"

He put the page in the drawer, slipped the key inside, too, and met Tommie on the way to the kitchen. "I was going to bring you some coffee, but I got distracted."

Her face brightened. "You found something, didn't you? What did you find?"

"Maybe Samuel didn't kill himself after all. I'll show you once you've had something hot to drink and I get a fire going."

"Sounds like a deal. I'll pour the coffee and meet you in Samuel's study."

I couldn't be certain what Odell was looking for when she was in the study, but I knew it had to be small. She wasn't looking for a large treasure—not in the places she was examining. I figured it was a key, and where do spies always stash the key? Taped to the back or bottom of a drawer. Duh! I wish I could take credit for being brilliant, but I'll settle for just taking credit for watching the right movies and finding the key.

Let me finesse opening this drawer. Aha! Just as I suspected. This is a key to a safety deposit box. Wetumpka has a number of bank branches, especially out on the highways. But my bet on Samuel is that he used the downtown bank, the Wetumpka National Bank. It's been a part of the community for many years and that appears to be where he had his checking accounts. I do believe a trip to town is in order right away.

There is much to do, and the renovation team will be out here soon. Then things will really get hectic. Here's Harley, bringing in an armful of wood for the fireplace. And Tommie will be right behind him. How to make them understand the key is to a safety deposit box. Oh, great! Here's a check book from the bank. That will do the trick nicely. And yes, they've snapped on to the key and the checking account. They're talking about going to the bank ASAP.

In the past two days, Tommie and Harley have become more and more adept at learning to comprehend me. They're quite intelligent for bipeds.

TOMMIE TOOK the coroner's report and sat at her great uncle's desk. Harley snapped on the bright desk light and pointed to the form where cause of death was listed. She saw it instantly. Something had been whited out and then neatly written on top of. They'd done a skillful job of it, but not skillful enough.

"Which means we need to get a copy of the original report from the state medical examiner," Harley said.

"I'll make a call." Tommie picked up the telephone on the desk and made a face. "The line is dead. I guess Britt Gordon had the land line disconnected. I need to check on the gas service and electricity." She pulled her cell phone from her pocket.

"You should," Harley said. "While you're doing that I'm going to check the game cameras I set up last evening. And we also need to go to the bank to check out that key."

"Where's Trouble?" Tommie asked. The black cat had simply disappeared. He was stealthy when he chose to be.

"He's in the house," Harley said.

"I'll keep an eye out. If he hasn't reappeared, I'll look for him after I make these calls."

Half an hour later, Tommie had taken care of her calls. She'd also saved herself a trip to the bank by calling and asking if Samuel had a safety deposit box. The answer was no. There was no box rented by Samuel at any of the other banks around Wetumpka either. The key was a dead end. Like so many other clues, it seemed.

She headed upstairs to look for Trouble. As much as the cat loved food, he wasn't hanging around waiting for breakfast and she found that a little strange. She'd made it to the second-floor landing when there was a knock at the door. She hurried down the central staircase to open the door to Hank Evans. Behind him was a five-man crew of workers.

"The supplies will be here in half an hour and I thought we'd get started if you're good with that." His smile was big and reassuring.

"You know where the kitchen is," Tommie said. Hopes for a quick breakfast disappeared, but she was too excited to care about food.

"We're just going to start working. Since you haven't restocked your kitchen yet, we'll begin with pulling out the cabinets and so forth. Once the space is cleared, we can talk about the next step."

Tommie nodded. This was exactly what she wanted, but she couldn't stop the butterflies in her stomach at the thought. "Just tell me if I can do anything to help." She stepped back and the workers filed past her, following Hank toward the kitchen. At the tail end of the procession, Harley came up to her, a worried expression on his face.

"What's wrong?" she asked.

"Of the five game cameras, three have disappeared. The other two hadn't been activated."

"They're just gone?"

He nodded. "Someone was here last night, and they took them. That's the only explanation."

He was right about that, and it was an explanation Tommie didn't like at all.

CHAPTER TWENTY-TWO

*T*ommie accepted the refill of her coffee as she sat on
Harley's porch. The demolition in the kitchen of the
manor had driven her, Harley, and even Trouble down to the
cottage. The October sunshine was warm, and the day incredibly
beautiful with the leaves of the hardwoods showing gold, red,
and orange and the sky a crystal cerulean blue.

"It's so beautiful here," she said as Harley put the coffee pot
on a trivet and sat down beside her.

"It's been a good five years for me, living here." Harley
cleared his throat. "I miss Samuel."

"I'll bet you do. I miss him and I never met him," Tommie
said. "Last night, as I was reading his book, I swear it was just
like he was telling me the story." Her laugh sounded strained,
even to her. "I still feel caught in a dream, or maybe at times a
nightmare. A month ago I was scrabbling for clients and
applying to set up a booth at craft festivals. Now, I'm renovating
a historic home for the biggest gamble of my life."

"To that end," Harley said, "you need to call the state medical examiner's office. We need to find out what was on the original death certificate."

"I will." She wanted to finish the coffee, grab just another moment of peace before she stepped into the mayhem of her day. "And we need to visit that fashion model friend of yours to check on the cloak and also check up on the Reverend Crystal Child."

"Yes, and find out what that key goes to. I could swear it's a safety deposit box. While we're out and about we can check with Hank and see if he needs anything from town," Harley said. "We can get supplies if he needs any."

"Thank you, Harley." Tommie had a sudden visceral memory of clinging to Harley as she came out of her night terror. He'd been so solid, so safe, so there for her. "Thank you for everything."

"No problem—"

His comment was cut short by the ringing of her phone. It wasn't a number she knew, but it was local so she answered.

"Ms. Sykes, this is Nancy Smith in the coroner's office." The young woman was whispering.

"Yes," she said, putting the phone on speaker so Harley could hear.

"I was just in the tax assessor's office running an errand for the sheriff and Paul Rider was in there. He was talking to the tax assessor about the value of your property. I don't know what he has up his sleeve, but I wanted you to know he's plotting something."

"Thank you, Nancy."

"Please tell Harley that I called you," she said. "I want him to know I'm helping."

"I'll make sure of that," Tommie said, working hard not to give Harley the "I told you so" look she wanted to throw at him.

"And thank you for the heads up." She hung up the phone and looked at Harley. "I told you she had a crush on you."

He only shook his head and laughed. "Let's head into town. We have things to accomplish and one of them is a visit with Paul Rider."

THE REAL ESTATE developer's office was just as Tommie had expected—all chrome and polished blond wood. The place was devoid of any family photos or personal touches. Abstract art adorned the walls. Bookcases, empty of books, contained real estate awards and a series of African masks.

"You must be psychic. I was planning to drive out to talk to you this afternoon," Rider said as he ushered Tommie and Harley into seats in front of his desk. He went to the door. "Beth, a tray of coffee and some cake, please. And don't dawdle." He closed the door. "So, have you come to put that old money pit on the market?"

"Loftus Manor isn't for sale," Tommie said bluntly. "There's no need to visit. In fact, there's no need to ask questions anywhere about Loftus Manor or me. I have plans for the property and I'll honor my uncle's wishes. The property isn't for sale."

"Everything is for sale, Ms. Sykes," Rider said. "Everything. The only question is the price."

"You heard her. Loftus Manor isn't for sale." Harley stood up to make his point. "Tommie, it's time we leave. We've delivered the message we came to give."

"Sit back down." Rider waved him into his seat. "Don't get emotional. I know you've lived there as a guest of Samuel for a while now and selling the estate would mean you'd be out on your ear, but this young lady has no ties to the property, and I can make her a very wealthy woman. Think about it, Ms. Sykes.

You can take your profit and go anywhere in the world, lead any life you choose. No one your age wants to be stuck in this backwater. Hell, there may be four eligible men in the entire county for you to date." He laughed. "And that's counting you, Harley, assuming you still have all your teeth." Rider smirked and he spoke to Tommie in an aside, "Most women wouldn't view Harley as much of a catch anyway. Way too much emotional baggage and too little ambition."

Before Harley could even frame a response, Tommie was on her feet. "I don't know who you think you are or what you hope to accomplish with this behavior, but I can tell you this right now. We came here as a courtesy. I wanted to make it clear to you that Loftus Manor isn't for sale. But let me assure you, should it become necessary for me to sell my family property, I'll find another real estate firm to use. You are a smug, arrogant ass."

"Now calm down," Rider said. "You can use another firm, but I'm the company with the bid from an out of the country interest. A bid that is in my hand right now. A very nice bid, if I say so myself. And I can tell you it's the best offer you're going to get." He picked up a piece of paper from his desk and whistled tunelessly as he studied the paper. He lowered it, slowly revealing his face. "How does three million sound?"

Harley watched Tommie's shock at the figure. It was a huge sum of money, and he realized what it might mean for Tommie if she simply took it and ran. He felt his stomach knot. Tommie would be justified in taking the money and leaving Alabama to build a new life almost anywhere else in the world. She was a California girl, used to a great climate and a state with a billion options for entertainment. That kind of money could buy her a storefront jewelry business in a district where folks paid top dollar for creativity and imagination.

"Mr. Rider, I have plans for a long future at Loftus Manor," Tommie said. "It's going to be my home, the place I eventually raise my family. It isn't for sale. Not now. Not next week. Please don't contact me with any additional offers or negotiations. This discussion is over."

She picked up Trouble and her purse and started for the door. Harley beat her there and opened it, unable to hide the big grin. "You served it to him hot and hard," he whispered as they walked out together, passing the receptionist who held a tray of coffee and cake.

"I'm so sorry," Tommie told her, but she kept walking.

When they were outside the building Harley couldn't help but laugh as he remembered the expression on Paul Rider's face. He had certainly underestimated Tommie Sykes. "You're a tiger when you're angry."

"He's lucky. I wanted to slap his face so hard his ears got whiplash." Tommie was frowning and Harley put a hand on her shoulder. He'd meant to say something, to compliment her on her courage and spirit. Instead, he kissed her without thought or planning. It was intense and brief as Tommie yielded completely to the kiss, but quickly broke it off.

"I apologize," Harley said. "I, uh, I didn't mean for that to happen."

Tommie smiled. "I'm glad it did."

At their feet, Trouble meowed as if he too was casting a vote of approval. Then he snagged her pants leg with a claw and pulled her toward the parking lot.

"Trouble says we have work to do," Harley said.

"And he would be right." Tommie's big smile was the only answer Harley needed.

. . .

"ARE you sure Ms. Murphy won't mind if I tag along?" Tommie asked Harley when they were parked in front of Patricia Murphy's beautiful home. The house was all glass and beautiful angles and it seemed to hang off part of the meteorite crater that was such a big part of Wetumpka's history.

"Patricia will be delighted to meet you," Harley assured her. "Come on." He held out his hand and she took it as they walked to the front door.

"This place is incredible," Tommie whispered.

"In her day, Patricia was the top fashion designer for Donatella Versace and a number of European labels."

"Why did she come back to live here in Wetumpka? Not that I wouldn't, but it must seem very tame after her days in the fashion business."

"I think maybe the stress of those runway days really made her unhappy. Here," he waved a hand, "she's surrounded by woods and nature and the wild creatures. I think it's peaceful."

Tommie didn't have time to say anything else because the door opened and a stunning woman in a flowing caftan took one look at Harley and raced into his arms. She gave him a bear hug and laughed. "It must be a Martian invasion to blast you out of Loftus Manor, but I'm damn glad to see you." She turned to Tommie. "And this, I'll bet, is the new heiress who is the talk of the town. She's every bit as pretty as the gossips say."

Tommie instantly liked Patricia and shook her hand with enthusiasm. "Harley said you were a fashion designer. He didn't say you were also beautiful." The woman in front of her was tall, slender, fit, and striking with her thick russet hair and pale complexion.

"Harley, take notes, darling. This is how you flatter a woman. If you can learn a few grace notes you won't have to spend your days alone."

Tommie couldn't help the laughter that swelled up and spilled out.

Harley laughed out loud. "I can see you're both going to double-team me. I expected nothing else. So abuse me as much as you want as long as you can help us."

Patricia finally took note of the black cat who stood perfectly still at Tommie's leg. "And who is your handsome familiar, Tommie? He bears an uncanny resemblance to the bookstore cat that solves mysteries."

"Because that's who he is," Harley said. "You don't miss a thing, Patricia. Well, are you going to ask us in or shall we conduct our business standing on the stoop?"

Patricia shooed everyone into the house and settled them in a den with a view of the meteorite crater that made Tommie feel as if she was in the foothills of the Appalachian Mountains. The fall trees swirled red, yellow, and varying shades of brown and green as if vibrant paint had been spilled down the steep incline.

"What can I do for you?" Patricia asked after they'd declined refreshments.

Harley brought the unusual button from his pocket. "We're trying to identify a cloak," he said. He watched as Patricia turned it over and over in her hand.

"This is an old, old button," Patricia said. "It's a star sapphire stone glued or forged into a bone button with a back shank. It belongs on an outer garment, likely feminine. The person who wore the garment would have been upper class, because a button like this would have been expensive."

Tommie brought the sketch of the cloaked woman from her purse. "This is what it looks like, with the three buttons. Have you ever seen anything like it?"

Patricia studied the button and the cloak. "It's a beautiful garment. I wish I could help you, but I can't. The design is striking, and the way the cloak hangs indicates it was made by someone who knows their business." She picked up the button. "Let me photograph this and see if any of my associates has better information. I have friends who've made a study of buttons."

"Thank you," Tommie said.

They chatted for a bit more before Harley and Tommie took their leave, Trouble following obediently out the door. When they were headed back to town, Harley suggested that they stop for some lunch. "You can't eat at the manor with the workmen in the kitchen," he pointed out.

"Meow!"

They both laughed. "Trouble takes his grub seriously," Harley said.

The black cat climbed up to the back of his seat and put a paw on Harley's cheek.

"He's warning you not to make fun of his appetite," Tommie said. "After all, he might eat a lot but he's still very svelte."

"Point taken, Trouble," Harley said. "Point taken."

CHAPTER TWENTY-THREE

*T*hey'd finished their lunch and were parked outside the local hardware store getting ready to pick up a few things for Hank and Katie when Harley's phone rang. He arched his eyebrows. "It's Patricia." He put the call on speaker.

"Harley, darling, that button has created a stir with my designer friends."

"Oh, really," Harley said as he winked at Tommie.

She felt a rush of warmth. They hadn't said a word about the kiss he'd planted on her, but she hadn't forgotten. It was impromptu and had caught them both by surprise. A fact she found she liked. They were both a little awkward dealing with the feelings that had developed between them.

"What are your friends saying?" Tommie asked, eager to hear the news.

"It seems that the star sapphire is a stone with a bit of a legend attached to it."

"This sounds intriguing," Harley said. "A good legend or a bad legend?"

"A bit of both," Patricia said. "I posted the photo in a group of designer friends and Angela Tessier Van, who is a costume designer in Hollywood, said she'd spent months hunting for star sapphire buttons for a movie she was working on. The script writer insisted that the star sapphires had magical properties."

"Oh, come on," Harley said, skepticism in his voice. "And you believe that?"

"What I believe doesn't matter," Patricia said. "I'm just telling you the lore. It's said that the glow of the buttons is a trapped soul in each stone."

"Like a ghost?" Tommie realized she sounded a tad unnerved.

"Exactly like a ghost," Patricia said. "It's said that the person who wears the buttons controls the ghost collected in each stone. She or he can set them free to do her bidding. I say she or he, but it's most always a woman in the lore. Usually women who practiced witchcraft. And the bone backing of such a button is always made of whale bone."

"I don't know what kind of bone this is," Tommie confessed.

"Run it over to Tuscaloosa," Patricia suggested. "I'm sure someone in either anthropology or one of the sciences can identify the bone."

"Great idea," Harley said to his friend then glanced at Tommie, saying, "I can do that when we get a chance."

"Any clue about the cloak?" Tommie asked Patricia.

"The style is what my friend called a wanderer's cloak, which goes along with the possibility of witchcraft or magical lore." Patricia's voice over the phone sounded very excited. "I'd give a lot to see the cloak."

"Thanks for the information," Harley said. "If you hear anything else, please let us know."

"Absolutely," Patricia said. "And Tommie, take care of yourself."

"I intend to."

"Me-ow!" Trouble cried out and everyone laughed.

"He always gets the last word," Tommie said. "It's one of his charms."

THEY THINK *I'm trying to have the last word, but I'm trying to let them know we're being watched. There's a woman behind the black pickup who's watching us closely. And I believe I've seen her before. Indeed, now that I've caught a full gander of her, it's Nancy Smith, the receptionist with the county coroner. She's the young lady with a crush on Harley. And thank heaven, here she comes. For a minute I thought Harley had a serious stalker—but since she's coming over to say hi, I have to drop the stalker part.*

It is clear she has eyes for Harley, and he is oblivious because he doesn't have any feelings for her. She's a nice-looking woman, but Harley can see only one woman right now, and that's the Loftus Lass. I can't complain about that either. My match-making intuition tells me they're perfect for each other. Both have been hurt in the past and felt betrayed. They've allowed that betrayal to fester and scar without real healing. If they're honest with each other—something it appears is very hard for the bipeds to do—they can help each other heal and thereby clear the hurdles to real commitment and deep feelings. My mission, and I do choose to embrace it, is to make them see what I see.

Ah, Nancy Smith is here. She's talking to Tommie, but cutting glances at Harley. She's trying not to be obvious, but Tommie sees what's going on and is being extra considerate to Nancy. Kindness is a choice, and I'm glad to see the Loftus Lass has a heart that allows her to choose it.

I'd better tune in to the conversation. I don't want to miss any clues, and Nancy Smith seems about to pop with information.

. . .

"I'M so glad I saw you here," Nancy said as she raced toward Tommie and Harley across the hardware store parking lot. "I have something important to share with you both."

"Thank you, Nancy. You've truly been a good friend to both of us."

"I don't like to see the big wigs in town try to bully the newcomer. And Paul Rider hates Harley for whatever reason. Paul is used to being the man every woman wants because he has money. The truth is, most women would prefer a man like Harley."

Tommie felt a stab of sympathy for Nancy, who so clearly had a bad case of wanting Harley. "You're absolutely right. I think most women value decency over wealth."

"And don't forget good looks," Nancy said, flushing profusely.

Harley too, blushed, which only made Tommie smile. Harley was a good man, and he was handsome, and he also had another attribute she valued—modesty. "Yes, Harley's a handsome man," Tommie agreed, delighted to see Harley begin to squirm from all the feminine praise.

"Did you find out something else?" Harley asked Nancy. It was clear he wanted to turn the topic of conversation away from himself.

"Paul Rider has listed himself as the realtor in charge of Loftus Manor, and he's received two offers. One locally and one from a foreign concern."

"How do you know this?" Tommie asked.

"Remember Paul's receptionist? That's the job I used to have, and Beth is my good friend. When I was quitting to go work for Mr. Moore, the coroner, I gave Beth a heads up. So I asked her about any offers and she told me." Nancy held up a hand. "She knows she shouldn't, but Paul treats her as bad as he treated me.

It's a little hard to work up a scrap of loyalty for someone who treats you like mud on his boots."

She was right about that. Tommie might not agree with it, but she certainly understood it. Spilling business secrets wasn't acceptable, but some people had to be paid in kind before they realized that brutish behavior only brought trouble to their front door.

"Do you know who the offers were from?" Harley asked.

"Beth wouldn't give me any names. She said one was a prominent woman in town and the other was a foreign concern. Chinese." Nancy bit her bottom lip before she addressed Harley. "I'm sorry I couldn't get that information, but Beth said she takes a paycheck from Rider and she didn't feel comfortable giving any more details."

"It's okay," Harley assured her, though he was scowling. "We appreciate this much information. Rider admitted to the foreign offer, but he didn't mention a local offer."

"I see by your expression that you're trying to work out who in town could bid on Loftus Manor," Nancy said. "Keep in mind it could be a consortium, not one single person. Folks banding together for an investment—that kind of thing. When I worked for Paul, I saw that a lot. Friends would get together and form a business, and then they'd build condos in a college football town, lakeshore developments, that kind of thing. If they picked the right project, they made a fortune."

"Well, Loftus Manor won't be one of those projects," Tommie said stoutly. "I'm going to make it into an inn. With canoeing and hiking and games like croquet or badminton on the lawn."

"Then you'll keep Harley on to help you with the grounds!" Nancy was almost breathless with relief. "That would be so great."

"Yes." Tommie fought the smile that wanted to spread across her face. "I hope to keep Harley on at the manor, if he'll consider staying. He's a vital part of the plan." She watched his pleased reaction to what she said. They'd never talked about it, but...in that moment she realized it was exactly what she wanted. Nancy was almost an angel for making her confront the truth and say it out loud.

"I do have some ideas for the recreational part of the inn," Harley said.

"I'm really glad you're going to help Ms. Sykes, but I'm a little surprised you're so willing to go along with changes to the manor," Nancy said. "I talked with Mr. Samuel often when I worked for Paul in the real estate office. Mr. Samuel was clear about the manor and how he didn't want any changes."

Harley pushed his dark hair back with his hand. "This might not be what Samuel wanted, exactly, but it keeps the manor house and the property intact, and now other people can enjoy the beautiful architecture of the manor. It is incredible. And the grounds are perfect for what I believe Tommie has in mind. When it comes right down to it, I think Samuel would be pleased that people are seeing and enjoying the beauty of it."

"I'd love to see it one day," Nancy said. "I've heard Mr. Samuel talk about it for years, but I've never been inside."

"Then why don't you come out for coffee or a drink tomorrow evening?" Tommie said. "It is a grand old place, and as you'll see, we won't be changing much of anything except the kitchen and dining areas. The renovation crew is already there working on it."

"Already?" Nancy said. "So quickly?"

"They arrived today. I hope to have it open and receiving guests by Christmas," Tommie said. "I'll need the income to keep things afloat, and with that wonderful renovation team in town, this was the perfect time."

"I see your point." Nancy smiled. "Now I have to get back to the office. Mr. Moore will be looking for me. I look forward to seeing the manor tomorrow evening. About eight?"

"Perfect. And thanks, Nancy," Tommie said as Harley came to stand beside her and waved goodbye to his friend.

CHAPTER TWENTY-FOUR

*D*r. Clyde Ashburn's office was filled with waiting patients, and Tommie and Harley took a seat as they waited to speak with the office manager. They'd had to leave Trouble in the car—they could get him into a lot of places, but not a doctor's office.

"Do you think they'll really give me Uncle Samuel's medical records?" Tommie asked. "I didn't have his medical power of attorney."

"I don't know," Harley said, "but we have to ask. If your uncle was really ill, I'll be more inclined to believe his death was a suicide. But if he wasn't, then I think we have to accept that it's possible we're searching for a killer."

"You think Nina Ahearn could have killed Uncle Samuel?" Tommie didn't like Nina; she was grasping and greedy. But Harley had assured her that Nina was good to Samuel, that she cared for him with some tenderness.

"I would never have thought so, but this whole foolishness about being his wife. I would never have anticipated that, either. Do you ever really know another person?"

Tommie was aware that question had depths to it that went beyond Nina. "I've been fooled before. I'm more careful now."

Harley's grin was lopsided and a little sad. "Me too. But lately I've been thinking that I don't want to hide from my feelings forever."

Tommie put her hand over his. "I'm thinking the same thing." The kiss had given her courage to let some of her defenses down.

"Ms. Sykes!" A nurse stood at an open doorway calling her name.

Tommie rose but stopped and motioned for Harley to go with her.

"Are you sure?" he asked.

"I am. We're in this together. I wouldn't have the nerve to pursue it if you didn't have my back."

Instead of a business office, Tommie found herself in the doctor's private office, and after a moment Dr. Ashburn came into the room and took a seat behind his desk. "You want to see Samuel's medical records," he said.

"Yes," Tommie said.

"May I ask why?"

Tommie studied the doctor's face. He was tired and harried, but he'd taken time to talk to her personally. "I'm Samuel's heir, and I don't want to believe he committed suicide."

"I see." The doctor turned to Harley. "You were friends with Samuel. What's your opinion?"

"I'm with Tommie. Samuel didn't seem sick, and he was perfectly fine when I left him the evening he died. No indication of depression or worry."

"What do you intend to do with any information you may dig up?"

Tommie was caught short. What could they do with it? Have

the cause of death changed. Maybe get the local sheriff to open an investigation. "I'm not sure," Tommie said carefully. "I don't want my uncle labeled a suicide if he isn't. But more importantly, if someone killed him, that person is still walking around free."

Dr. Ashburn nodded as he spun his chair to open a filing cabinet drawer. "I told the coroner I disagreed with the cause of death, but I wasn't allowed to examine the body. Moore said he was required to send it to Montgomery to the state medical examiner."

"That's true," Harley said. "But there's an issue with the cause of death on the death certificate. It may have been changed."

Ashburn stopped rifling through the files and turned to them. "Not supposed to happen." He pulled out a file. "Here are Samuel's records. He was in great health for his age. I saw him only a few months ago and he was spitting fire and talking about how he had to beat you at a game of chess, Harley. He valued your friendship."

"And I his," Harley said. "I miss him."

While Harley and the doctor chatted about Samuel, Tommie went over the medical chart. As Dr. Ashburn had said, Samuel was in great shape for his age. There was no indication of anything that should have worried him.

Tommie closed the file. "Thank you, Dr. Ashburn."

"What are you going to do?" the doctor asked.

"Keep digging," Tommie said. "I'm almost certain my uncle didn't hang himself. And now, it's up to me to find out what really happened."

"Be careful," Dr. Ashburn said. "Remember if someone did harm Samuel, they won't hesitate to do the same to you."

"Anyone you'd care to warn us about?" Harley asked.

Dr. Ashburn hesitated. "The last time I saw Samuel, he was

physically fine. His heart, his respiratory system—he was in great physical shape. But I was worried about him. He was so angry at Paul Rider, the real estate guy. He said Rider was harassing him because there was a client who desperately wanted to buy Loftus Manor. The client had some idea that a treasure was hidden there."

Tommie shot a glance at Harley, who nodded.

"Did Samuel say who this client of Rider might be?" Tommie asked.

"I did ask Samuel, but he brushed it off. He said he'd stopped by to tell Paul that Loftus Manor wasn't for sale and would never be as long as he lived."

"But Paul couldn't let it go?" Harley asked.

"That's what Samuel indicated. He was annoyed with Paul and said he was mad enough to press charges for harassment. Paul had some buyer that was determined to at least talk to Samuel in person to make an offer. Samuel refused."

"You don't recall the potential buyer?" Tommie asked.

"Samuel never said a name, and I didn't press. Perhaps I should have."

"No, thank you, Dr. Ashburn," Tommie said. "As you've indicated, Samuel seemed in good health."

The doctor stood up. "I hope you do pursue this. I've never felt comfortable with letting Samuel's death simply fade away. Like you, I want to find the person responsible, if there is such a person."

Tommie and Harley thanked the doctor and then left. When they were outside, Tommie stopped beneath a sycamore tree. The yellow leaves drifted slowly to the ground with each gentle breeze. "I think Uncle Samuel was murdered." Tommie didn't want to believe it, but her heart told her it was true.

"I think so too."

Tommie felt a prick on her calf and looked down to find Trouble staring up at her. "Me-ow!" The cat let his concurring opinion be known.

"What are we going to do about it?" Tommie asked Harley.

"Find out what the hell is going on at Loftus Manor. If it's someone looking for a treasure, they may have killed Samuel. I'm hoping your renovators have some explanation for the appearances and disappearances of that figure we've all seen. Let's head back to the manor."

Tommie put a hand on his arm. "How far is Montgomery from here?"

"Under an hour if the traffic is light," Harley said. His face lit up. "You want to visit the medical examiner and check on that report."

"I think we should," Tommie said. "If it was changed, we need to report that and begin to find out who changed it."

"Good idea. Let's take care of that."

They'd barely buckled their seatbelts when Tommie's phone rang. "It's the renovation team," she said before she answered.

"Tommie, can you get back to the manor?" Katie Evans asked. She was slightly breathless.

"Is someone hurt?" Tommie was instantly on alert.

"No, but Hank found something. You really need to see this."

"What is it?" Tommie asked.

"You'd better take a look for yourself. I'm not trying to be mysterious, but...just come back as fast as you can."

"We're on the way," Tommie said as Harley put the vehicle in gear and sped toward the manor.

THE BIPEDS HAVE UNEARTHED some actual clues—a refreshing turn of events. The problem is that none of the clues add up to a picture of what's going on. We have a star sapphire button, unusual and intriguing. We have a carefully changed death certificate and a real estate developer who seems determined to buy the manor. And we have a newly minted wife, who may or may not be the wife. And now I won't find out today. I was hoping when in Montgomery to lead the humanoids to investigate the Reverend Krystal Child, alleged minister and unifier of bipeds in wedded bliss. As Sherlock would say, a boast that defies logical deduction.

But it sounds as if there's something amiss at Loftus Manor, and our attentions are better focused there. With my keen feline hearing, even though Tommie didn't put the conversation on speaker, I could detect the excitement, and perhaps trepidation, in Katie's voice. The renovation team has found something of great interest. My curiosity is piqued, and as we all know cats and their curiosity are fodder for the triteness mill. I've never known a cat that was actually killed by curiosity. And just to lay the old saw aside, we do not have nine lives. Two scores settled rapidly.

And we're turning down the drive to the manor. Harley has a lead foot but he's slowing as he sees Katie and Hank sitting on the front steps with the workers scattered about the lawn taking a break. Whatever they found has halted the renovation dead in its tracks.

My case is about to take a turn.

CHAPTER TWENTY-FIVE

ommie pointed the flashlight into the shallow recess of the kitchen wall and gasped. She'd been warned, but even so she wasn't prepared for the horror of the eyeless skull angled up at her. Long stripped of any flesh, the human skull sat atop a pile of bones. Once upon a time, it had been a human being.

"I'd better call the law," Tommie said to Harley.

"I already have," Harley admitted. "This is a little too much Edgar Allan Poe, and while Samuel might find this thrilling, it's a matter now for the police. Keep in mind, we can't touch anything."

"The minute we saw it, we stopped work," Katie said.

"Who is it?" Tommie asked everyone there, though she didn't expect an answer. The bones had once been a living person, but who? "Did Samuel ever say anything about someone going missing?"

Harley coughed. "No. And trust me, if there'd been a missing relative or any idea of a skeleton walled up in the house, Samuel would have been telling tall tales about it all over town." He picked up a piece of rubble that had been removed from the wall. "Looking at the mortar in those bricks Hank knocked out, I'd say this body has been back there at least a hundred years."

"I agree," Hank said. He put his arm around Katie. "We've found some strange things renovating old houses, but never a skeleton. I pulled the camera crews out, but..." He looked from Tommie to Harley to Katie. "It would make some incredible television."

"Oh, dear goodness," Tommie said and sank into a kitchen chair. "I'm not so sure that's a good idea." Her first thought was protecting her uncle and Loftus Manor.

"But it could be," Harley said, his face alight with inspiration. "Think about it, Tommie. If whoever is in this house is looking for a buried treasure, release of this information may draw them out into the open. Surely with a skeleton, there's bound to be something worth killing for."

"We don't know this...person was murdered," Tommie said. "Maybe he or she died of natural causes."

"Not likely," Hank said. "I agree with Harley. This could be a golden opportunity. And if we can solve the mystery of the corpse while we're filming or before we finish production, we'd be happy to forgive *all* the renovation costs. This would garner our TV show an incredible bite of the audience, which translates into profits for us so we wouldn't need to charge you."

Tommie closed her eyes briefly. It was a tempting offer, but the bones looked so helpless and defenseless. They had once been somebody. And Hank and Harley were right. It was likely the person had been murdered. Folks didn't normally wall up a person who died of an illness or accident. This body had clearly been hidden.

"It might also help the law find the person responsible," Katie said. "I mean surely there are stories or rumors of someone who went missing from these parts. And with the time-frame back in the 1800s this didn't involve Samuel at all. It's ancient history with a lot of audience appeal."

"It could be a win-win," Hank added. "At any case, let the crew document what we've found, and if you don't want the footage to air, I swear to you I'll delete it and never say a word."

Tommie swallowed. Trusting others wasn't her strong suit. She'd just begun to trust Harley, and now here was a huge matter where misplaced trust could come back to bite her for the rest of her life. "You swear you won't use the footage?" she asked.

"We promise," Katie said.

"Go ahead." She stepped back as the camera crew rushed forward to set up lights. In a matter of moments they were ready to record, and Tommie realized that the law officers would instantly shut down the filming when they arrived. Hank and Katie were taking advantage of every second of time.

"One of our first renovation projects at Loftus Manor is to open the kitchen area for bigger commercial appliances and also to take out the smaller pantry, breakfast nook, dining area, and one of the small storage areas to make room for the additional dining space that will be needed when Loftus Manor is an inn," Hank explained to the camera.

"Unfortunately," he continued, "when Rudy and I took out this wall," he pointed with a crowbar, "we found a lot more than we bargained for. A human skeleton." The camera crew moved in for close ups of the body in the wall.

Harley signaled Tommie to walk out into the foyer with him. "I'm glad you let them film it, and I believe you can trust them to honor their word to you."

"I hope so. I don't want this footage showing up all over the internet when I'm trying to book Christmas rooms. This could kill my business. If I ever get a business going." She felt despondent.

"Or it could increase your business. Haunted houses are big bucks," Harley said, putting a protective arm over her shoulders. "Look, this was bound to get out no matter whether Hank and Katie use it or not. How many of those workers do you think have cell phone footage of that find? And it'll be all over town once the law arrives. This way, at least you can control the major narrative."

Harley was right about that. A skeleton walled up in the notoriously haunted Loftus Manor was going to be big news in Wetumpka and surrounding areas. The gossip would fade, eventually, and a good way to stay on top of the story and how it was reported was by working with Hank and Katie, who could actually normalize the macabre find. For a man who'd spent the last five years as a virtual hermit, Harley had a good handle on marketing and promotion techniques. He was a man with surprising gifts.

As the sound of sirens drew closer, Tommie squared her shoulders and prepared to do the necessary things to have the skeleton removed and to cooperate with the local law enforcement.

When the patrol car pulled up in front of the manor, Tommie was surprised to see it was a city cruiser rather than a county sheriff's car. The handsome man that stepped out of the vehicle had to be Aiden Rivers, the man engaged to marry Trouble's human mother, the bookseller.

"Aiden!" Harley greeted him with affection. "I thought the sheriff would come out?"

"I asked to take this," Aiden said. "It's an interdepartmental cooperation thing. Sheriff Havard has all of his men at a double drowning on the river. Terrible tragedy. I was happy to check this out for the county."

After an introduction, Aiden followed Tommie into the house and through to the kitchen where the gaping hole in the brick wall was impossible to miss. Aiden took a long look. "Mr. Moore, the coroner, is sending a team to remove the remains. I'm sure they'll send the bones to Montgomery." He turned to Tommie. "Our medical examiner doesn't have the skill or equipment to evaluate a skeleton. The state facility is far more sophisticated."

Tommie nodded. She still had some questions for the state medical examiner about Samuel's official cause of death—a pressing matter that had completely been derailed by the discovery of a skeleton.

"We'll have the remains removed as quickly as possible," Aiden said. "I'd like a chance to examine the area where the body was stored, get some detailed photographs, and then you can resume the renovation. Not a lot of forensic evidence left to gather, I fear."

"Do you have any idea who it might be?" Tommie knew she sounded melancholy, but she couldn't help it. "Will you be able to tell cause of death?"

"I don't know is my answer to both questions," Aiden said. "I'll talk to Tammy. She knows a lot of people in the area who know a lot of history. Surely there must be some kind of story if the bones belong to a local person. We'll do what we can. I promise."

HARLEY GLANCED over at Tommie as she talked with Aiden, waving at the hole in the wall and finally taking Aiden into the small study where Samuel had died. Harley wanted to be with her, but he knew Aiden preferred talking alone with Tommie, and Harley had something else he needed to do.

Apparently, the black cat had his own ideas about the next step to be taken, too. He fell in with Harley as he went out the front door and walked around the manor to the wood shed. From an assortment of tools, he picked up an axe, a sledge hammer, and a crowbar.

Hank and Katie had instantly stopped work the minute they'd discovered the skeleton, but when the employees from the coroner's office finished up with the body removal, Harley intended to take out more of the wall. There was more to the body's hiding place than just a convenient dumping site. Harley had done some arithmetic based on the conversation he overheard between Aiden and the coroner's men, which seemed to indicate the skeleton was at least a hundred years old, as they had guessed. Which meant the bones had been encased in the house long before Samuel moved in. Had Samuel known of any rumors of a body walled up in the manor, he would have conjured scary stories with great flair. The skeleton in the wall was far too reminiscent of "The Cask of Amontillado" for Samuel to resist repeating. No, the dead person had deliberately been walled up. If this was not a murder, then it was a cover-up of a death.

That kind of story was macabre, but it could help boost tourists for Tommie's inn. It could also attract the bad element of people who would seek an opportunity to destroy and dig up the property. Someone would need to keep a close eye on the grounds and house. Harley stopped himself, because he was already visualizing filling that role. He'd agreed to stay until Tommie was settled, so it was foolish to play out fantasies of a long-term stay. He had feelings for Tommie, but emotions were a long way from a commitment. He needed to step back.

The black cat was sitting in front of him, watching with that intense green gaze that seemed to read Harley's mind. He chuckled at the thought and bent down to pet the cat. Trouble responded with a loud purr and then darted off to the servant's door of the house. With everyone focused on the skeleton, now was a good time for a little more exploration of the manor.

In the back of his mind, Harley had been flipping over the possible ways the uninvited visitor was gaining access to Loftus Manor. Like the cat, he'd settled on the servant's entrance. When he tried the door, it was locked, as Tommie had insisted. She checked and locked the doors at least once a day, sometimes more. He was about to go back to the front when he noticed an area around the lock that had been chipped, as if smacked with an ice pick or some sharp device. Harley rattled the door and then slid a credit card down the lock. The door clicked open and he stepped inside, the cat right with him.

Instead of going to the kitchen, Trouble headed up the narrow stairs that led to the second floor, and then the attic. Harley and Tommie had briefly toured the attic, but they'd put off an extensive search until the renovators were on site.

"Me-ow!" Trouble blinked his green eyes at Harley. "Meow!"

"Show me," Harley said to the cat.

Trouble bounded up the stairs and kept going until he was at the attic door.

A chill swept over Harley as he pushed the door open and stepped into near total darkness. There were several small windows around the large room to allow for ventilation, but they hadn't been cleaned in years and the light that filtered into the room was muted.

He stood for a moment, getting his bearings and trying to understand why his heart was beating at triple pace. In the far-right corner of the room, a shadow moved. It wasn't just his imagination, because the cat saw it too and reacted. Trouble leaped on top of a covered sofa and from there to a table top and a bureau. The attic was a graveyard of abandoned furniture.

Harley rushed toward the area where he'd seen movement, but without a flashlight, he stumbled several times. By the time he got to the area, it was empty. Thick dust on the furniture was undisturbed. He chuckled softly. Finding the skeleton in the wall had really put his imagination into overdrive. He blew out his breath and felt his heartrate slow. If someone was in the attic, they could find hiding places with ease, but based on the dust, no one was here. It had been a trick of light or the branches of a tree outside moving in the wind.

"Who's up here?" he called out. He didn't expect an answer. "When I find you, I'm going to march you right downstairs to the police." He waited, but there was no response.

The only answer came from the cat, who leaped over the top of the furniture that was such a stumbling block for Harley.

"Meow!" Trouble called out, urging Harley to follow him.

He obliged, wondering why the cat had been so insistent on coming to the attic. When he made it to the opposite wall, he found himself in front of some framed portraits. Judging from the dust on the cloth that covered them they hadn't been viewed in many years. Harley had no interest in disturbing them, but the cat had other plans. Trouble slid between several of the paintings and sent a whole stack of them toppling over.

"Watch it, Trouble," Harley said. He didn't know if the art was valuable or sentimental, and he didn't want to find out. "Come on, cat, let's go back downstairs." He hadn't meant to leave Tommie alone for this length of time. She'd seemed okay, but finding a body in the walls of your home was enough to shake up even the most stalwart person.

He started to turn away, but the cat was at his leg. Trouble reared up and put his paws on Harley's leg. When he dug his claws in, Harley realized the cat meant business. "What's going on?"

When the cat had his full attention, Trouble went back to the stack of paintings. He patted one with his paw.

"You want me to look at this painting?" Harley asked, and didn't feel in the least foolish talking to the cat. Trouble comprehended plenty.

Trouble slowly blinked his big green eyes that were luminous in the dimly lit attic.

"Okay, then." Harley began picking up the fallen paintings and moving them aside until he came to the one Trouble had indicated. He lifted it up and removed the brown paper wrapping—which had partially been clawed away—that had been used to protect the painting. He couldn't stop the gasp that escaped him.

The woman who stood at the edge of a woods wore a dark cloak with three star-sapphire buttons on the left shoulder. The hood of the cloak covered most of the woman's face, but not enough to hide her identity. Rachel Loftus stared back at him from the painting. She was young, vibrant, and so beautiful that Harley fully understood Samuel's lifelong devotion to his bride and wife. But why was she wearing the cloak?

CHAPTER TWENTY-SIX

*T*ommie saw the awe and appreciation on the faces of Kate and Hank as they viewed the portrait Harley had found in the attic. While they'd been occupied with the removal of the skeleton in the wall, Harley had brought the portrait downstairs, removed a pastoral scene that had hung above the fireplace, and hung the Rachel portrait in the main library—all before he'd called everyone in to see it.

"The time period makes it look like she lived in the 1800s," Katie said. "And that cloak! It's almost as if I can see a wind riffling the edges of it."

"It's an extraordinary work of art," Hank agreed. "Why was it hidden in the attic?"

"I have no idea," Tommie said. Looking into the eyes of the woman wearing the mysterious cloak with three buttons on her shoulder—buttons that glowed with an inner light—Tommie still felt as if she'd been kicked in the stomach. The old lore that the glow of the star sapphire was a trapped soul made her slightly nauseated. Aside from that, the painting was an incredible work of art. She couldn't help but think that as much as Samuel reportedly loved Rachel, this vision of her should have been prominently displayed. Not hidden away in the attic.

"Samuel never mentioned this painting," Harley said. "I don't understand why not. It's incredible."

One look at the beautiful woman in the portrait and Tommie knew the cloak played a role in her family history, and in the mystery of the hidden painting. More of a role than she'd ever believed. Remembering the vision she'd seen—the woman in the cloak in the back garden—she felt frustration. She had so many parts of the puzzle, thanks to Harley and Trouble, and yet she still couldn't piece together what was happening in Loftus Manor.

"That's definitely Samuel's wife, Rachel," Harley explained to Hank and Katie. "Samuel was always showing me pictures of her. He was dedicated to her and his love for her never faltered. I could have sworn he was deeply in love with her until the day he died." He looked over at Tommie and caught her eye. "He was always showing those same pictures to Nina."

His implication was clear to Tommie. "Do you have any idea why Rachel is wearing that cloak?" That was pretty much the only thing she could think about.

"I don't. We'll have to find that out," Harley told her, his hand on her shoulder offering reassurance and support. "It's a great clue, though."

Tommie started to respond, but she remained silent. Her frustrations wouldn't help anyone find answers. She was momentarily distracted by Trouble, jumping to the mantel below the portrait. The cat was so athletic and graceful, he landed between several candles and a vase of silk flowers without disturbing a single thing. He sat down and turned to watch everyone.

"The portrait is a great find, but it doesn't help us identify the body in the wall," Hank said, reminding them that their biggest priority was to solve the identity of a dead person. "Aiden's FBI training will come in handy finding the facts."

"I'm glad the body is gone," Tommie said. Aiden had overseen the coroner removing the bones for transport to Montgomery. Forensic coroners could work miracles with DNA and other technology—or so she'd been assured. "Surely there are missing person's reports or...something that will give us answers." The idea that the bones would go unclaimed forever was intolerable.

"Aiden will have some answers for us tomorrow," Harley assured her. "For right now, why don't we take the rest of the day off from the renovation. You look done in."

Tommie saw the worry that floated over his expression. She stepped closer to the painting. "Are you one hundred percent sure this is Samuel's wife?"

"It's Rachel," Harley said, his tone tender and kind.

"But the woman in the old photo we found in the book can't be Rachel," Tommie said.

Katie put a hand on her arm, her face suddenly alight with an idea. "Wait a minute! Call Tammy Lynn. Hank, do you remember Tammy telling us about some big costume ball that Samuel held years ago? He and his wife hosted this gala event as a fundraiser for a city charity."

"I do," Hank said, his expression excited. "It was a huge success. According to Tammy, the ball was the event of the decade. Everybody who was anybody attended. Lots of celebrities, including Louise Fletcher, back home in Alabama after her first movie role. And Harper Lee, who'd just won her Pulitzer. And E.O. Wilson—they all attended. There were politicians and sports figures and musicians. It was a homecoming for a lot of Alabama talent in many fields."

Tommie shot a questioning look at Harley. Even in the middle of the terrible mess they found themselves in, she had an idea that a do-over of the ball would be the perfect way to announce Loftus Manor as an inn. "Do you know anything about this?"

"I never heard a word," he said, "but Loftus Manor would be the perfect location for such a party. I can see it. And I can see Rachel coming dressed as some historical Loftus relative, which is exactly what I think happened."

"It was a costume party," Katie said. "And from what Tammy said, everyone came as a historical figure. Maybe this was Rachel's costume."

It was almost like a click in Tommie's brain. "Rachel came as someone from the past, someone linked to Loftus Manor. But who *is* the woman in the cloak?" she asked, musing aloud.

"You sure have a lot of mysteries at this old house," Hank said. "Skeletons in the wall, mysterious paintings and what should prove to be a narrow passage in that wall that we'll explore tomorrow. Today, I think we're done. I sent the work crews home already. If it's okay, we'll be back tomorrow at seven."

"That's fine," Tommie said. She was eager to explore the area behind the wall even further, but after the day she'd had, she didn't want to do it with dusk stealing over the sky. Tomorrow was, indeed, another day.

"I'll see Hank and Katie out," Harley whispered in her ear. "Sit down on that sofa. I'll bring in more firewood and when I get back, I'll give you the best foot massage you've ever had."

Tommie couldn't help laughing. She'd never have taken

Harley for a foot massage kind of guy, but it sounded perfectly divine. "You're on."

She listened to the renovators and Harley chatting as they made their way to the front door. Even though she felt she was shirking her hostess duties, she was exhausted. Her shoulders ached from the tension. When Trouble jumped into her lap, she cuddled him against her, glad for his loud purr. "You found the portrait, Trouble. You added to the puzzle while at the same time you're helping to solve it."

The cat leaped from her lap and, in one long bound, was back on the mantel. With great care and control, he stood on his back legs and reached his front paws up, up, up the portrait until he patted Rachel's décolletage.

"Be careful!" Tommie jumped to her feet. Trouble was always very careful, but his claws could easily ruin the painting.

"Me-ow!" His cry was demanding, and he gently patted the canvas again.

"What is it?" She knew the cat was trying to show her something. She got a chair and moved it to the fireplace so she could get closer to the painting. When she was beside the cat, he gave the painting one more pat and jumped down.

A thin gold chain on Rachel's neck winked in the light from a western window. A tiny gold key was tucked in the crease between Rachel's breasts. "The key!" She recognized the size and shape instantly.

Harley opened the library door and entered with a load of wood just in time to see Tommie jump to the floor. "It's the key," she said. "The gold key!"

"What are you talking about?" he asked.

"The key you found behind the desk drawer. We thought it was a safety deposit key for Uncle Samuel, but when I called the bank, he didn't have a box, remember?"

"Sure." Harley put the wood down and tossed a couple of logs on the fire. He moved to examine the portrait more closely. "It does look like the same key." He bent to rearrange the wood.

"It was never a key to Uncle Samuel's safety deposit box." Tommie grabbed his arm and stopped him so that he faced her. "Think about it."

Harley inhaled. "Because it was the key to a box in Rachel's name."

"Exactly! I'll bet Samuel was paying the rental on Rachel's box all of these years." Tommie was almost hopping up and down. "We have to find out what's in that box. Now."

"Raincheck on the foot massage," Harley said, excitement in his voice now. "Get your coat, Tommie. We're going to the bank."

"Right now?" Tommie was more than ready to go, but the bank would be closed in only a few minutes.

Harley checked his watch. "We have fifteen minutes to get there and ten minutes to do our business."

"We can make it happen." Tommie abandoned the library and ran down the hall to the small study where Harley had found the key. Trouble was already there ahead of her, using his paws to pull open the drawer where Harley had placed the key.

"You are one smart cat," Tommie told him as she scooped the key up in one hand and the cat in the other. "Let's make tracks."

THE PROCESS OF DEDUCTION, *as elucidated by the inimitable Sherlock Holmes, led me to connect the key hidden in the back of the desk drawer with the key in Rachel's portrait. Visual stimulation—coupled with keen observation, as Sherlock tells us. Very satisfying, indeed.*

Now, as Harley drives like the proverbial bat out of hell toward Wetumpka's oldest and most stately bank, I hope I will not be proven wrong. The Loftus Lass easily came to conclude what I did ---the keys are one and the same. But I am the one who led her to that belief. For both our sakes, I hope I'm correct. And for heaven's sake, we need an end to the negative things happening at the manor.

Tommie has a life and future with her inn and jewelry making, and Harley, I hope, sees his future here as Lord of the Manor to help Tommie realize her dreams. I do believe that Harley loves the estate as much as Tommie will grow to. He belongs here. With her. If he will only open his eyes and see the truth.

Tommie is telling Harley that she hopes she isn't wasting their time with this deposit box idea. Oh, my. I find this sudden indecisiveness—and self-doubt—to be mildly amusing. And to my shame I realize that I feel some of the same emotions. This is not my normal self-confidence, which I delight in putting on display. I think the Loftus Lass makes me feel especially vulnerable. She's so eager to do the right thing. And she's so willing to doubt herself. She needs a little more feline attitude, which I realize is up to me to demonstrate. And so I shall.

Here we are at the bank. In fifteen minutes it will be closing time. I see that Harley and Tommie have no interest in waiting until tomorrow. They're barreling right into the bank and I'm hot on their heels. When the young woman steps in front of me and tries to block me, I give her a growl and a hiss, as if to say, back off! Yes, I can and will be assertive—to show the humanoids how it's done.

Tommie turns to me in astonishment, but I breeze past them all and head toward the vault. It's a beautiful old bank building, and while I'd love to take time to explore and investigate, it's almost closing time.

"Meow!" *I call to them.*

"That is one bossy cat," *the bank employee says, and not with admiration.*

"But he is insanely smart," *Tommie assures her.*

Harley is asking to see the safety deposit boxes. When the bank manager starts to protest, Tommie shows him the will, leaving everything from the Loftus Estate to her. Soul heir. Bingo, we're all headed into the vault. At least one of the many mysteries of Loftus Manor is about to be resolved!

CHAPTER TWENTY-SEVEN

*H*arley stepped back from the table where the very
annoyed bank employee put the big safety deposit
box that matched the key. He'd wanted to remain in the lobby,
but Tommie had insisted that he accompany her into the vault.
Somehow, Trouble had also managed to slip in. The cat had given
the young teller a hard time, and then he'd disappeared. The
feline could make himself virtually invisible when he chose.

The teller left the room and Tommie put her hands on the
lid of the box. She looked at Harley and inhaled. "Here goes
nothing."

When she flipped the lid back, she reached into the box and
brought out a sheaf of papers. There was also a small jewelry box
and some assorted mementos. As she leafed through the
contents, she let out a soft exclamation and held up a square
card. "Oh, Harley, look at this. It's an invitation to a costume ball
at Loftus Manor. Look! A sketch of one of the star sapphire
buttons had been used as the centerpiece on the invitation. It's
the party Katie and Hank were talking about."

Tommie held the papers and motioned Harley over so they

could look at them together. He stepped forward, and Trouble jumped to the top of the table.

"A costume ball. I hope there's more information about the cloak in there." He nodded toward the teller who was standing impatiently in the doorway.

"It's time for the bank to close," Tommie said. "Maybe we should take this stuff with us. We can bring it back tomorrow."

"Good idea. Let's do that."

"I wish I'd brought an envelope or folder," Tommie said. "But I can just hold it as we leave." She closed the box, returned it to the wall, and called the young woman back to lock it. The teller eyed the bundle of papers in Tommie's hand, but she didn't say anything.

"Thanks for letting us in," Tommie told her. "Sorry we were so late."

"It's just now five," the young woman said. "No problem at all."

When they stepped back into the lobby, Harley gently grabbed Tommie's shoulder. He pointed to a man striding across the parking lot. "Is that Paul Rider?"

"Yes," the young teller said. "He was here but said he forgot something and would come back tomorrow. Thank goodness. He always has a lot of things to do and I'm ready to go home."

"And we thank you again," Tommie said, heading straight for the door with Harley and the cat.

Once they were outside, she turned to face Harley. "Do you think Paul Rider was spying on us?"

Harley, who'd thought exactly the same thing, nodded. "He bears watching. Now let's get home."

He handed Tommie into the passenger side of his car and opened the back door for Trouble. "Hop in, Detective Trouble. So far, you're the best thing we have going for us in figuring out what's going on at Loftus Manor." When the cat was on the back seat, he closed the door.

Daylight was fleeing from the western sky, and Harley's inclination was to press hard on the gas pedal, but he slowed his speed. The headlights illuminated the road, but it was twisty and sometimes filled with deer during the fall and winter months. Often when he was driving back to the manor he'd see does with their fawns. He and Tommie had accomplished what they needed to do. There was no need to rush.

Darkness was beginning to settle over the road as the sun dipped into the horizon, and Harley felt a sinister sensation creep over him. His body was on red alert. He slowed even more and checked behind him as he came up on the turn off to the manor. This narrow road carried little traffic, but it was the quickest way home. Normally, he wouldn't give it a second thought.

He took the turn and had traveled less than half a mile when he noticed headlights behind him. They were coming up fast. Too fast. He watched for a moment, his alarm growing at the other car's speed.

"Tommie, reach in the glove box and hand me that Glock."

"What?" Tommie shifted to face him. In the glow of the dashboard, her face was filled with worry. "What's wrong?"

"We're being followed. Could be nothing, but I don't want to be caught unprepared."

She found the gun and gingerly handed it to him.

He admired that she didn't question him. She'd come to trust him, as he'd begun to trust her. "Everything will be fine. Like I said, it's probably nothing. We'll just let them pass us." Still, he wrapped his fingers around the gun, very aware of the trigger. To be prepared, he let his driver's window down, the whole time he drove and watched his rearview mirror.

"Meow!" Trouble said from the back seat.

"We have it covered," Harley assured the cat, though as the car pulled right up on their bumper, he was less certain. This stretch of road was dangerous in the daytime, when the twists and dips could often hide on-coming traffic. Now, with a large car right on their bumper, the danger was increased. In the best-case scenario, someone was jacking with them. It could be a carload of kids unaware of how very dangerous tail-gating could be.

Whether it was meant to be annoyance or scare tactics—or worse—he couldn't say. But he was ready for whatever happened.

The car swerved suddenly into the passing lane and put on a burst of speed until it was abreast of Harley's vehicle. The light had almost gone for the day, but the last ray of the sun glinted off the gun's barrel as it came out of the passenger window of the passing car. It wasn't a joke, as he'd hoped. This was serious trouble.

Harley slammed on brakes. He'd been ready and prepared, and he punched the brake, turning the wheel simultaneously, spinning his vehicle but keeping it on the road instead of running down into a ravine. The assault car flew past them as a gunshot exploded from the barrel. Harley's car skidded and spun, ending up crossways in the road.

"Get down," Harley ordered Tommie. She crouched on the floorboard.

Harley stopped the car, jumped out, and dropped to the ground where he fired three shots after the disappearing car. He thought he heard one hit metal. Before he could do anything else, the car disappeared around a sharp curve in the growing darkness.

He heard Tommie's door slam shut and in a moment she was kneeling beside him. He could feel her trembling, and he wanted to pull her into his arms and comfort her, but this wasn't the time.

"Who was that?" she asked.

"I don't know. There wasn't a tag on the car, and the windows were too dark to see in. All I can tell you is that it was a black Tahoe. There was a driver and a passenger."

"They meant to kill us," she said, her voice small and breathless.

"I think they probably wanted to hurt us," Harley agreed. "I think maybe the intention was to run us off the road and down one of the ravines. Make it look like an accident."

"Do you think this is because of Loftus Manor?"

Harley didn't want to make her more fearful, but he couldn't lie. "What other reason could there be? No one here knows you and I can't imagine why anyone would be after me. I don't have anything or know anything worth killing for." He stood up. "Tommie, let's just get in the car and get out of here." He looked around, realizing that if the attacker came back, they were not in a great defense position. He only had a limited number of bullets left in the clip. It was too dark to examine the area for any clues. That would wait until daylight when professional law officers arrived and could truly evaluate the scene.

Tommie didn't ask more questions. She and Trouble, who'd joined them on the asphalt, hurried back to the car. Harley maneuvered the car around on the narrow road, and they drove back toward town. He had no intention of ending up in an ambush. "There's a back way to Loftus Manor. Several, in fact. But let's grab a bite to eat in town. I know you're going to say you can't eat, but let's do this. For safety's sake." He handed Tommie his phone. "And this time, we're calling the law. Aiden can meet us at Tantee's Restaurant. His number is in the contact list."

CHAPTER TWENTY-EIGHT

*A*iden walked into the restaurant and gave Tommie and Harley a nod as he sauntered over and took a seat. He looked longingly at the vodka tonic Tommie sipped—at Harley's insistence to calm her nerves—but he shook his head when the waitress asked for an order. "I won't be here long," he said.

"Stay and have a bite to eat," Tommie said, knowing that Aiden was doing them a favor by meeting at the restaurant rather than asking her to meet him at the station.

"Too much to do," Aiden said. "I want to check out the area of the road where this took place. I'm still giving the sheriff's department a hand, and Tammy asked me to keep an eye on you two. She's worried."

"We'll come with you to the scene," Harley said, pushing back his chair.

Aiden held up a hand. "Please, just stay here and have something to eat. I know exactly where it is. If I were going to plan some kind of assault, that's exactly the patch of road I'd select."

"I wish this would stop," Tommie said, and to her surprise, she heard the tears in her voice. She blinked them back from her eyes. "I don't want to take anything that belongs to someone else, but I do want what Uncle Samuel wanted me to have."

"A reasonable request," Aiden said. "I'm just wondering if this has anything to do with you inheriting the manor, or what someone perceives is hidden at the manor. I've kept the discovery of the skeleton totally under wraps. I threatened the renovation crews, and Hank and Katie promised no one would talk. You two aren't talking. Let's just keep that body to ourselves. The coroner took one look and realized it was out of his abilities, so the bones have gone on to Montgomery."

"I think it was a woman," Tommie said. "The bones looked delicate."

"We'll know more soon," Aiden said, and he patted her hand on the table top. "I do have some news for you two. I had some of my men search around the manor and we found your damaged game cameras. We also reviewed the ones that worked, and there was nothing recorded. The broken ones—we couldn't recover anything at all. I'm sorry. But I also ran a check on Nina Ahearn's presiding clergy at the wedding. I wouldn't worry about that. The woman is a fraud and it's my belief that the purported marriage is a fraud."

"So Nina is not Samuel's wife?" Harley clarified.

"Correct. She is nothing to Samuel or to you, Tommie. I don't know where she got that hare-brained scheme to pretend to be legally wed, but I talked with the police chief and he says if you want to press charges, he's ready to do it."

Tommie felt both men watching her. Even Trouble was waiting for her to respond. "No, don't prosecute right now. I can do it later, right?"

Aiden nodded. "Yes, but don't wait too long."

"Nina and the woman pretending to be his daughter, Odell Rains, were put up to this by someone else," Tommie said.

"That's the person I want to get. If I don't press charges, I can hold it over Nina's head maybe. Convince her to talk. Or I guess technically it would be blackmail her into talking."

Aiden grinned. "Not a bad strategy for a young heiress. If you decide to forgo the inn, maybe you'd take some training in law enforcement."

Tommie rolled her eyes. "Truly, it's your girlfriend's cat," she pointed at Trouble, "who is the prime detective. He's pretty amazing."

"He sure is," Aiden said. "One day, when we all have time for a drink or a cup of coffee, I'll tell you all about how Trouble solved the biggest case of my life and also pushed Tammy into my arms."

"Sounds like you and Uncle Samuel have a lot in common—storytelling," Tommie said.

"Your uncle was a terrific man. Few people know the things he did for the community. There were families he supported for years, helping with college educations for at least twenty young people that I know of. The local humane society has a shelter because of him. He was very generous."

Tommie couldn't help the swelling of pride, even though she hadn't known Samuel. "The more I hear, the more I like him. I wish I'd known him before he...died."

"By the way," Aiden said, "I'm looking into the altered death certificate. I'll have some answers on that too."

"Thank you," Tommie said, and she meant it. "Thank you for handling that. It's all so technical and..."

"You're more than welcome. We'll get to the bottom of this." Aiden stood. "Now I've got a team out on Brindza Road looking into the scene of your attack. We'll do a cursory investigation tonight and tomorrow we'll be there as soon as it's daylight. I'll be in touch."

When he was gone, Tommie heaved a sigh of relief. "What is going on here, Harley? Who would want to hurt us?"

"We need to look at the papers we took from the bank."

Tommie slapped her forehead. "I'd forgotten. In all of this madness, I just forgot I had them." She reached into the inner pocket of her jacket and brought the bundle of papers out. She divided them into two piles and handed one to Harley. "No time like the present. And I truly am not hungry. This drink hits the spot."

"I'm not sure that's the wisest choice, but..." Harley signaled the waitress for another round of drinks. "Your wish is my command. Let's get busy looking for clues."

The pile Tommie kept had a sleeve of negatives and photos and she brought out the prints, which had faded with age but were still clear. The night of the costume ball was depicted in all its splendor. Banked arrangements of flowers, tables of exquisite food, a champagne tower, the faces of laughing men and women —no one Tommie recognized—indicated that the ball was a smashing success. When she found some photos of Samuel and Rachel together, she could almost feel the love between them. Harley had spoken the truth about their commitment to each other. It was clear to see.

"Look, she's wearing the cloak." Tommie pushed a photo over to Harley. Trouble, too, examined it.

"They look so happy," Harley said.

"They do."

She continued going through the photos and stopped. In one snapshot of Rachel and Samuel standing at the bottom of the beautiful staircase, there was something above them—a wispy film. The more she looked, the more the image looked human. But it wasn't a person; it was an entity. It hovered above the stairs, an ethereal being caught on film. "Oh, dear," Tommie said.

"As Melinda in the TV show would say, 'We are with ghost at the manor.'"

She held the photo out to Harley, who looked shocked. In return, he handed a piece of thick, aged paper to her. "And treasure," he said. "I believe it's a map of where the Loftus fortune has been hidden."

CHAPTER TWENTY-NINE

*W*hile Tommie and Harley pore over the treasure map—and they are deeply puzzled by the seemingly indecipherable legend of the map—I'm keeping an eye out for anyone in the restaurant who might display too much interest in what the humanoids are doing. I would caution the bipeds to use more care in their actions, but it's been a tragic, stressful day and it's good to see them plotting together. Funny how sometimes life hands us the exact person who can give us what we need. And when the exchange is beneficial to both, this bears the fingerprint of the gods. I can almost see the high walls of defense both Tommie and Harley have built beginning to fall, brick by brick.

All well and good for the romance department, but if someone here in Tantee's Restaurant has an untoward interest in what's going on with the Lofton Lass and Loftus Manor, I need to be aware of it. Harley is normally an eagle-eye for trouble. Case in point the expert driving he did on Brindza Road to keep us from getting shot or wrecked. But right now, he is besotted with Tommie. Give the kids a little room for pleasure. Life is too short, even for a feline with nine lives. Take a moment of joy when it knocks at your door.

Ah, Harley is coming to his senses and looking around the restaurant.

He cautions Tommie to whisper. Good work. But so far, I don't detect any enemies near us. A needed break in the constant drama of Loftus Manor since Tommie arrived.

To my great delight, when Harley ordered coffee, he also included a small portion of the grilled rainbow trout for me. The dish comes with a light cream sauce, which I adore. I give him a big wink to let him know how much I appreciate his thoughtfulness. I have to say, Tommie needs one of those dolls that cry and raise hell if you don't feed it or change it. I would suggest handcuffing it to her wrist or else she'll leave it somewhere and never notice. She's a lovely lass, but when she isn't hungry, she forgets that I have a very small stomach and expend vast amounts of energy in helping her. But no biped is without sin. They'll be hard pressed to equal the perfection of the average feline, not to mention the truly superior perfection of...yours truly.

Now that Tommie and Harley have eased back from the so-called treasure map, I can take a gander. At first it seems to be nonsense, but it is definitely a map of something. Treasure? I'm not certain. That is the first assumption, of course. But why wouldn't Samuel have found the treasure? Or at least why wouldn't he have left directions to Tommie on how to access the treasure? Why give her the manor but not the means to support it—if those means truly do exist?

I'll need to really think about this map, but to be honest, it appears to be something more interesting, at least to me. This seems to be dead space within Loftus Manor. Passageways. And that one in particular seems to reveal where the skeleton was found. I can't be certain until I get back to the manor and check it out, but what if Rachel knew about the passageways and decided to leave a detailed map for someone else. And what if Samuel wasn't aware of these hidden means of moving about the house? Which leads to the bigger question. Did Rachel know details of the person sealed in the wall from a century ago? None of this seems to have a direct flow of logic. Sherlockian deduction demands logic. I daresay this would drive the Baker Street sleuth to his well-documented indulgences.

Ah, my fish is here. The aroma has me salivating. And oh, yes, so worth it. This is divinely scrummy. And if I play my cards right, I'll have a dollop of cream for my afters! Thank you, Mr. Brawny.

HARLEY WATCHED the cat eat with pleasure. One thing about Trouble, he knew what he liked and he ate it with relish. And the cat did have refined taste. No doubt about that. When Trouble sat back from his dish, Harley signaled Tommie that he was ready to go. He'd made no progress with the map, and by now wasn't convinced it was even a real treasure map. There were curious notations—numbers and codes—about the entire thing. And while it vaguely resembled some of the interior of Loftus Manor and grounds, drawn out like an architectural plan, he couldn't be certain. Too bad he didn't know a cryptologist to ask for help. The numbers and notations were small, and he couldn't connect them in any way to the architecture of the house.

"What does 18 narrow mean? Do you think we'll figure this out?" Tommie asked him, exhaustion in her voice.

"I don't know, but we will put it all together." She needed to believe, and that he could give her. Sometimes hope was the only thing that kept a person going. Tommie had had quite a week since she'd moved to Alabama.

When they left the restaurant, Tommie stumbled slightly and he caught her, bringing her into his chest to stabilize her. Which turned into a warm embrace. She was so exhausted, all defenses were down, and they stood outside the restaurant in the parking lot, just holding each other while the cat gave them a knowing look. He could almost swear the cat approved of the growing feelings between them.

When Tommie and the cat were safely in his vehicle, he texted Aiden to let him know they were headed back to Loftus

Manor. Aiden had mentioned that several deputies would be on alert along the roadway. Harley was good with that. He could protect himself—but Tommie and the cat were another matter. He wouldn't risk them. He was glad to have the help from Aiden and the other officers.

Tommie fell asleep as soon as the car was in motion, and Harley drove carefully, alert for danger from any side. Trouble hopped into the front seat and helped him keep watch. They made it back to the manor without incident.

The minute Harley pulled up, though, his heartrate increased. The front door was wide open. Again. He thought of the photograph of the "spirit" Tommie had found in Rachel's lock box. It was either a spirit or someone who had a key to the manor. Tommie had locked the door. He was certain of it.

She awoke as he parked at the front door.

"Stay in the car," he urged her. "Please, Tommie. I'm better able to investigate if I don't have to worry about you. Here, get behind the wheel and be ready to drive off if anyone comes out of the house. And give Aiden a call." He reached over to the glove box and got his gun before he handed her his phone. "This is going to end, one way or the other."

"Be careful. Nothing is worth getting hurt."

"I'll be safe. And you take off if anyone other than me comes out that door."

"I promise." Tommie slid beneath the steering wheel. She kept the car running.

Harley was aware Trouble was waiting for him at the open door. Funny but the cat gave him a lot of confidence.

TOMMIE CHEWED her bottom lip as she watched Harley and Trouble disappear in the doorway of Loftus Manor. She'd given her word, and she intended to honor it, no matter how much she wanted to go inside the manor. She had to accept that Harley was better trained in this than she was, and it was true she could endanger him or herself by sneaking inside. She would wait.

She tried to relax in the driver's seat, but she couldn't. The brief nap had given her a new surge of energy, and she watched the front door, praying that Harley and Trouble were safe and both would come out in a moment to wave her into the house. Or even better, Harley would catch whoever was playing with them and hog tie them until the law could arrive. If anyone could do it, Harley could. She had faith in him. Especially with Trouble on the scene to help.

No matter how she stared at the doorway, though, it remained empty. She was so focused on that one location that she almost missed the movement in an upstairs window on the side of the house where her room was located. In fact, it was one of the windows of her room—a woman was standing there, looking down on her. She couldn't see her features clearly, but the outline of her form, the narrow waist and fuller skirt, the hair piled on her head. It was definitely a woman and one she'd seen before.

She got out of the car slowly and hesitated, locking the doors to protect the paperwork she'd taken from the bank. She wanted to call Harley, but he'd given her his phone. She had no way to reach him, but she couldn't let the woman escape.

"Damn it." She ran up the steps and into the house. Should she call out? She decided not to. Instead, she rushed up the stairs to the second floor and headed to her room. She was going to confront the intruder now, once and for all.

There was no sign of Harley or Trouble, and she made it down the landing to her bedroom on silent feet. The door was open and she slipped into the room, aware of the scent of heavy perfume. In the dim light cast by a single lamp she realized the room was empty. She was too late yet again.

She heard footsteps, moving fast, headed toward her. "Harley?" she called out, not wanting to catch him off-guard.

"You were supposed to stay outside," Harley said as he and the cat entered the room.

"I saw someone in the window. She's gone though."

"I saw her in your uncle's study," Harley said. "Well, Trouble saw her first. I caught a glimpse as she left the room. She disappeared down the hall, up the stairs, and by the time I got up here, I didn't see her. I went to Nina's old room first. I assumed, if it had something to do with the inheritance of the house, whoever it was might go there."

"Instead, she came to my room." The truth of her statement sent a chill over Tommie. "Did you get a sense of whether she was...real, or a ghost?"

"Real," Harley said with decisiveness. "There was mud tracked into Samuel's study, by the desk where we found the key. And someone had riffled through his papers. Someone, a very much alive someone, has been coming and going here. They have to be here in the house still." Harley stepped forward and went to the window. "We've overlooked the method of entrance and egress, but we have to find it."

They both noticed that Trouble had jumped onto the windowsill. The cat reached up with his front paw and began tapping the glass panels. Tommie knew he was seeking something, but she couldn't figure out what. A person couldn't disappear into glass any more than bricks and mortar. Still, the cat was determined. He stood on tiptoe, seeking the top of the window with his front paws.

Tommie stepped up to the window and began feeling along the top of the panes where the windows locked. Her search led her to more closely examine the framework of the window. Loftus Manor had been built of heavy limestone rocks. Time would leave little mark on the old home. But as thick as the exterior walls were, and compensating for wood framing, something seemed off about the dimensions of this particular area.

Tommie slid her fingertips along the wood, feeling for what her eyes couldn't see. She found a small, hard nub. Acting on instinct, she pressed until she heard a click, and a part of the window frame pushed back, revealing an opening barely big enough for a person to step into. A small person.

Tommie shifted her shoulders into the opening. "I'll see where it goes."

Harley gently grasped her hand. "Look." He pointed toward the woods near the back of the house. A woman fled into the trees.

"Should we follow her?"

Harley thought a moment. "No. She's likely hidden a car down by the river. She'll be gone before we can get there. Let's find out where this passage goes."

"You won't fit," Tommie said. It was just a fact that Harley's shoulders were too broad, his frame too tall. The passage would accommodate only a small-framed woman. "Go after the woman! Even if you can't catch her maybe you can get a glimpse of her car."

"Let me get a flashlight for you. Or we can wait until Hank and Katie get here tomorrow. Just in case you get stuck."

"I have a light on my phone. Go! I won't get stuck," Tommie said. She had a sudden revelation. "Harley, those numbers, on the map of the manor. They're measurements of the areas where the walls are thicker, where there's a space to move between the walls. If I remember correctly, there's space on this wall down to the ground floor and extending into the yard. There must be some kind of tunnel or underground passage that opens into the woods." Tommie could barely suppress her excitement. "We've figured it out, Harley. Or at least a part of it."

"Except we don't know who that woman was."

"Now that we know how she's getting in and out, we'll be able to figure out the rest. Go, please! See what you can find out."

Harley put a hand on her shoulder and squeezed. "I don't like you going in there alone. What if someone is waiting in there?"

Tommie nodded at the cat, who hopped into the opening in front of her. "I won't be alone. Trouble will be with me."

CHAPTER THIRTY

*C*hoosing wisely is the mark of a true detective, according to Sherlock. I've chosen to stay with the Loftus Lass as we penetrate the dark confines of this crawlspace. There's plenty of room for me, but I can hear the labored intake of her breath. She's scared and close to hyperventilating—a righteous case of the collywobbles. I understand. The air in here is damp and musty. Each step beyond the light could be off a steep ledge—impossible to tell. She is moving tentatively, but she is marching forward with all the courage I expect. I'll rub against her legs and give her some comfort and confidence, I hope.

If the ghostly marauder who haunts Loftus Manor can get up and down this passage, so can we. The steps do go at a rather steep angle, but at last we've come to a level part of the passage. I can't discern what is ten feet to the right or left of us, or even above or below us. We are in a black hole, moving steadily, but to what destination? I can only stay a few feet ahead of Tommie so that if there is danger, I can sense it first.

Her cell phone does a fair job of illuminating the area immediately in front of us, and I see now there are names and marks carved into this wall that indicate a number of people have passed through here. She's documenting the passageway with photographs. Smart girl. Loftus

Manor is relatively isolated. Why would anyone be forced to use this elaborate system of passages and what is obviously a tunnel? Why not just walk across the lawn—if my presumption that we are moving away from the manor is true.

It's a curiosity for certain. But wait! Look at this! I must get Tommie to see. I bump her shins, catch her leg with my claws and at last, she is looking where I point. Her gasp is exactly the proper response.

I sense a bit of fresher air. I hope we're coming to the end of this tunnel and freedom! I feel like a mole, and let me say that moleishness is not greatly appreciated by cats. If we'd been intended to plow underground in dark and fetid tunnels, we would have been designed with little webbed hands and feet for digging. Ugh! What a foul situation.

We've come to the end of this passage. If my calculations are correct, we are in the spot where we saw the woman appear. Which means we need to push against the ceiling of this tunnel to see if we can find an exit. The idea that we might have to travel back the way we came is beginning to freak even me out—and I am not a feline who rattles easily.

But ah, yes, there is a small step stool. It's wooden and handmade. Very old but sturdy, and it indicates these tunnels have been in use for a long, long time. Probably since Loftus Manor was built. The Loftus Lass is climbing on the stool and pushing against the ceiling.

Sweet heaven, a blast of fresh air! Yes. And one can only hope Mr. Brawny is there to help us out of this hole. Or perhaps that won't be necessary. Here's a ladder. That will work perfectly to deliver us into the fresh air of a gorgeous October night.

WHEN HE SAW the slight upheaval of the ground and leaves, Harley rushed to help Tommie push open the trap door not far from the back corner of the manor. Tommie's assumption had been correct, there was an underground passage that led away from the house. Harley was eager to put Tommie's feet on solid ground. When he pulled her free of the hole, she clung to him for a long moment.

"Boy, am I glad to get out of there," Tommie said, shuddering, but still able to control her tears. "Whew, thank goodness I'm not claustrophobic. That tunnel isn't intended for someone with space issues. There were places where my shoulders rubbed the sides of the walls." She blew out her breath. "I'm not normally afraid of tunnels but I kept thinking, how old is this passage, has there ever been an earthquake in this area, who built this and why? I was getting a little freaked out when I came to the end, thank goodness."

It made Harley nervous just hearing about it. "Did you see anything in the tunnel? Or the passage?"

"I did!" Tommie held out her phone. "And I took photos."

"Smart girl!" Harley was elated. "What did you find?"

"Look." She went to her camera icon and into her camera roll. "There are marks on the walls. Some of them are made by someone my size, but there are other marks that look to have been made by someone the size of a child. And then this." She flipped to one photo where Trouble was clearly pointing to some writing on the wall. The letters J I X had been scratched into the stones. "That's the name of the little ghost in your uncle's story. Her name was Jacquelyn, but she was called Jix."

For Harley, the pieces shifted into focus. The long history of the manor, the ghost stories, the tunnels, the disappearing forms at the windows. It all made sense if viewed from a historical angle. "I have a theory about Jix and these passages."

"What?" Tommie asked. She was busy closing the trap door and recovering it with leaves. "Did you identify the woman we saw?"

"Yes, but first things first. In the story you said Jix had to stay at the manor. She could never leave. She didn't go to school."

"That's right," Tommie said. "I assumed she was sick or something. Some reason she didn't go to school with Ada. And then I thought it was because she was a ghost."

Harley couldn't help the thrill of excitement he felt. Finally, something was beginning to make sense. "I think Loftus Manor may have been a way station on the underground railroad to help slaves flee north to freedom. I'll bet there are more tunnels that extend farther into the woods. We can check with Katie and Hank. Think about it. This passage leads into the woods, and not half a mile away is the Coosa River. They could have had a boat waiting to take them upriver, or possibly even just followed the river north, through Tennessee and on toward Illinois." His voice softened. "I think Jix was a little girl, a young slave, who stayed with your ancestors. I think they gave her a home, for whatever reason. She may have been too sick to continue, or perhaps she had no one to watch after her."

TOMMIE FOUND it difficult to breathe. Harley was right. She knew it in her bones. "So Samuel wanted to honor Jix and keep her as part of Loftus Manor so he wrote a ghost story about her."

"Yes, he memorialized her in his story," Harley said. "That is so like Samuel. Somehow he learned her story and he didn't want her to be forgotten."

"Will we ever find out why she didn't go north with the others who surely kept moving away from Alabama?" Tommie asked.

"That's another mystery, and it may have to do with the person in the wall. You said it was a smaller skeleton. Female, you thought. What if it was Jix's mother or her big sister or someone she was traveling with. It makes sense, if the older woman died of some illness and the owners of the manor at the time had to get rid of the body—for whatever reason they couldn't dig a grave and bury her. Perhaps they were being watched all the time. Or it's possible there were pattyrollers all in the woods, watching for slave sympathizers. Folks back then didn't tolerate those who fought against slavery or attempted to help slaves gain their freedom. A burial might have been too dangerous."

The sadness that touched Tommie's heart told her that Harley had hit upon the truth. Perhaps they would be able to prove it, or not, but in her gut she believed Harley's theory to be true. A chill brushed against her left check, as if the touch of a cold hand had drifted over her. She looked toward the manor, and for a moment she thought she saw someone standing in her bedroom window. For a split second, it looked like a young girl, staring longingly out into the grounds.

Trouble, too, was fixated on the window and he let out a low, pitiful meow.

But in a moment the figure was gone, possibly an accident of the lighting in the bedroom, perhaps the flutter of her curtains where she—or someone else—had left the window open. The image of a human was there and then gone. It was Jix waving goodbye, Tommie thought, and the sadness intensified.

Harley picked up Trouble. "Let's go back to the manor."

"Harley, before I take another step you have to tell me. Did you see the woman who was in the house? Did you recognize her?" Along with being unnerved by the adventure in the tunnel, Tommie also felt a sense of dread. "Was it someone we know?"

"I'll tell you everything shortly," Harley said. "We still haven't talked to the genealogist in Knoxville. Let's head down to the manor and go through some records and find his name. Then we'll move to the cottage, where we have better phone reception. We're going to figure every bit of this out, and then you can take up residence in Loftus Manor without anything from the past hanging over your head." He took her arm and gently urged her forward.

Trouble sprang out of Harley's arms and began running toward the manor.

"Look, Trouble is already on the way. That one fact gives me a lot of comfort," Tommie said. "We're going to solve this."

TOMMIE SAT in the rocker on the porch. She held her cell phone in her hand. She had three bars of service, but still she didn't make her call.

On the small table beside her was a Lynchburg lemonade and a note with the name of the Knoxville genealogist Samuel had consulted with on it. She hadn't dialed yet—Harley still had to reveal what he'd learned in his pursuit of the intruder. He'd urged her to sip her drink and calm down before they talked. He was worried about her, and she could understand since her breathing was shallow and her heart racing.

The sounds coming from the kitchen told her Harley was busy making them something to eat. He'd promised to divulge his findings once Tommie ate something hot.

Waiting wasn't Tommie's strong suit, though. She *couldn't* wait any longer. Time was an eel, slithering through her fingers. And no matter how she chided herself for being foolish, she felt the danger closing in on them. Action was required.

She dialed the Knoxville number and waited for Marlin Lovett to answer. She found him to be a kind, compassionate man who willingly answered all of her questions—with surprising clarity, but few new facts. He recalled Samuel's interest in the underground railroad and the role Loftus Manor—like many other anti-slavery homeowners—played in ferrying slaves to freedom. By the time Harley brought out a tray of food for her, she'd finished her conversation and was waiting to tell him the news. The delicious smell of beef stew teased her appetite. She hadn't been hungry at all until she smelled Harley's cooking. The man was good with the pots and pans.

"I'll tell you what I found out from Mr. Lovett, but first, what about the strange woman you chased? Quid pro quo." She wasn't going to tell Harley another thing until he came clean.

He sat in the rocker beside her, his own tray at the ready. When he put a bowl of tender beef on the floor for Trouble and the cat dug into it with great appetite, he sighed. "Okay, I know who she was. I recognized her car, though I can't prove she was driving it."

"And you're going to tell me *her* name this instant, right?" Tommie was ready to stand up and snatch the truth from him.

"I am. But I don't want you to react right away. You have to eat, and then we have to decide how to proceed."

"Okay?" Tommie felt like she was pulling teeth. "Who is it?"

"Nina Ahearn."

Tommie was a little surprised by the fact that she wasn't surprised at all. Nina Ahearn made perfect sense. And now that they knew what she was up to... "We should call the cops on her. I've had enough. We already know she didn't marry Samuel and the whole fake marriage thing is a sham. Now she's trying to make me think I'm crazy or the house is haunted." She reached for her phone. "I'm done with this."

"Not yet," Harley said. "That's why I wanted to give you time to think about it. Nina has already lost her bid for any part of the inheritance. She should have followed Odell Rain's lead and left town. But she didn't. And for whatever her reasons, she's been tormenting you with her ghost appearances, her prying. If there's no money in this for her, what's the motive?"

"I don't know, which is why we should call the police," Tommie said. "I can't keep hanging back and being tentative. This is going to end, and it's going to end badly for Nina and all who are behind this."

"Completely agree, but—" Harley's eyes were a deadly gray. "But why don't we see if we can't use Nina for our own good."

Trouble looked up from the food he was intently consuming. "Me-ow!" He held up a paw as if to high five Harley.

"How?" Tommie asked.

"We let her find something. Something that she'll take back to the people she's conspiring with. That way, we can get her *and* the head of the snake."

"I like that idea," Tommie said. "I like it a lot."

Tommie had just finished the last bite of her stew when car lights came down the long, winding drive.

"Oh, dang. I forgot all about this. It's Nancy Smith. I invited her for a drink and to see the house. She's been so helpful to us." Tommie regretted the invitation but it was too late to rescind.

"Let's make it a short visit," Harley said. "We both need to talk and plan our next move. As well as get some sleep."

The way he looked at her lips made Tommie think sleep might not be on his mind. And that was perfectly fine with her. They left the cottage and started walking at a fast clip toward the manor where Nancy's taillights burned bright red in the dark night.

CHAPTER THIRTY-ONE

"I hope I'm not early," Nancy said. She got out of her car and waited for them as they walked down the drive.

Tommie noted with amusement and a bit of sadness that Nancy had changed from her work clothes into something she might wear on a date. It was touching. She was so clearly smitten by Harley.

"Not at all," Tommie said. "I'm looking forward to showing you Loftus Manor. I can't believe you've never been here before now. Samuel was remiss. And I have to warn you, Harley is quite the accomplished bartender."

"I expect Harley is very good at any job he turns his hand to," Nancy said.

They were standing at the entrance to the manor, and Tommie grinned at the blush that colored Harley' cheeks. Nancy sure got to him with her adoration, and it was a joy to watch. Harley's bashfulness told her a lot about him.

"Come in, Nancy, and name your poison."

"What?" Nancy stepped away from Tommie, shock on her face.

"Tell us what you'd like to drink," Harley said. "It's just a saying because, you know, alcohol is a poison."

"Oh, right!" Nancy laughed. "Sometimes I can be naïve."

"Nothing wrong with naivete," Tommie said. "In fact, it's refreshing."

"I'll mix the drinks while you show Nancy around," Harley said.

"Perfect," Tommie agreed. "Let's start upstairs."

There really wasn't much to see upstairs except the beautiful décor and the array of antiques that the Loftus family had acquired over the years, but Nancy took her time, exclaiming over a headboard or highboy or the drapery fabric. She took such pleasure in her tour that Tommie couldn't begrudge her the time. Harley joined them with drinks—lemon water for Tommie —and they sipped and walked as Harley took over the narration about the house. He was far better versed in Loftus history than Tommie, though she was catching on fast.

"I can see how you got the idea to turn the manor into an inn," Nancy said. "I would never have thought of such a thing, but actually, it will be perfect. Samuel would talk about the reno-vations he and Rachel made to the house when they were first married and came here to live. They really modernized the place. That's when they put in the bathrooms for the bedrooms." Her face softened with a smile. "Samuel said he was scandalized by the changes, but that Rachel insisted that everything—home or human—had to be renovated to keep up with the times. Those who fought modernization were crushed." Nancy's mood suddenly turned melancholy and she blinked back tears. "He really loved his wife. I wish I'd known her."

When they were done on the second floor, they started in

the main library. Tommie stood with her back to a warm fire as Harley gave some of the historical information about Samuel's book collection. Again, she was amazed at the breadth of her uncle's interests. He had a true joy in learning.

She'd forgotten about the portrait of Rachel in the cloak until Nancy exclaimed, "That's incredible. Wow. Samuel talked about that painting once or twice. He hated it."

"What?" Tommie asked, surprised. "It's beautiful. Rachel looks like she stepped out of one of Samuel's stories."

"That was the problem," Nancy said. "The cloak. He was very annoyed with the cloak. It had a dark history and he said it belonged to someone from the past of Loftus Manor."

"And why would Rachel wear a cloak that upset Samuel?" Tommie asked.

"There was a huge costume ball and Rachel had found a photograph and had the cloak copied for her outfit. She meant to please Samuel, is how I heard it. She went to great detail." She pointed to the buttons on the shoulder. "Samuel said those incredible buttons each held one lost spirit. He said something like the cloak was symbolic of things that had gone wrong at the manor."

"Did he think Rachel collected souls or spirits?" Tommie was horrified.

"No," Nancy said and then laughed. "But you know how Samuel loved his ghost stories. He hated the idea of trapped spirits, and those buttons really set him off."

"The concept of spirits trapped in any stone is disconcerting," Tommie said.

At Harley's gentle urging, Nancy moved along with the tour. "I want to hear all about the renovations," she said. "Gossip in town is that Hank and Katie said they were starting in the kitchen and dining area." When she saw the hole in the wall, she rushed toward it. "What is this?"

"Hank is removing a wall to open more dining space. Katie said it might have once been storage, like a pantry, that was walled over." Tommie was only glad the bones had been removed. Nancy was a very nice person and had been a kind friend, but a skeleton in the wall would have been too delicious not to repeat.

"Is this a secret passageway?" Nancy put her head in the hole, trying to see.

Harley laughed. "You've listened to too many of Samuel's tall tales."

"But it looks like a passage. How exciting. This really is like one of Samuel's stories." Her eyes teared up. "I miss talking to him. Sometime, if he was having lunch with Nina, I would just sit at their table and listen to him tell about this house and his ancestors. He was very private, you know, but once he started talking about Loftus Manor, he never tired of it. It was difficult to tell what was true and what was made-up." She laughed softly. "That was the fun of Samuel. He could pull you into a true story or a totally made-up yarn and no one could tell the difference."

"He was a fine storyteller," Harley agreed. He subtly checked his watch.

"I've overstayed my welcome," Nancy said quickly. "Could I see the room where he died? I know it sounds morbid, but he talked about 'his little study' so much. And playing chess with you, Harley. You were a blessing in his life." Nancy walked back to the hole and sighed. "If it isn't a passage, it could be a hidey hole. During the Civil War, some landowners would build false walls so they could hide their valuables in case Yankees came to raid them. I've heard stories about a lot of treasures like that, hidden and forgotten." She smiled. "And some of those stories I heard from Samuel. He just loved to get people going. I'm not being morbid, honest. I just want to see the room where he...left us."

Tommie was taken aback by Nancy's request, but she led the way to the small study. She didn't elaborate, and Nancy stood at the open door, looking in. "I don't think he committed suicide," she said. "He wasn't the type."

"What do you think happened?" Harley asked.

"I think someone killed him because of the stories about hidden treasures. Robbery gone wrong." She sighed. "I hope you catch the person who did this." She put a hand over her mouth. "I am so sorry. I didn't mean to say anything that might upset you."

"It's not upsetting," Tommie assured her. "And it's not the first time we've heard that sentiment."

"Did you happen to see the original coroner's report on Samuel?" Harley asked.

"No. I'm sure it's in his file, but I never saw it. My boss is picky about the forms and things. Was something wrong?"

"No," Harley said quickly. "It's just hard to believe it was ruled suicide. I agree with you. Samuel wasn't the type, nor did he seem to have a reason."

"Are you searching for his killer?" Nancy was wide-eyed.

"Hardly that," Tommie said, brushing the topic aside. "I don't need the stigma of a murder attached to Loftus Manor if I'm going to have an inn here. It's over and done. Best to let sleeping dogs lie, as the saying goes." Her gaze connected with Harley and he nodded. They didn't need to start any rumors, and as nice as Nancy was, the desire to gossip was part of human nature.

"We're focusing on the renovations and getting the inn open by Christmas," Tommie said. "That's ambitious enough."

"Thank you for the tour and the drink. Both of you. I should leave. It's getting late and the road here is tricky, as I'm sure you've discovered."

"I hate to ask, Nancy, but have you heard anything more from your friend who works for Paul Rider? About what he may be up to? And doesn't he drive a big dark SUV?

Nancy frowned. "I can't remember his vehicle, but I haven't talked to my friend. Not really. But I'll keep an ear out. I can call her—"

"No, please don't bother." Tommie put a hand on Nancy's shoulder. "Thank you for the offer."

Nancy's smile was wide and radiant. "I'm just so excited that Loftus Manor is going to become the show place of Wetumpka. If you have parties here, maybe I'll be invited."

"Of course," Tommie assured her.

"That's so exciting." She put a hand on Tommie's arm. "I know Samuel loved the manor, but by turning it into an inn, everyone in town can enjoy the beauty of the place. Now I really must go."

They walked her to the door and as Tommie watched her taillights head down the long, dark driveway, Harley put his arm around her shoulders.

"You good?" he asked.

"Tonight, I'm better than good."

"Really?" He pulled her closer and tipped her face up to his. "Why?"

"Because I have you in my life." The words were easier to say than she'd ever anticipated. With Harley, admitting how she felt came naturally. "Let's go inside."

"An invitation I'd never turn down," Harley said.

Laughing, they called Trouble to follow, ran into the house, up the stairs, and into Tommie's bedroom. When Tommie closed the door, she felt her heart thudding. It wasn't the idea of a ghost but the anticipation she felt for Harley's touch.

The light clawing at the door made her hesitate. She opened it and found Trouble sitting there. Instead of walking into the room, the cat gave her one loud meow and then turned and sauntered down the hallway.

"I do believe Trouble just gave us his blessing," Tommie said.

"Then there's nothing holding us back," Harley said with a wicked grin.

He picked her up in his arms and gently kicked the door closed.

THANK HEAVENS *the bipeds finally got over their trust issues. Now they're canoodling, and from what I can determine by eavesdropping, with great...fervor. A happy ending for those two is what I can easily predict. While Tommie came here with the intention of being alone, I think fate has conspired to give her love. And she's a lass with a lot of bottled up passion, much like Mr. Brawny. Ah, there's nothing like a little knee trembler to take the edge off at the end of a hard day.*

Best to leave them to their own devices while I, as lead detective on this case, continue with the work of the investigation.

I think it's up to me to explore the passageway that Hank opened up. I'm the only one who can conveniently fit in the space, and I also have superior night vision.

Up and over, and I'm inside the wall. This space is dry and far more pleasant than the tunnel, but that's because I'm still in the house proper. I'm going slowly, making sure I don't overlook any clues. Peculiar, but this passage dead-ends. Literally. There's a brick wall here. By my calculations I'm still in the old dining area. There's nothing to see here. Just dust and the debris of old houses. Unlike modern homes, Loftus Manor is all wood and stone. That makes the walls solid, and try as I might, I can't find anything here except some...balls of hair, as in animal hair. Ah, I see. Amazing that humans thought to include horsehair in the wall plaster. For all of their awkwardness, all reared up on two legs, they do have a creative disposition. At least some of them.

Now that I'm out of the hole in the wall, I think I'll ease down to the little study where Samuel died. There's something about that room that just troubles me. Why did he pick that room to die, if indeed he died by his own hand?

This old manse is beautiful, but I have to admit, it has the demeanor of a sad and haunted house. Tommie might not appreciate my assessment, but it's true. It's almost as if the house were aware of us, of what we're doing. I know that sounds slightly mad, but it's how I feel. Honoring one's suspicions is the mark of the very best detectives. The trick is to respect that feeling, and to balance it out with evidence and common sense. Humanoids, in particular, find that equilibrium difficult to maintain. Felines, though, come by it naturally.

There's nothing amiss down in the kitchen area. I overindulged in that delicious beef stew Harley whipped up, but now I've walked off the feeling of being uncomfortably full. I think I'll stake out Samuel's little study as the place to sleep. Tommie's bed is full, I think, and I don't begrudge her a tot of it. I've noticed a few slinky kitties around Wetumpka who caught my fancy, but my job keeps me on the road. I hate to start a romance if I'm going to be working. I'm a little sensitive to the "tom-catting" trope that follows an elegant black cat around.

I'm sorry the fire has gone cold. The night really isn't unpleasant, but there's something about the crackle of a fire that lulls a cat to sleep. And even without the fire, I feel myself embraced in the arms of Nyx, that fearsome goddess of the night.

But wait, I hear something. A clicking. But it comes from no specific place. It moves. I chase it hither and yon, but I get no closer to finding the source. And now it's gone. An old house settling, perhaps. That's what *people are often told when they hear things in the night. Still, there's the sense that I'm being watched, though that's impossible.*

Or is it?

Harley discovered the old caregiver, Nina Ahearn, wandering around Loftus Manor. Tomorrow, he and Tommie will confront her and if necessary, file charges. But while Nina is gone, who's to say that there isn't someone else in the walls or hiding around the attic. Normally I can sense intruders—the little odors and noises they produce. But Loftus Manor has been a strange experience for me. There's often the heavy smell of perfume, but that's it, and it leads to a dead end. And, of course, the visuals—that female image standing in the window. We can presume that's been Nina Ahearn, moving through the halls and passageways she learned about when she lived here. But what if it's someone else? Someone we've overlooked?

While I can't locate the source of the clicks or the perfume, I am burdened this night with a sense of foreboding. So far the attempts to oust Tommie from this house have been centered on fear. Let us hope it doesn't descend into violence. I shall keep a vigilant watch.

CHAPTER THIRTY-TWO

ommie awoke at the first pinkening of the sky. She
was wrapped in contentment and a sense of safety, and
when she turned and saw Harley's profile on the pillow, she
knew why.

She noted the laugh lines at the corners of his eyes and
mouth. Though he wasn't a man who laughed a lot in public, he
had a keen wit and was quick with a private smile. His eyelashes
were thick and curled, something any woman would envy, and
when he was awake, they framed his serious gray eyes. Now, they
brushed his cheekbones and emphasized the straight nose that
led to lips that knew how to kiss a woman. Harley might be on
the shy side, but somewhere along the way he'd learned the
talents of a kind and considerate lover.

His lashes moved up and he turned to look at her. His hand
instantly cupped her face. "Good morning, beautiful."

"Yes, it's a very good morning." She stretched and felt the
pleasant tightness of her muscles.

"Katie and Hank will be here early," Harley said, pulling her
snuggly into his chest.

"I know. As eager as I am to get the renovations done, I'd love to take this morning off. Just for us."

"And I would love that too, but it's not to be." Harley threw back the covers. "I'm going to the cottage for a shower and some clean clothes. Meet you there—I'll put coffee on."

Since the manor kitchen was in total disarray, meeting at the cottage was the perfect solution. She slipped from beneath the warm covers, chill bumps dancing over her skin. The minute Harley opened the bedroom door, Trouble scampered across the room and jumped in the bed.

"You and Trouble come down to the cottage after you've had a shower. We've got a lot of loose ends to tie up."

Tommie stretched, giving him a tantalizing view of a long thigh as she moved one leg out from under the covers to the floor. "It's cold."

"I'll turn on the heat in the bathroom before I leave."

"You're a good man, Harley Jones."

"I try to be."

Tommie checked her watch. "I'll be down in thirty, if Trouble lets me out of bed." She pulled the cat to her.

"If I have to come get you both, I'm going to have fun doing it," Harley warned her.

"We'll see who gets the short end of the stick on that." Tommie loved that she could now tease Harley and they both enjoyed the game. "Now be gone! I need coffee and something wonderful to eat. Trouble is hungry too."

Harley gave her a sharp salute and left. She heard him go into the bathroom, no doubt to turn on the gas heater, and then clatter down the stairs. The front door slammed.

"No rest for the wicked," Tommie told Trouble as she stroked him and then slipped from the bed. "We have mysteries to solve, my fine black friend."

"Me-ow!" Troubled replied, as if to say, "Indeed we do."

She loved that the cat seemed to converse with her. He was a truly special feline, and one she was lucky to have in her corner. And it also seemed he wanted her to follow him. In fact, he was downright insistent, tugging at her slipper.

"Shower first," she insisted, and the cat reluctantly released her slipper. The minute she was out of the shower and dressed, he was back at her, using his claws to gently pull at her jeans.

"Okay, okay." She followed him down to the kitchen area where he hopped into the hole that Hank had made.

"We're going to explore that later today, when the workers are back." Tommie tried to reason with the cat, but he was insistent. He ran from the hole in the wall to a sledgehammer lying on the floor, then back to the hole. It was clear he wanted her to enlarge the hole. And nothing other than action was going to settle him down.

"Okay. I'll give it a try." She lifted the sledgehammer and began to swing. The plaster shattered and the old bricks behind it gave way with far less effort than Tommie had anticipated. As the hole widened and the dust settled, Tommie stepped back. What in the world had the cat been so determined to find? She'd come to a section of wall that appeared to end the hidden area. The brick to the left of her hole was solid, without any space for anything, even a cat.

"That's the end of the road, Trouble. I don't want to go any further. I don't know which walls support the second floor. We have to wait for Hank and Katie." She checked her watch. "And they will be here soon. Now we have breakfast waiting at Harley's."

She bent over to scoop the cat into her arms but he leaped free and disappeared into the hole, meowing for her to follow. She knew it would be simpler to do his bidding than argue and she found a flashlight and leaned into the hole. Had the cat not cried out and called her attention to the small carved box tucked into the bricks, she would have missed it completely.

Her heart rate increased as she crawled halfway into the small area and reached to grab the box that was shaped like it might contain jewelry. Was it the long-hunted Loftus fortune sealed in the walls? She finally drew it forth and sat down on the floor outside the hole. The box was light in weight and when she shook it, there was no noise. It didn't sound like jewels and gold coins would be heavy. She started to open the box but hesitated. This was something she needed to share with Harley. He was as much a part of this as she and Trouble were.

HARLEY PUT the coffee pot on and some bacon in a frying pan as he dialed Aiden River's number to get an update on the recent attack that could have ended with grave injury to Tommie or himself. He'd downplayed his real concern in front of Tommie, but now he had a chance to really talk to Aiden.

As the phone rang, he found he was smiling to himself, thinking about Tommie and the night they'd shared. He hadn't expected intimacy—hadn't wanted it. But now it was like the most precious gift he'd ever been given. Once the strange activities at Loftus Manor were explained and any other false claims settled, he and Tommie were going to have a fabulous time preparing the inn for occupancy. He admitted to himself he wanted to stay, to be a part of it. To be a part of Tommie's life in any way he could.

When Aiden answered, he laid everything out—the disappearing figure, Nina Ahearn slipping in and out of the manor, Paul Rider's keen interest in selling the manor, and the tampered with death certificate. That, along with the skeleton in the wall had Aiden worried.

"Can you convince Tommie to leave the manor. Maybe move into a hotel?"

"I can try, but it's going to be difficult. The renovations have started."

"I was going to call you today anyway. I sent a deputy over to check out Nina Ahearn's vehicle. It appears her car has been grazed by a bullet. You said you fired several shots. I can't say for certain, but it's worth checking out. We'll need to run some forensics to be sure, but I'm willing to bet that was the vehicle that tried to run you off the road."

"Nina's been a busy bee," Harley said, feeling the anger surge at the thought of how easily Tommie could have been harmed.

"This isn't definite, and we need to investigate further. I sent some officers to check out the car, but it was gone. Nina's been staying at a local hotel, and they said she'd checked out. Just wanted to give you a head's up."

"Thanks, Aiden. We'll be on the lookout for her."

"As soon as I get a report on the skeleton, I'll be around to visit with Tommie. Maybe I can convince her to at least leave the property at night. Until we resolve this."

Harley chuckled. "Good luck with that." He saw her and the cat coming down the drive. "Be in touch, Aiden. And thank you."

He was draining the bacon on paper towels when Tommie and the cat arrived with an ornately carved box in hand. Tommie held it out to him. "Trouble found this in the wall, where the skeleton was. It's too light to be gold, but it could be the Loftus family jewels that are supposed to be hidden in the house."

"You didn't look?" Harley found that the fact she'd waited to include him touched him deeply. "And Trouble didn't make you look? Curiosity killed the cat, you know."

Trouble jumped on the table and reached up to put his paws on the box.

"He's dying to know what's inside," Tommie said. "And so am I."

The box, which was beautifully carved with an eagle soaring over a forest, was simply made. There was only a hinge. No lock or means of securing the box. Harley handed it over to Tommie and waited for her to open it.

She lifted the lid and pulled out a sheet of paper covered in black India ink. Harley knew instantly it was old, and he relaxed when Tommie settled on the table top so she could use more care unfolding it.

She waved him over and together they opened the large page of beautiful calligraphy. Harley immediately noticed the signature of Farthwright Loftus. As he scanned the document, Harley realized how valuable it was—and how at the time it was written it could also have sent a number of people to the gallows.

"It isn't jewels or treasure that was hidden at Loftus Manor," he said, "it's a map of the underground railroad stops for slaves as they made their way to freedom. It lists every farm that's safe for them to approach and how to get there. This map would have taken runaway slaves all the way through Tennessee. From there, someone else would have helped them continue."

"The people who did this were very brave," Tommie said, her finger stroking the page softly. "Do you think this was left behind by the woman in the wall?"

Harley sighed. "I do. I think that was her most valuable possession. She must have been the leader of a group of slaves moving through this area."

"What could have happened to the rest of them?"

"It was against the law for a slave to know how to read. I suspect they memorized every single detail of this document and then they traveled on by what they'd committed to memory. Taking the actual document was too risky. If the document had fallen into the wrong hands, a lot of people would have been hanged."

"So you think this was the big treasure of Loftus Manor?"

Harley watched her face closely. Tommie seemed strangely elated. While she could have used a fortune in jewels, she seemed excited about this find.

Harley put his arm around her. "I do. I'm sorry it's not money."

"I'm not." Tommie looked at him. "I have the best slogan for my inn: Loftus Manor, on the road to freedom. This will only enhance the future of the inn."

Harley hugged her close. She never disappointed him. "Perfection."

Trouble wasn't willing to be left out of the celebration. He hopped to the table, grabbed a slice of bacon, and started his breakfast.

"I have an idea," Tommie said, her eyes sparkling. "Let's use the carved box to lure those working against me out of hiding."

Harley instantly saw her point. "We can announce we've found the Loftus treasure and then pretend to leave the manor."

"They'll come, hoping to find additional treasure," Tommie said. "I think it might work."

"It's worth a try. Hank and Katie will help us. They can take the box to town and show it around. Word will spread like wildfire."

"That's exactly what we want."

"Me-ow!" Trouble gave his unblinking green-eyed approval to the plan before he grabbed more bacon.

CHAPTER THIRTY-THREE

t last, the case is coming together—and not in the way any of us anticipated. Harley and Tommie make a great team. And they share a set of values that will stand them in good stead in the future. In that regard, I am satisfied with my work of the romantic kind. That is not the case with the felonious mishaps of this mystery. As to pinpointing the culprit, I can't definitively name the prime suspect. This is unpleasant for me and I'm tempted to sack myself. Felines are never indecisive, unless we are toying with the bipeds, and then it is only for show. I must confess there have been a few times when I would cry to come inside and then stop at the threshold and look around, just the tip of my nose inside. I am amused to see how long Tammy will allow me to prevaricate. Then I turn around and walk off, wait for five minutes, and cry at the door again. It's a petty game but still somewhat amusing. Somewhat along the lines of humans dangling catnip-stuffed cloth parakeets for cats to chase. Silly but fun.

Me, I'm waiting to find out who the elusive "ghost of the manor" will turn out to be. We know Nina is involved, and her knowledge of the property has been a real asset to her liege lord. But she isn't the master-mind. I suspect Paul Rider, the pushy broker, plays a role, but that is yet to be determined. Perhaps it's just that I don't care for his bullying ways. In case you don't know, cats despise being bullied. And I don't care to see my biped friends put in the grinder by a bully either.

But now we're heading up to the manor to photograph the hole and anything else that will help bait the trap. We'll move the vehicles and pretend to leave the manor unattended.

While the cats are away, I hope the mice do come out to play.

HANK AND KATIE were all in for the plan to publicize the "treasure find," a fact that gave Tommie even more confidence. She sent photos to the two renovators of the hole and the elaborate box she'd found inside. The ancient map, which was of extreme historic value if not monetary, had been carefully put away. She'd have the document evaluated and preserved as soon as possible. Harley had even mentioned donating it to a museum, which really appealed to her.

To make the treasure story enticing, she'd decided that the box contained a fabulous emerald and diamond necklace and matching earrings—fodder for the rumor mill. Hank and Katie would rave about the beauty and value of the jewels. When their audience was salivating with a desire to see the "found" treasure, they would show a photo of an incredible necklace that Tommie had found on the internet and "borrowed."

Once the fishes had snapped at the bait, the renovators were to tell whoever would listen that the work crews would be back at Loftus Manor bright and early the next morning to continue tearing out the wall. They would add that all indications were that more treasure would be found in the secret hidey hole as they opened the enclosure. And Hank and Katie would casually mention that Tommie and Harley had been called away from

Loftus Manor on some kind of family emergency. They would be gone over night.

Tommie was on edge to hear if their plan was working at all.

When Katie called Tommie at lunchtime, the renovator was elated with the success of the plan. "Everyone is talking about the treasure," she said. "People are coming up to us, asking questions, wanting to know what you're going to do. Will you tear down the manor to search for more treasure? The town is abuzz. And we did exactly as you asked. We indicated we believed more treasure would be found once you returned from your emergency trip."

"Thank you so much." Tommie felt tears threaten. The Evans had been more than true friends to her, and she barely knew them. After years of feeling mostly alone, she'd found a niche in Wetumpka and people who genuinely seemed to care about her. And one very special man in particular.

She glanced at Harley and he put his arm around her shoulders, drawing her in for a gentle hug as she thanked Katie and put the phone away.

"This is going to work," Harley said. "We're going to find the guilty party and put an end to this so that your dream of an inn can become a reality."

"Had I not met you, I don't know that I would even have a dream," Tommie admitted. "You made the dream seem possible."

DARKNESS HAD FALLEN over the manor, and Harley felt the rush of adrenalin that warned him danger was imminent. Tommie had drifted into a fitful sleep on the old sofa they'd found in the attic, where they'd set up their base camp to catch the person trying to run Tommie away from Loftus Manor.

Harley had restaged the game cameras and connected them to his phone so he could watch the driveway to the manor and also the woods that led from the river. Only two of the cameras still worked and he hadn't had time to purchase new ones, but at least he had a visual of the two primary ways to reach the manor.

They'd driven their vehicles deep into the woods down a trail that eventually connected with the road to town. It was overgrown and almost unusable, but the paint on the vehicles was hardly a concern for either of them.

Harley wanted to pace but more than that he wanted Tommie to sleep while she could. They had a lot of work to do if anyone took the bait they'd so carefully set.

Harley checked his phone, which he'd put on silent. Aiden Waters had been alerted, and he and some of his officers were ready to arrive on the scene, sirens blaring, if anyone showed up. Harley texted the police officer just to be on the safe side and got an instant response back. All was in place. Now it was a waiting game, and Harley was glad Tommie had found some rest. Even Trouble was snoozing beside her.

In the quiet of the house, Harley thought about Samuel and the wonderful times they'd shared in Loftus Manor. Never in a million years would Harley have thought that Samuel would die, and that his heir would prove to be such a wonderful person and companion. Harley had accepted that his heart had been frozen by the past, but he'd been wrong. Tommie had thawed it. The more he learned about her, the more he cared. And amazingly, he looked forward to deepening his feelings for her. Instead of running away, he was headed straight into her arms and he didn't want to put on any brakes.

He settled into an old club chair, checked the cameras again, and checked his watch. It was only eight o'clock at night, but Loftus Manor was isolated and the darkness wasn't mitigated by streetlights. It was just the moon and the stars, which were actually brilliant. Harley stood up and slipped over to the big window that gave an excellent view of the front of the manor. His breath caught at the sight of the woman standing in the middle of the oyster shell driveway.

She wore a hooded cloak, and she made no effort to hide herself. She stood silently looking up at the manor, almost as if she were communing with the house. Harley felt the goosebumps move down his arms. He wasn't afraid, but the figure was a little creepy. He looked over, thinking to wake Tommie, but when he looked back, the driveway was empty.

Phantom or human? It was the same old question.

He felt something brush his legs and he looked down to see Trouble staring up at him. The cat jumped to the window ledge and looked out.

"Time to move," Harley said softly, stroking the cat. "Wake Tommie, please."

Trouble jumped down and ran to the sofa. In a moment he was purring and head-butting Tommie awake.

"What happened?" she asked, sitting bolt upright when she realized she was in the attic. "Did I miss something?"

"We have company. A woman in a cloak."

"Who?" Tommie was on her feet.

"I couldn't see. The hood."

"Is she coming inside?"

Harley considered. "I don't know. She was in the driveway and then she was gone."

"We have to lure her inside," Tommie said. "Then we can catch her. And I'm going to find out who's been tormenting me the whole time I've been here."

"To be honest, Tommie, I didn't anticipate a female." Harley

had truly pointed the finger of guilt—if only in his own mind—
at Paul Rider, the real estate man.

"I know," Tommie said. "But whoever she is, she's trespassing. And I'm not going to believe she's some wayward spirit.
She's flesh and blood and therefore we can get her. And then we
can make her talk."

Harley smiled. He loved her spirit. "And that's exactly what
we should do. Remember the plan?"

"I'm to make some noises up here, like a ghost would make.
Too bad we don't have some chains to rattle."

"Lock the attic door behind me. I'm going down the
servant's stairs and see if I can find her. Just stay safe, Tommie.
Whatever happens, you stay here with Trouble. And call Aiden if
you hear anything that concerns you. I don't think this woman is
alone in this, so there's likely someone else on the property."

Harley went to the attic door. He was armed with a flashlight
and a wooden baseball bat he found in a corner of the attic. And
his cell phone camera, which would document what happened.
Tommie had a bat, too, and a flashlight. He didn't feel good
about leaving her, but she also had Trouble. Something told him
the cat would protect her to the death. Trouble was just that
kind of feline. Thank goodness.

When he heard the dead bolt slide into place, he started
down the steep stairs. Now that he knew the true history of
Loftus Manor, he couldn't help but wonder how many slaves had
slept in the attic and made their way down these stairs in a bid
for freedom. He could almost hear the ghostly echo of their feet,
shuffling softly down the worn boards.

Assisting a slave to run away was a capital offense that often
resulted in hanging. But somehow he wasn't surprised that the
Loftus family had been involved. Samuel was a man who stood
up for what he believed. Harley thought of Tommie and shook

his head. She was a chip off the Samuel block, for sure. And soon the true story of the manor would be told by Tommie and the guests who came to her inn. There was something very satisfying in that.

He'd made his way to the ground floor when he stopped to listen. The woman in the cloak had to be somewhere on this level. He would have heard her on the stairs or in the upper hallways. She was likely in the kitchen area, looking for the hole where treasure had been found.

Now he had to use extreme caution. His goal wasn't to confront the woman, but to spy on her. To see what she went after. And hopefully to discover the other people involved in tormenting Tommie. Trespassing was at least one crime they could be charged with, though pretending to be a ghost wasn't a real crime. Aiden, though, would have a better handle on the legal charges that could be brought—and he intended to make sure every possibility was thrown at them.

As he eased from the back of the house toward the kitchen, he heard a soft whisper of a voice.

"I'm in. There's no one here. I left the front door unlocked."

Harley recognized the voice—he'd heard it before, but the timber of the whisper made it hard for him to pinpoint the owner. He eased closer to the door, hoping to sneak a peek. If he could just catch a glimpse, he'd know who she was. But he also couldn't get caught or the plan would be foiled. He cast a quick glance into the room and saw the cloaked figure. The woman was tall and slender, but with the hood up and from the back he couldn't even determine the color of her hair. When she started to shift to face him, he ducked back into the hall.

He checked his impulse to peek again and slipped away. As he'd anticipated, the intruder was poking around the hole in the wall that Hank had created and Tommie had widened. There was nothing else to be found, but the intruder didn't know that.

He slipped back to the servants' stairs. According to the plan, his job was now to follow the intruder wherever she went, hoping she would lead him to her confederate. But he had a niggling worry about Tommie in the attic. She'd promised to stay there and stay safe, behind the locked door. There was only that one way into the attic, and if she stayed there she should be okay.

A terrible thought came to him. One that almost froze him to the spot.

What if there was a secret passage that ended in the attic? What if Tommie was a sitting duck for someone who intended to get her out of Loftus Manor. One way or the other.

CHAPTER THIRTY-FOUR

I applaud Mr. Brawny for managing to keep the Loftus Lass safe behind a locked door, but I have to point out that surely he knows her well enough to realize she won't stay up here for long. She is already pacing. Her nerves are stretched too thin and she is ready to pop a gasket, as the seamstresses of White Chapel would say.

Hark! I hear something that sounds like a mouse rustling in the northern corner of the space. Tommie hears it too. She's not the kind of lass to wallop a rodent—far more likely to trap it in a kindness cage and set it free in the woods. But she is heading in the direction of the noise with her bat raised and her flashlight at the ready.

I'm a cat with a lot of skills, but I admit, I wish Mr. Brawny were here now. He's a lot bigger and stronger than I am, though I do have a few moves in the martial arts department, should that become necessary. Pouncing cat, leaping tiger. I can do some damage if I must.

The noise is getting louder, and Tommie is sussing out the source. It seems to coming from...the back wall.

Oh, no! This isn't a mouse. It's a rat. A big human rat. One who has been tormenting Tommie the whole time she's been here. Well, the villain is about to be unmasked. At least we'll know who it is, which may not

*save our lives, but it will satisfy my curiosity. A cat should never die
with curiosity unfulfilled.*

TOMMIE'S first instinct was to unlock the attic door and run
downstairs and out into the cold night. But there wasn't time.
She swung her flashlight to the north wall of the attic where the
heart of pine wood was slowly opening into a passage. Standing
in the passage was a woman in a hooded cloak.

Tommie couldn't stop the sharp intake of her breath, which
drew the figure's attention to her in the attic's gloom. The hood
sheltered the person's face from view, but Tommie knew she was
a woman.

"Who are you?" Tommie asked. She was too stunned to try
to run. She held the baseball bat loosely in her left hand and the
flashlight in her right.

"Why couldn't you just leave?" The woman threw the hood
back and Nancy Smith stood in the passageway. From beneath
the cloak she drew out a gun. "All you had to do was leave for a
week or two. That's all I needed to find the treasure. But no, you
had to start renovating, tearing out walls. You had to be so
greedy. You have no claim on Loftus Manor. None at all."

Tommie heard the fury in Nancy's voice, but she didn't
understand where it came from.

"You have no idea how many times I listened to Samuel brag-
ging about this manor, about what was hidden here, about the
riches he intended to distribute in Wetumpka to all the people
who'd shown him kindness. And what did I get? Not one
damn penny."

"You expected to be paid for befriending an elderly man?"
Tommie knew she shouldn't, but she couldn't stop herself.
"What kind of soulless person are you?"

"The kind who is going to do what's necessary to get you out of my way. You should never have come here. You should have left when the ghosts warned you to go. Why did you have to be so damn stubborn? And then you drew Harley to your side to help you. He should have been helping me. He should have been kissing me, not you."

Tommie shifted back, but Nancy came forward, closing the gap. The intimidating tactic sent a flash of temper through Tommie, but she wisely stayed silent and let Nancy talk.

"You think you deserve all of it." The skin around Nancy's eyes was white with fury. "The house, Harley, the treasure. Your uncle strung me along for years, hinting that I would inherit. He did the same to Nina. You think she'd spend all that time out in the woods with a freaking old man just for a paycheck?"

"Uncle Samuel paid her handsomely." It was the first thing that came to Tommie's mind. "He was good to her. She was well paid for her time, and she could have left whenever she wanted."

"Except he teased her with hints of big money at the end. He led her to believe she was going to benefit in a significant way."

"He did leave her money," Tommie said. If she remembered correctly it was twenty-five thousand, but she didn't name the sum.

"Not enough for what she gave him." Nancy looked around the attic. "This place was where we got the inspiration for our plan. When Nina found the portrait of Samuel's beloved Rachel, the cloak made everything so much easier. You could see us, but the cloak concealed our identity. And you couldn't be sure if we were real or ghosts. It was perfect. Samuel would have highly approved of our ingenuity, taking his storytelling to the perfect conclusion."

Tommie had never met her uncle, but from everything she'd been told by Harley and others, this didn't sound like him.

"Samuel liked to entertain people with his stories, not torment them. I don't believe for a minute he'd approve of what you and Nina are doing. What I think is that you and Nina were so consumed with greed and jealousy that you heard what you wanted to hear. And then you roped that poor girl, Odell, into the scheme. She was smart enough to run before I sicced the cops on her. I see you're not that smart."

She saw the anger flair in Nancy's eyes and realized that she was truly dealing with someone who didn't have a grip on reality. Truth held no ground in Nancy's brain. Facts didn't exist to her. Everything was filtered through her own need, grief, trauma, and pain. The view of events she maintained had nothing to do with reality. Because of that, she was incredibly dangerous. And she was holding a gun.

"I'm not going anywhere," Nancy said. "But you are." She motioned toward the locked door. "You're going downstairs and tell Harley to give it up. He can't save you anymore. Odell should have finished you off on the street, but she just didn't have the killer instinct. Something I don't lack."

"If you truly deserve part of the inheritance, I'll share with you." Tommie decided to try reason as a stall for time.

"I deserve all of it, you stupid twit. You're the interloper. Not me. I've been here all along, keeping that lowlife Paul Rider from moving in on Samuel when your uncle was lonely and vulnerable. I'm the one who has protected Loftus Manor all these years. Not you. You don't deserve a thing."

"Maybe you're right," Tommie said. She was being edged closer and closer to the attic door. Once it was unlocked, she intended to make a break for freedom by running down the stairs. It was a dangerous ploy with Nancy, so unhinged, holding a gun. The staircase went straight down to the ground floor without any twists or turns and no place to hide. Tommie could almost feel the bullet in her back. But staying in the attic with Nancy, so angry and aggrieved, was not an option.

"Meow," the black cat said, and Tommie had the sense he understood her plan. He would help her if he could. She slid her gaze toward him, and the cat blinked twice, slowly. Tommie had no doubt the feline understood the danger of her situation, and possibly his too. Nancy didn't strike her as a person who had any great affection for cats, dogs, or anything alive. How had she not seen this earlier? She'd foolishly felt sorry for Nancy, even inviting her to the manor. Of course, Nancy and Nina had been in and out of the house whenever they wanted.

Samuel must have let on to Nina about the passages and Nina had clued Nancy in. The two had been double-teaming Tommie and Harley since the beginning.

"I don't smell the perfume you normally wear," Tommie said, hoping a change of subject would alleviate the murderous tension Nancy displayed.

"That was Nina's idea. Truly brilliant. I know you searched for the source, but you never found it. Tiny little atomizers in the passages so we could trigger them with our cell phones. We really had you going. Harley, too. He's not as smart as I thought he was." She grimaced. "That's a disappointment."

"Harley thinks you're very special." That was exactly the wrong thing to say, Tommie realized instantly.

"Get down those stairs. Your precious Harley has been taken care of by now. I wonder how you'll feel when you see him, dead."

Tommie almost cried out, but the black cat gave her leg a swat. Instead of showing weakness, the image of Harley injured —or dead—was exactly what she needed to fling back the bolt on the door and throw it open. She was just about to hurl herself down the stairs when Nancy charged. She had the gun pointed at

Tommie's face as she screamed and ran forward. Before Tommie could do anything at all, Trouble stepped in front of the rushing woman.

The world seemed to go into slow-motion as Nancy's momentum threw her out the open attic door and headlong down the stairs. She landed at the bottom in a heap that indicated multiple broken bones.

"Oh, no!" Tommie started down the stairs but Trouble was ahead of her. When he got to Nancy's body, he edged the gun away from her limp hand.

Tommie checked for a pulse, but it was clear Nancy's fall had killed her. Her eyes were wide-open, staring up at the ceiling, unseeing. Tommie wanted to close them, but she dared not. She had to find Harley. He couldn't be hurt. He had to be okay.

Trouble led the way toward the renovation area and Tommie almost wept when she heard Harley's voice.

"I would never have suspected you. Never. I thought you were a friend." Harley said. There was a small cry of pain and then Harley added, "This should hold you until the law gets here. Aiden is on the way."

Tommie peeked around the doorframe and saw Harley tightening the ropes on a person in a navy-blue cloak who sat in a chair and struggled against her bonds. Another cloaked woman. It had to be Nina.

"Harley!" Tommie rushed toward him and he caught her against his chest and held her.

"It's okay," he said. "I got her. But you should have stayed in the attic."

"I meant to, except Nancy Smith had other ideas. She's dead." She told him briefly what had happened. "Nina and Odell were lured into this. Nancy was the mastermind."

Harley blew out a long breath. "Nancy had some help, I'm

afraid. We underestimated those women. This isn't Nina." He pulled the hood back to reveal the lovely woman who'd once been a model, the one who had promised to help them with the blue cloak and star sapphire buttons. Patricia Murphy glared at Tommie.

"You should never have come here. Samuel should never have learned about you. We had everything in place with Nina claiming to be his wife, even though she was Jell-o, quaking at every event. She wanted the money but she wasn't willing to do the work."

"Why?" Harley asked her, and his voice showed the betrayal he felt. "We were friends. Samuel adored you. And you don't need the money. Why would you be involved in this, Patricia?"

"We didn't intend to hurt anyone. At least I didn't. I swear it. Nancy was the one who gave Nina the drugs to give Samuel. I really don't think she knew it would kill him." She shrugged. "But Nina didn't know and neither did I. That's why we staged his death to look like a suicide. I swear this is the truth. I only wanted time to get in the house and look for the treasure Samuel was always telling us about. We didn't want to take anything from Tommie or anyone else. We knew the marriage or daughter claims wouldn't hold up for long, but Nina had been scoping out the house for months. We only needed a little time. But Tommie couldn't wait. She had to hire those renovators and we knew if we didn't do something she would find the treasure. And she did."

Harley scoffed. "Treasure? There was no real treasure. We found a map that detailed the role Loftus Manor played in the road to freedom for slaves. Back in the day, the owners could have been hung for helping men, women, and children who only wanted to be free. That was the treasure. The map the runaways memorized to move north."

"But the necklace—" Patricia looked from one to the other.

"Was something we made up," Tommie said. "A photo from the internet. We never found any jewels or money. Only things that Samuel held as more valuable than money."

"We didn't intend to harm anyone," Patricia said. "I ran up some debts. I had to settle them or lose my home. Nancy knew all about the hidden treasure that didn't really belong to anyone. We only wanted what was hidden. Nothing else."

"And you all felt entitled to Samuel's things, especially the hidden treasure. And you truly didn't care who you hurt. You shot at Harley and me. We could have wrecked and been seriously injured or killed. Now Nancy is dead. She fell down the stairs." She felt the tears coming on but she blinked them back. "I'm alive because Trouble saved me."

Harley picked up the cat and scratched him under the chin. "His name may be Trouble, but it's always trouble for the bad guys."

In the distance Tommie heard sirens. At long last, the haunting of Loftus Manor was done.

CHAPTER THIRTY-FIVE

*H*arley hammered the last nail to hold up the garland of fir fronds and colored lights over the door of Loftus Manor. The sign, Loftus Manor Inn, was already decorated in glittering white lights and tinsel. And even better, the inn was completely booked. Tommie went to hold the ladder for Harley to climb down and she couldn't resist kissing him. Loftus Manor was a magnificent place to live, but Harley was the true inheritance her uncle had arranged for her.

"The champagne and cranberry juice to make Poinsettias arrived, along with the cheese and other canapes. Our first festive Christmas Eve in the manor." Tommie did a little spin. "Tammy is coming and bringing Trouble and Aiden." She kissed Harley again. "I can't thank Aiden enough for getting the case into Samuel's death reopened. He's not listed as a suicide any longer. Thank goodness Nancy Smith admitted to killing him. He can rest in peace and so can we. The past is now truly settled."

"It hurts my heart to think Samuel died at the hands of

someone he trusted." Harley kissed the top of her head. "But he wasn't a suicide and I'm glad that's been set straight."

"I wish I could have met him. I've been going through the genealogy he collected and it's fascinating, Harley. Maybe only to me, but the Loftus family covered all the territory, from horse thieves and gamblers to teachers and philanthropists. I love knowing all of this. And those ghost stories! I'm so glad he wrote some down. I still think about Jix."

"If the manor has to be haunted, I hope it's Jix," Harley said.

"As long as Katie and Hank got all of those passages repaired so we can safely use them in our tours, I don't think we have to worry about any more ghosts." Tommie had considered sealing the passages and blocking them, but it was a fascinating part of the house's history as well as that of the region. And she was proud of her ancestors and the role they'd played in changing the world for the better.

"I'm glad the other houses marked on the map to freedom were agreeable to being part of the underground railroad network," Harley said. "Too many of the homes had been destroyed, but the four left have been terrific about working with us to re-create the road to freedom for smuggled slaves."

Harley was right about that. They'd connected the trail from a home in Dothan, Alabama up through Wetumpka and on into Huntsville and finally Tennessee. The four homes still in use had been excited to join in the "freedom trail." Three were already inns or B&Bs, and now the fourth one had begun renovations. Hank and Katie had signed on for the job as part of their TV show continuing what they'd started in Wetumpka. The connection to the freedom houses had been good for everyone.

A car pulled into the driveway and Tommie ran to greet Tammy, Aiden, and Trouble! Tammy had a platter of tiny cupcakes decorated as Christmas presents, and Aiden held a tray of deviled eggs. "We're here to help celebrate the grand opening of Loftus Manor Inn," Tammy said. "We thought we'd come early and help."

"Thank you." Tommie was delighted to see her friends. They'd become very close in the last two months.

They turned back toward the house and Tommie noticed that Trouble froze, staring into the big window in the front parlor where the lighted Christmas tree could be seen. She saw it too, the image of a young girl standing at the window. Jix was smiling. Tommie nodded to her and gave her a welcoming grin. Perhaps all the ghosts weren't gone, but this one would be a pleasure, not a problem.

So Tommie and Harley are not alone in the manor—and of course there are the guests, all waiting inside for the Christmas Eve party to begin. I understand there will be grilled salmon bites with dill sauce just for me. The managers of Loftus Manor Inn know how to treat a feline guest.

This case has left me exhausted. I even lost five ounces, mostly because Tommie and Harley don't understand the importance of regular meals. Let's hope they advance their nutritional knowledge before they decide to have a baby. But as Trouble the Great Prognosticator, I predict it won't be long before there are wedding bells and then baby rattles. Those two are so much in love they are almost...humorous. But it's a good humor.

I'm glad to see Jix has remained on the premises, freed now of the past and the loss of her mother. Now that her mother's bones have been found and properly buried on the estate, Jix is free to stay or leave. For now, she's here to look out for the bipeds. That makes me feel good because I understand my services are needed on a new case. The burden of popularity grows heavy at times, but I am a cat fit to carry the weight. Now for some simple pleasure. Food, cream, and the joy of my bipeds. It's indeed a grand holiday season.

ACKNOWLEDGMENTS

The books in the Trouble Cat Mysteries are a collaboration of a number of authors who all work together to bring these creative and fun books to readers. Trouble was my creation, because I've had a number of so wonderful black cats, as have many of the other writers. Long ago when I wrote Harlequin Intrigues, I created another black cat detective, Familiar. He was so popular, with his Humphrey Bogart thoughts and observations, that we decided to start a new series with Familiar's son, Trouble.

Trouble studied his craft under this father, but he was also addicted to watching Benedict Cumberbatch as Sherlock Holmes on the telly, and so at times, Trouble pops out with a British phrase or saying in his thoughts (he doesn't talk). But like his father Familiar, Trouble is a superior creature, especially when compared to the "bipeds" he endlessly tries to help.

Along with his superior sleuthing skills, he is also something of a devotee to Cupid. In that role he pushes his charges to see the romantic potential that is right in front of them.

Each book is a standalone mystery with a completely different cast of characters, but they all share the cat.

We currently have 13 full-length novels, 2 anthologies of short stories, and 2 digital novellas with plenty more to come!

Last March of 2020, as the pandemic wreaked havoc on people's lives and jobs were lost, we Madcatters, as we call ourselves, decided to give away the entire series of books for those stuck at home, worried, and without income to buy books. We gave away over 61,000 free downloads of the series. We were thrilled at the interest and hope people loved our books and will continue to read the new books in the series.

I want to acknowledge my partners in crime—the Madcatters who work so hard to bring readers entertaining stories with a hint of romance and a lot of mystery, with the bonus of that sassy and superior Trouble.

I want to thank our Beta Readers who volunteer to go over our manuscripts to cull out the typos, punctuation, nonsensical errors I make (and putting in the wrong name—oh how I HATE doing that. Brain collapse).

And I really want to thank Priya Bhakta, the star of KaliOka Press, who formats the books, puts them up, keeps up with the millions of details, keeps me straight (soon she will be spoon feeding me if my brain doesn't snap back to work) and who NEVER has an unkind word for anyone. Priya also creates terrific promo materials for us to post on FB and other social media and in ads and newsletters.

I'd also like to acknowledge Jennifer Williamson, who does our accounting and makes sure the authors are paid royalties on time. (Never, never put me in charge of money! I lose it!) My agent, Marian Young, who got us a terrific audio deal with Tantor Books.

And Cissy Hartley with Writerspace, an author promotional service. Cissy does our covers and helps get the word out about our books. She goes above and beyond.

And most importantly, thanks to our readers who gave a new series a chance and have now become our best ambassadors to spread the word about Trouble, the black cat detective.

ABOUT THE AUTHOR

Carolyn Haines is the *USA Today* bestselling author of over 80 books. In 2020, she was inducted into the Alabama Writers Hall of Fame. She was the recipient of the 2019 Lifetime Achievement Award from the Alabama Library Association and the Mississippi Writer's Guild, the Harper Lee Award for Distinguished Writing, the Richard Wright Award for Literary Excellence, as well as the "Best Amateur Sleuth" award by *Romantic Times*. Haines writes in a number of genres, from cozy mystery to horror and short fiction. She got her start in publishing in romantic mysteries with one savvy black cat detective called Familiar. She's delighted to bring back the first *Familiar* stories—and to introduce Trouble, son of Familiar, in a delightful new Trouble Cat Mysteries series which features a number of talented authors (and cat lovers!)

www.goodfortunefarmrefuge.org

Thank you for reading this book published by Good Fortune Farm Refuge, a 501(c)(3) animal rescue. 100% of all proceeds from the sale of this book will be donated to the GFFR which helps pets receive loving homes and medical treatment.

www.carolynhaines.com
carolyn@carolynhaines.com

f   facebook.com/AuthorCarolynHaines

🐦   twitter.com/DeltaGalCarolyn

📷   instagram.com/carolynhaines

a   amazon.com/author/carolynhaines

BB   bookbub.com/profile/carolyn-haines

g   goodreads.com/CarolynHaines

ALSO BY CAROLYN HAINES

SARAH BOOTH DELANEY MYSTERIES

Them Bones

Buried Bones

Splintered Bones

Crossed Bones

Hallowed Bones

Bones to Pick

Ham Bones

Wishbones

Greedy Bones

Bone Appetite

Bones of a Feather

Bonefire of the Vanities

Smarty Bones

Booty Bones

Bone to Be Wild

Rock-A-Bye Bones

Sticks and Bones

Charmed Bones

A Gift of Bones

Game of Bones

The Devil's Bones

A Garland of Bones

Independent Bones

SARAH BOOTH DELANEY SHORT MYSTERIES

Shorty Bones

Bones on the Bayou

Guru Bones

Jingle Bones

Bones and Arrows

Clacking Bones

Enchanted Bones

PLUTO'S SNITCH

The Book of Beloved

The House of Memory

The Specter of Seduction

A Visitation of Angels

FEAR FAMILIAR

Fear Familiar

Too Familiar

Thrice Familiar

JEXVILLE CHRONICLES

Summer of the Redeemers

Touched

Judas Burning

NOVELS

The Darkling

The Seeker

Revenant

Fever Moon

Penumbra

Deception (originally published as Summer of Fear)

AS R.B. CHESTERTON

The Hanged Man (short story)

TROUBLE ON THE MOUNTAIN

Trouble Cat Mysteries #14

REBECCA BARRETT

Chapter One

TROUBLE ON THE MOUNTAIN

Rebecca Barrett

*C*hildren are not my thing. Noisy little buggers. They're tolerable, I suppose, from a distance. Which is exactly what I plan to do... distance myself from this pack of little ruffians before they decide that rolling down a grassy slope toward a precipitous drop down the mountain isn't entertaining enough.

The Red Head is the leader. He's showing off for the little girl with a Scottish terrier sitting at her feet. His attempts to produce a smile from her have been unsuccessful for the past fifteen minutes. I suppose you must give him credit for effort. That said, I will climb another branch higher in this dogwood tree. In my experience, the biped attention span in males of this age has never been of long duration. I don't plan to be his next challenge.

It's beyond me why adult bipeds bother to drag their offspring to places of educational value before the age of adulthood. These little boys are probably no more than eight or nine, an age when the historical significance of FDR's Little White House is a bore. Especially since, I believe, the school system has not yet freed them from the current term.

With summer and the promise of freedom only days away, who would think a trip to a museum a good idea?

Ah, they have tired of playing at Federal agents shooting villains trying to storm the doors of the Little White House. One races across the drive toward the servants' cottage near where I perch. He brandishes the bit of tree branch he is using as a gun at his colleagues-in-terror as he turns to stand his ground at the door to the garage beneath the living quarters.

A woman comes hurrying from the direction of the administration building higher on the hill. She arrives on the spot just in time to prevent the troop from storming up the stairs to the servants' apartment in their game.

She pushes an errant blond curl back from her face. "Where are your parents?" *she inquires as she physically blocks the doorway.*

The Red Head glances toward the little girl then steps forward. "We want to go up."

"I'm sure you do. But you can only go with adult supervision."

"We don't need supervision." *He puffs out his chest, the challenge clear in his eyes.*

Dear, dear. The little ruffian is going all out to impress.

The blonde, obviously an employee of the museum, tries to hide her amusement.

The front door of the Little White House opens and Tammy Lynn steps out with her sorority sister, Amelia, in tow. She looks up the sloping hillside and sees the confrontation.

"Lila!"

The blonde turns, shades her eyes against the angle of the sun, and smiles. "Tammy! I didn't know you had arrived."

Tammy hurries up the walkway to the guest cottage and servants' quarters. Amelia follows on her heels. They catch the blonde up in a three-way hug as they jump up and down and squeal like little kids.

Well, this is certainly a side of Tammy that I haven't seen before.

"Oh, Lila! It's so good to see you!"

"I've been looking forward to this week. Why didn't you ask for me at the admissions office?" *Lila's cheeks are pink with enthusiasm and the smile on her face changes her attractive features into something altogether quite stunning.*

"We knew you were working and didn't want to disrupt your day. Besides, it's been ages since I took the tour of the site."

The little boys begin sword fighting on the bricked patio that connects the guest quarters and the servants' quarters. Lila sighs. "Excuse me for a moment."

She shushes the boys and with hands on hips, demands, again, to know where their parents are.

The gang of four look at each other and shrug.

"Well, I guess you'll just have to wait for them at the admissions office with me. Surely they'll come looking for you at some point." *She takes her cell phone from her pocket and presses a button.* "Oscar, could you join me at the guest house, please?" *She puts the phone back in the pocket of her skirt. Stares the boys down and says,* "Don't move."

The moment Lila turns back to her friends, the quartet sprint toward the guard houses further up the rise, over the bumper gates, and are last seen racing toward the avenue of the states' stones.

Lila sighs and laughs. "I'll have to send Oscar after them."

"They're just being boys," *Tammy says.*

"I know and I hate to have to discipline them but this is a museum and it's my job. It's one thing to enjoy the outdoor elements but they were getting out of hand. And, as usual, the parents are nowhere to be found." *She gives a wave of her hand.* "But forget about them. Come on and let's do the exhibit." *As she links her arm with Tammy, she sees the little girl and the dog.*

"Teagan, I didn't know you were down here." *She motions for her to come forward.* "You remember my friends, don't you? Tammy and Amelia?"

Teagan smiles shyly but says nothing.

"We're going to my office to have a cup of tea and make plans for our week-end. Want to help us?"

Teagan looks at Lila then up the tree where I'm perched.

"Ah," *says Tammy.* "I see you've met Trouble."

Upon hearing my name, Teagan gives Tammy a sharp, quick look to see if she's teasing.

"Well," *Lila says,* "you and Fergus can stay here with Trouble but don't tease him."

Fergus. What kind of name is that for a dog? Obviously, he doesn't seem to mind as his ears perk up and he wags his short tail. Dogs are so easy.

I hope he and Teagan don't think I'm here for their entertainment. In truth, I'm not sure why Tammy decided to bring me to Calloway Gardens on this annual gathering of her sorority sisters. I have no doubt that I'll be bored stiff.

The female of the biped species is even more inexplicable than male humans. But they do have the advantage of opposable thumbs which can come in handy. And, I must say, the food at the Lodge has been splendid so I shall tolerate Tammy's whimsical decision to bring me along.

Tammy and her friends head up the hill toward the main building of the museum complex, talking over each other in their excitement to be together. I climb a branch higher as Fergus barks. He doesn't seem particularly friendly.

No sooner than Tammy and company are out of sight, the gang of pre-adolescent males reappear like a locust plague.

The Red Head has a look of purpose in his eyes. Denied the stairwell a few minutes earlier by the park ranger Tammy calls Lila, he has returned with his motley crew to storm the bastille of the servants' cottage.

As the boys clatter up the wooden steps, the Scottish terrier rises to his feet, his body aquiver with indignation. Very admirable, I dare say, for a dog.

The little girl, Teagan, stands her ground for a moment longer until the cries of jubilation from the boys change to a note of surprise, then outrage.

"Hey, you!" *It's the voice of the Red Head.* "You can't do that!"

The words, "I'm telling," *ring out from another juvenile male and Teagan and the terrier run up the stairs as one of the boys scampers down. With a quick look over his shoulder, he races off in the direction of the main building of the museum.*

A sharp bark from the terrier brings me down from my perch high in the dogwood tree as two more boys clamor down the steps. Obviously, it's time for cool heads to prevail. Mine, of course.

The moment I cross the threshold of the doorway leading onto the stairs, I know something foul is afoot. Not only am I a sleuth of great renown, but one who possesses all the finely honed senses of my species. Yes, I am that cat, son of Familiar, disciple of Sherlock Holmes, and my sensitive nose tells me a body lies above.

On the small platform at the top of the stairs, Teagan, the Red Head, and Fergus stare through the plexiglass barrier that prohibits tourists from entering the display. From this vantage point, the living room with a pot-bellied stove, a small kitchen annex, and a bedroom with a single bed are clearly visible. Also visible is a man lying on the bed on his side, facing away from us to the far wall of the bedroom. A dark stain on the pillow tells the tale.

"He's not supposed to be there. No one is supposed to be there," *the Red Head protests indignantly.*

Teagan is quiet for a moment. Her gaze travels over the surface of the protective barrier. "How did he get in?"

I look up at her with a smidgen of admiration. Crikey, if she isn't a cool one, and sharp. A budding junior detective, perhaps? She is correct in her observation. There is no discernable means of access into the preserved space of the living quarters. The barrier is floor to ceiling so not even I could slither over or under it. So, how did the killer get the body into the room?

I sniff along the base of the barrier. It's a custom fit. Designed, no doubt, to not only keep foot traffic at bay, but to preserve the old furnishings from the elements of Georgia's often muggy weather and varied vermin species. Surely there is some way for the rangers who staff the museum to gain access. I must discover how.

Adult voices signal the approach of Lila, Tammy, and a male. The intermingled chatter of high-pitched pre-pubescent males clamors for supremacy. The cavalry has arrived.

"HOW COULD THIS HAPPEN, Oscar? How did he get in there?" Lila Sanderson schooled her voice to hide the panic she felt. The man lying in the middle of a museum display was definitely dead. If the lack of movement from their attempts to get his attention wasn't enough, the dark reddish stain on the pillow confirmed his status.

"Why are you asking me? I'm not in charge of the displays." Oscar was clearly distancing himself from any responsibility for a breach in the museum's security. "All I do is keep an eye on the tourists when we're open."

Lila had her cell phone out and had already punched in the number for Warm Springs Police Department. Clay Bishop answered the phone and Lila mentally rolled her eyes. The patrolman had been trying to get her to go out with him for several months. He was good looking and knew it. Her refusals had only increased his determination.

"Hi, Clay, it's Lila over at the museum."

"Well, hello, Lila. Change your mind about the Memorial

Day picnic?"

"We have a dead body at the museum."

Clay chuckled.

"No, seriously, Clay. There's a dead body on the bed in the servants' quarters above the garage. I think there's blood."

She heard the change in his voice. "Are you sure?"

"Well, no. I mean he might be alive but he's not moving. He doesn't respond when we call out to him."

"Have you checked for a pulse?"

"No, Clay. He's behind the plexiglass barrier. We're waiting for someone to bring the key down here." She hesitated. "But I think he's dead. There's something about the stillness, you know? I can't explain it."

"Right. I'll be there in ten minutes. I'll have Patti call an ambulance. Don't open the display until I get there."

SCOOP JACKSON WAS at his desk in Atlanta, browsing through a brochure on deep sea fishing off the coast of Cancun, Mexico when he got the call. The Warm Springs Police Department had a dead body right smack dab in the middle of the FDR state museum. In a sealed room. A real Agatha Christie who dunnit.

His gaze dropped down to the bottom of the brochure and the deadline for cancellation. He had three days. Doable, he decided. How complicated could it be in a small town like Warm Springs, Georgia?

He lifted the receiver of his desk phone and dialed. Birdie answered on the second ring.

"Saddle up, Birdie. We're off to Warm Springs."

"Yeah? What's the case? Accident? Poachers? Vandalism?"

"Colonel Parker in the pantry with the cleaver."

"Murder?"

"In a locked room, no less."

"Hot dog!"

"I'm glad you find your work so rewarding."

"A locked room, Scoop. This is what every forensic scientist dreams of."

"Well, stop dreaming and assemble the team. See what kind of accommodations are available in Warm Springs. We have to wrap this up in two days."

"Ah. Fishing over the long week-end?"

"Better than that. Deep sea fishing off the coast of Cancun."

The team consisted of Scoop, Birdie, and McFadden. As the lead on the case, Scoop felt the talents of the three of them would be sufficient to wrap things up quickly.

Accommodations were an issue in the small town. Since it was crucial to be as close to the museum as possible, Birdie booked them into the Warm Springs Bed and Breakfast in the heart of the small business district.

The hour and a half drive from Atlanta to Warm Springs took two hours. Late afternoon traffic on I-85 was a beast. Scoop drove straight through the crossroads of the town's business district on Highway 27 to the turn-off onto Little White House Road.

Two patrol cars and a hearse sat in the parking lot at the end of the long, winding lane that led to the secluded complex that had been Franklin Roosevelt's retreat. There were three additional cars parked together well away from the main museum building. One had a government issue tag. The staff, Scoop decided.

A patrolman stood at the top of the steps leading up from the parking lot to the entrance to the museum compound. A little girl sat one step up from the bottom of the stairs. A black scotty sat at her feet.

As he approached, the child looked up and squinted at him as she pushed a strand of long blond hair behind her ear.

"Are you the FBI?" she asked.

"No. I'm Scoop Jackson with the Georgia Department of Natural Resources Law Enforcement team." He took his identification badge from his pocket and showed it to her. "You were expecting the FBI?"

"It's a dead body. He was murdered."

"Yeah? How do you know he was murdered?"

"The room can only be locked from the outside."

"I see."

The police officer made his way down the steps just as Birdie joined Scoop and the little girl.

"Who's this?" Birdie set her heavy crime scene bag on the bottom step and put her hand out to the scotty to sniff.

"That's Fergus." The little girl stood.

"And what's your name?"

"Teagan."

The policeman broke in. "She's the assistant director's daughter." He looked from Birdie to Scoop. "You're the team sent to deal with the body?"

"That would be us. Scoop Jackson." Scoop shook hands with the patrolman. "This is Birdie and bringing up the rear," he glanced over his shoulder at the third member of their team crossing the parking lot, weighed down with various cases of equipment, "Is McFadden."

"Clay Bishop," the officer replied. "I was first on the scene."

"Who discovered the victim?"

"A bunch of kids."

All eyes went to Teagan. The terrier stood and moved closer to her, his body aquiver from nose to tail.

Scoop crouched to bring himself down to Teagan's level. "Well, now, I can see why you were expecting the FBI." He glanced up at Clay Bishop then returned his attention to the little girl. "Where's you dad?"

She buried her fingers in the dog's hair. "He's dead."

"I thought—" He looked up at the patrolman.

"Her mother, Lila Sanderson, is the assistant director."

Scoop felt the anger rising but he kept his voice calm as he spoke to the child. "How did you find the body?"

"It was the other kids. The tourists. They were playing at sword fighting and ran up the stairs to the servants' quarters. They thought the man was sleeping."

"But you didn't?"

"No."

"Why's that?"

She thought about it a minute. "He didn't move." She kneaded the dog's fur. "You could tell he wasn't breathing."

Scoop had received only the broad strokes of the scene with the initial phone call. Had there been blood? He had been afraid of what the child might have seen. But stillness, that was a very discerning observation.

Clay Bishop seemed to appreciate that he was losing ground with the investigative team. He cleared his throat. "We took statements from everyone who was in the park at the time. Got all their contact details. Shirley's going through the receipts for the day, checking credit cards to identify folks who were in here earlier. So far, we've only found three who paid with cash."

The door of the museum opened and a redhead stepped through with a black cat at her heels. "Teagan! Your mother is looking all over for you." She hurried down the steps. "You were supposed to wait..." The redhead stopped as her gaze fell on

Scoop. As she continued on down the steps, she said. "You were supposed to wait in the office with Shirley."

"She was busy."

"Oh, sweetie." She hugged the child to her and turned to Scoop and his entourage. "Tammy," she said. "Tammy Lynn. I'm a friend of Lila's in town for the weekend." She gestured toward the main building. "You'll find her inside to the right. She's expecting you."

"Thanks." Scoop started up the steps and Teagan tried to fall in step with him.

Tammy held her back. "No, sweetie. You need to stay with me."

"But I found the body."

"I know, but Oscar and your mother can show them where."

"They need to take my statement."

The look of disappointment in her expression made Scoop stop for a moment. "Tell you what, Teagan. When we've had a chance to look things over, I'll review your statement with you. I wouldn't want to miss any important details."

She sighed then reluctantly nodded her head.

As he continued up the steps, he could feel the gaze of the redhead boring into the back of his head. He looked over his shoulder and she quickly lowered her eyes to the child.

End of excerpt from *Trouble on the Mountain*
by Rebecca Barrett
Trouble Cat Mysteries #14

TROUBLE CAT MYSTERIES

Please join our Trouble Cat Mysteries page on Facebook:

fb.me/TroubleCatMysteries

www.troublecatmysteries.com

Familiar Trouble | Carolyn Haines

Trouble in Dixie | Rebecca Barrett

Trouble in Tallahassee | Claire Matturro

Trouble in Summer Valley | Susan Y. Tanner

Small Town Trouble | Laura Benedict

Trouble in Paradise | Rebecca Barrett

TROUBLE'S DOUBLE CONTEST WINNER
Reggu

I'm a smoky black cat called Reggu and this is the tale of one kitty's quest for finding a forever home and a good life ever after. I believe to be more than five but less than ten years young. My kittenhood is a bit of mystery even to myself. I rather not reminisce those days. Happier times came along when I was taken to a rescue centre from the streets, where I was found wandering alone.

I had a warm bed and plenty of food, but I was still yearning for a home of my own. One day a nice young lady visited the shelter to look for companionship. Beware of my eyes! I mesmerized her with my stare and off we went. She was an avid Harry Potter fun and named me after Regulus Black, a handsome young man.

We had couple of lovely years together until the call of her destiny meant that she had to move abroad. That made me very sad, but as luck would have it, I had been looked after from time to time by a dedicated cat lover. She had lost her beloved cat and was willing to adopt me for good.

The rest is the history as they say. Mummy and I have been together now for over 3 years and love each other to the moon and back. You don't hear me meow, but I'm not a mute cat. I have an expressive purr, soothing like the sound of a trickling brook my hooman auntie says, which is often in use. Sometimes I let out a little squeak to call somebody to play with.

Mummy mistakenly thinks that my troubled past caused me to lose my voice. As a mentalist I have more subtle ways to communicate with hoomans. My mission is to teach telepathy to Mummy, so she could understand me like I understand her. Just wish she was more natural. *Sigh!*

Mummy says that I am kind, modest and loving. I try not to scratch things she likes. Holy Kittens, that really requires a mind control.

Getting groomed, chasing and being chased, running through my leopard tunnel, meditating on my back and snoozing on top of Mummy when she sleeps, these are the things I love. Birdwatching is always interesting. Observing people is also enjoyable. Hoomans are ever so whimsical.

My motto is "Silence is Golden".

You can read more about me on instagram **@ecotactiledesign**, **#RegguTheCat**. I'd be delighted if you visit me at **instagram.com/ecotactiledesign**.

Paws up, Reggu the Mentalist

— MARITTA STURT

CPSIA information can be obtained
at www.ICGtesting.com
Printed in the USA
LVHW090809030721
691833LV00019B/495